The dry ice ... and the wat ... the longest ninety seconds in the history of time, the golden cage with its jeweled padlock emerged from the water.

The wardrobe assistants rushed forward with towels, then, as one, fell back with terrified shrieks, sounding the first notes of the horror chorus we all became when we saw what they'd seen.

Where Rikka's vertical eyes had been, gaped empty sockets.

Her nose, the left side of her face, and her entire throat were missing.

"Piranhas!" Shelly's scream rose above all the rest. Then she fainted dead away.

★

FASHION
Victims

SOPHIE DUNBAR

W🌐RLDWIDE®

TORONTO • NEW YORK • LONDON
AMSTERDAM • PARIS • SYDNEY • HAMBURG
STOCKHOLM • ATHENS • TOKYO • MILAN
MADRID • WARSAW • BUDAPEST • AUCKLAND

Dedicated with love and honor to the original Survivors,
those who have passed and those still present:

Michael and Molly Markman
Selma Rivlin
Grescha and Lola Gersony
Jack and Anya Buvitt
Seymour Buvitt
Helen Luria
Jascha and Pauline Levenson
Rosl Hackmeyer

FASHION VICTIMS

A Worldwide Mystery/April 2002

First published by Intrigue Press.

ISBN 0-373-26418-6

Printed in U.S.A.

Ezekiel 37: 1-10

ONE

IT HAPPENED so fast.

One minute, Frank and I were standing together. The next, he had been swept completely out of sight by a dark, churning funnel cloud of egos and cleavage vying for maximum exposure.

My goodness, this certainly wasn't Encino anymore. No, it was Beverly Hills, and the grand opening of trendy clothing boutique, Bonsai. It was also the night of the first murder, but that came later.

So far, the action had been much your routine Hollywood codependent feeding frenzy of paparazzi upon paparazzee, except more of both species had turned out than I personally would've counted on for something that wasn't a movie premier or the launching of yet another celebrity cartel restaurant.

As cameras snapped, crackled, and popped like acid-laced Rice Krispies, at least half of everybody you've ever seen on the TV tabloids either tried desperately to get their pictures taken, or tried desperately to pretend they didn't want to get their pictures taken.

I was scanning the crowd in vain for a glimpse of Frank, when Davida Yedvab's trademark donkey bray rose effortlessly above the other animal cries. "Just can't seem to hang on to those husbands! Huh, Ava?"

With thick, black curls springing haphazardly around a strong-boned olive face, Davida looked every inch the Sabra warrior woman she had, in fact, been. After her husband Boaz disappeared in his fighter jet somewhere over the Sinai, she decided to emigrate from Israel to L.A., retiring a well-notched Uzi to wield an equally lethal zoom lens.

During the eighties, Davida and I worked for the same public relations firm. Since then, we'd moved along on parallel tracks, which, while rarely converging, provided us with a certain sense of continuity. Her dig about hanging on to husbands dated back to our mutual PR days when I was just a little flak catcher who caught the eye of a Famous Client.

Of course, the marriage was over in an L.A. minute—which has been described as a New York minute that's been lying out on the beach for three hours—but I got a fond farewell plus some lovely parting gifts. A substantial divorce settlement, too, since during the time we were married he starred in a huge box office success. But that was almost immediately embezzled by my accountant, who also happened to be my second husband. It was a rebound thing.

Now Davida's teeth gleamed in a pearly grin as she joined me, a cluster of cameras hanging from her muscular body like baby possums.

"I'll have you know Frank Bernstein and I are forever," I told her. "Like they say, the third time's the charm."

The wattage of her smile dimmed and I knew she was thinking of Boaz, the love of her life. During the last twenty years, Davida had indulged in some serious affairs, but in her heart, she was still married to Boaz Yedvab. *Zo ad olam,* as the Hebrew vow goes.

"You guys here to work?" she inquired, sharp brown eyes roaming the room, perpetually alert for the juicy shot that could mean thousands of dollars to a hardworking mamarazzi.

"I hope so. We sure need the money. And we might have a good chance. Once upon a time, back in New York City, Frank and Barry Lehr were at each other's bar mitzvahs and graduated from high school together."

Davida arched a thick, cynical brow. "Hmmm."

"Not to mention Sonia and Morrie—that's Barry's parents to you—still play bridge every week with Frank's aunt Henny. That's why we got invited to this bash in the first place."

It meant a lot to Henny, who'd raised Frank from age eight, to feel that she had some sort of input to our existence three thousand miles away. She constantly monitored the news media for all the terrible things that were going on in California, an activity which inspired a steady stream of long-distance phone calls, filled with dire warnings against earthquakes, cocaine, and the Israeli Mafia.

"Now, I'm impressed!" Davida laughed. "Your production company has definitely got the inside track to shoot the Bonsai television commercials. Barry's mother and Frank's aunt will see to that."

Barry Lehr was the architect-turned-clothing-designer behind the wildly successful Bonsai style. The debut Bonsai line had been such a hit in expensive stores on both coasts, Barry was now feeling confident enough to take the plunge into his own retail operation. A marketing survey concluded that a flagship store on Rodeo Drive, even in these economically unstable times, offered the greatest potential profit center for his quirky, Japanese-inspired fashions.

"Exactly how does Barry define the Bonsai look?" Davida speculated mischievously. "Jewpanese, perhaps? Japaraellli?"

"I tell you how I define it!" a whiney voice snapped viciously. "As theft!"

"Thanks, Woo." Davida addressed the man who emerged from behind a support column where he'd been eavesdropping. "It makes us feel so very special to know we're among the five thousand people you've shared that particular thought with.

"And by the way. Woo Kazu, do you know Ava Bernstein, in whose presence you just committed slander?"

The designer and I were deciding that we had sorta, kinda, met somewhere, when Davida remarked in a bored tone, "Oh surprise, surprise. There's Kato. It was too much to hope for that he wouldn't show up. Can you believe they still want snaps of him? Back in a minute, guys." She began to elbow her way through the crowd, leaving me alone with Woo.

As Frank says, everybody's got a shtick. In Woo Kazu's case

it was a chopshtick. Two chopsticks, actually, stabbed at dramatic angles into the twisted knot of shiny black hair on top of his head.

While my private idea of a great designer outfit is finding more than one piece of Donna Karan in size 4 on sale, I have to stay up on the fashion scene because of my work. That's how I happened to know that Woo Kazu was one of the original Vietnam boat babies, born to a Japanese pearl merchant and the daughter of a high official in the Nguyen Van Thieu government.

He was six months old the night his grandfather was assassinated by Ho Chi Minh spies, and his parents made a desperate escape with just the clothes on their backs and all the pearls they could carry.

Inevitably, their boat was captured by the merciless Thai pirates who cruised the Pacific, preying on defenseless refugees. True to their terrible custom, they raped the women, then robbed the boat of everything remotely valuable. Everything, that is, except the cache of priceless pearls Woo's parents had concealed in his dirty diaper.

As a consequence, his family had begun its new life in Los Angeles with a literal "shitload of pearls," a W interview quoted him as saying.

Woo Kazu was brilliant, erratic, bisexual and triracial, being Japanese on his father's side, Chinese on his mother's, and Vietnamese by birth. He initially gained fame by designing a line of very high-priced workout gear with a distinctly Pacific Rim flavor, which quickly went international after becoming a hot commodity in the United States among affluent gym bunnies.

WooWoo Wear had since expanded to include casual street clothes, and most recently, an evening collection. His style had been praised as a cross between the delicacy of a Japanese watercolor and the knife edge of an Asian gangster, and if there was any resemblance between WooWoo and Bonsai, I certainly couldn't detect it.

When I said as much to Woo, he tugged agitatedly at his scraggly Fu Manchu goatee. "Of course you can't see it!" he shrilled, "because when I realized what Barry Lehr was up to, I couldn't present some of my own designs. He would've accused me of copying him!

"Besides," Woo continued in a calmer tone, "Barry couldn't design his way to the next room by himself. It's that wife of his. She used to work for me, you know."

"Oh, really?" I murmured, exactly as if I'd never heard firsthand from Cherry Rose herself about the two torrid years she'd spent as lover and employee in Woo Kazu's Venice Beach atelier, which ended with his rejection of her personally and professionally.

"But...gee, that must've been a long time ago, Woo. I mean, haven't Barry and Cherry Rose been married about five years now? And Bonsai's only been on the market for three seasons." Oh, puhleeze! Was this guy kidding? Sketches allegedly stolen by Cherry Rose back in the early nineties would hardly be on the cutting edge of the Third Millennium.

Woo definitely caught my implication. He adjusted the drape of his quilted charcoal silk jacket and huffed defensively, "Well, but designers always work multiple seasons ahead."

This was no doubt true, but failed to explain why Woo hadn't just gone forward and produced whatever he was accusing the Lehrs of ripping off before they could beat him to it. He'd certainly had plenty of time between his breakup with Cherry Rose and now.

Woo's baleful obsidian eyes took on a sheen of cunning. "Don't be too shocked if the empire de Bonsai suddenly withers away," he remarked obliquely. "I've got an inside track...." On that discordant note, Woo Kazu thrust the long, sharply pointed ebony chopsticks more firmly into his topknot, and angled off toward a tiny Japanese girl with a crewcut who was beckoning to him imperiously.

Davida reappeared a moment later, cameras clanking as she approached. "Ava! What did you do with that little dim sum? Emphasis on the dim."

"And here I thought Asians were supposed to be so inscrutable," I marveled.

"Oh, some of them definitely are," Davida said flatly, all traces of amusement suddenly gone. "One in particular. He was so inscrutable that up until a couple of months ago, I actually thought..." She bit her lip, shrugged, and began to deftly reload one of her dreadfully expensive cameras which did specific and esoteric things, don't ask me what. As far as I'm concerned, a box of film that takes its own pictures ranks right up there with salad-in-a-bag and liposuction as one of the greatest inventions of all time.

"Davida!" I enthused. "There's a new man in your life?"

"Was, Ava," she corrected, shutting one camera and flipping open another. "And for the first time, I didn't feel haunted by the ghost of Boaz. It was almost as if he had, well, given me to...this person."

Since she avoided mentioning "this person's" name, I guessed it was fairly famous. Since there weren't that many well-known Asian male stars in America, I couldn't imagine who she meant. Sammo from *Martial Law* perhaps?

Davida continued. "He had been trying to persuade me to marry him. And then, just when I was finally getting used to the idea, he stopped asking." She gave an ironic snort. "In fact, he stopped. Period."

"What happened?"

"Nu, what else? Another woman!"

I said inadequately, "Oh, Davida, I'm so sorry."

"Hey!" She shrugged again. "Hard come, hard go!" Her brisk tone warned me to drop the subject.

"Listen, Ava. I've got a few more shots left on this roll. Let me use it up on you, okay?"

I was delighted. While I am among the rare exceptions that look ten years younger and fifteen pounds lighter on TV, my bone structure morphs perversely in still photos. The last good pictures I had of myself were the ones Davida took at my first wedding. I was more heartbroken about throwing them away than I was about the divorce itself.

"Smile, Ava!" Davida ordered, and I obeyed, knowing my deceptively simple black silk crepe tuxedo, with jet-beaded vest to match its lapels, was doing far better things for me than those sleazy rubber sausage skins currently in vogue were doing for some of the chickiepoos half my age. Not to mention the ones that weren't. They, poor deluded dears, looked like an audition for *Bride of Michelin Man*.

Davida followed my gaze. "You'd think a girl could at least count on rubber to smooth out those pesky lumps, bumps, and bulges. But, nooooo!" She chuckled, gleefully firing a few rounds of Fuji at one of her favorite targets, an overripe, fiftyish blonde who must hold the record for turning up in a certain tabloid under "Fashion Flops."

Tonight, she was tortuously stuffed into something slick and fuschia, like a psychedelic kielbasa. She must've been breathing through gills.

Spotting Davida's busily strobing flash, the blonde strutted and posed, blissfully unconcerned that she was destined for "Would You Be Caught Dead in This Outfit?"

Unfortunately, she wasn't the only one.

TWO

HOW DO I KNOW fluorescent lighting was created by a misogynist? Because just one glimpse at her reflection in a public restroom is enough to send practically any woman spiraling into deep depression since her face is clearly decomposing right before her eyes. It should be a law to have CAUTION: OBJECTS IN THIS MIRROR ARE FAR MORE ATTRACTIVE THAN THEY APPEAR! etched into the glass.

Bracing myself for the inevitable, I joined the ladies frantically performing CPR upon themselves in front of the Bonsai powder room mirror, but for once, it wasn't quite as bad as I'd expected. Largely because of my new haircut, which Frank describes as "Carol Brady, 2001," although those expensive blond highlights, so artfully applied, now seemed about as subtle as a paint-by-number portrait.

Things went downhill from there. My intriguing combination of Joan Crawford eyebrows and Bette Davis blue eyes was distorted into a one-woman *What Ever Happened to Baby Jane?* enhanced by a pair of dark circles á la Uncle Fester. And the emphatic parenthesis around my mouth could've been carved with an ice pick. (Even in more flattering light, I'm self-conscious about this feature, but Frank assures me he adores parenthetical statements.)

The only advantage to fluorescence besides cheapness is, if you can get yourself looking halfway alive in its ghastly glow, you're bound to feel like an incredibly fabulous and stunning creature anywhere else.

I finally spotted Frank, just as I started to descend one of the two flights of metal steps that connected a loft area containing offices, the femmes convenience and storage space with the Bonsai showroom. He had been backed into a corner by the same pint-sized Japanese chick who'd earlier lured Mr. Kazu away from my charms, and he was wearing that expression of polite desperation he always gets when somebody propositions him.

My six-foot-three, curly-haired, cleft-chinned, brown-eyed husband sincerely doesn't understand why women make passes at him when he only wants to be friendly and what's more, never appears in public without his wedding ring, a wide band of European rose gold that once belonged to his father. To Frank it's not just a symbol of commitment, but a kind of talisman, as if it contained the power to ward off predators like a crucifix turned upon Dracula. He can't seem to grasp that to some females, a wedding ring is more like a red flag to a bull.

Furthermore, he does not subscribe to the generally held theory that his total gorgeousness might contribute to the situation. Living with that face every day for fifty-plus years (he barely looks forty) has bred an honest indifference.

In all truth, I never yearned to marry a handsome man, knowing too well what vexation it can bring upon the guy's wife. In my sinful youth, I had more than once been the source of such vexation. Most of us would agree that indeed we do reap what we sow.

Too bad more of us don't remember this before we do the actual sowing.

It was taking me much longer than it should've to reach Frank, because the narrow staircase was jammed with people yakking on their portable phones. About three quarters of the way down, I got stalled behind an extremely hefty redheaded woman wearing purple chiffon, who was barking and spitting gravely Russian at somebody on the other end of her Nextel.

When she abruptly snapped the phone shut and surged forward, I was carried along in her majestic purple wake by sheer momentum. The crowd in front of her had no choice but to part like the Red Sea, or be crushed to a pulpy mass.

Frank saw me coming when I was yet afar off, and waved with flattering fervor. "Ava, baby!" he roared in that husky baritone, which even after five years, still packs the power to move me.

The girl spun to look, crew cut bristling with hostility. Possibly she didn't actually plan on burning me with the cigarette smoldering at the end of her jade holder, but I did a defensive sidestep, just in case.

"Miko Hayashi, this is my wife, Ava," Frank told her, sliding an arm around my waist.

"Hello, Ava," Miko said, with a smile as cold as the little claw she reluctantly offered.

"Miko's going to be managing the store for Barry," Frank explained, "and I was just telling her that you're the writing half of our team."

Miko curled a disdainful lip. "How sweet," she said, then turned her back on me and spoke exclusively to Frank. "Listen, I have to go now. But I'll be calling you first thing in the morning about the lunch meeting."

As she moved off to intercept an android of her acquaintance, I was struck by her very apropos resemblance to a bonsai. Spiky, stunted, and somehow twisted.

"What lunch meeting?" I demanded irritably. The pounding of hammers and wet cement smell were beginning to get on my nerves. When it came to chutzpah, Bonsai was way out in front, daring to stage a grand opening while still actively under construction. Those were authentic carpenters hard at work up there, perched on tall ladders that soared into the rafters of the hangarlike room.

Frank gave me a soothing ear nuzzle. "Miko's going to get Barry to bid us for two regional commercials. They're thinking music video."

"Such originality!" I sniped, although music videos were the main reason B-Pix, our production company, remained solvent while others had gone belly-up.

When Frank was still executive producer at Agency X, I was hired as group head at Agency Y and ordered to create a breakthrough commercial for dry cat food. "You're supposed to be funny," they said unsmilingly. "Give us another Meow Mix."

The problem was, they didn't have Meow Mix. They had Kitty Bitties, and no commercial on earth could change the fact.

At that point, Frank and I had technically been married three years, though with separate employers and shooting schedules, we'd managed to spend only a total of about eighteen months actually together. But unbeknownst to us, things were soon to change.

Miraculously, we were both free to attend our third anniversary, which definitely called for a celebration, so we splurged and went to the fanciest place in town. This was back when all the trendoids were swathing themselves in grunge—hideously expensive (and often just plain hideous) outfits born of an unholy alliance between a sixties thrift shop and an Army surplus store. I wouldn't have expected to see somebody try to get away with grunge at this particular restaurant, but she did—emerald green velvet strategically ripped to provide tantalizing glimpses of the peach-colored lace slip that showed unevenly below her hem, accompanied by the obligatory Chanel combat boots.

"I've got to admit, it works for her," I conceded generously, secure in strapless larkspur blue moiré, with Frank's anniversary gift, sapphire and diamond earrings winking coquettishly in the candlelight.

"And to think," Frank marveled, "not so long ago, only a bag lady would've appeared in public wearing stuff like that!"

"Oh, well. Like they say, fashion flows up."

"Fashion flows up," Frank repeated thoughtfully.

The idea hit us both at almost the same moment and we began to talk it out, not realizing how loud our voices were getting until we noticed a distinguished man at the next table was staring at us intently.

A few minutes passed, then a waiter glided up, bearing two fragile balloons of cognac and a business card upon his silver tray. "Compliments of the gentleman," he murmured, indicating the man who'd been watching us.

Frank and I raised our glasses to him in bewildered thanks, then I glanced down at the card to learn our mysterious benefactor's identity. I nearly fainted. Silently, I passed it to Frank, who jerked up his head in astonishment to gape at the man. He was observing us with amusement, and made a distinctly European gesture of invitation.

Numbly, we joined him at his table.

"I see you know of me," he chuckled, after learning our names. The man was a fashion designer, his name an international household word. Households like palaces, villas, chateaux, and schlosses on the Danube.

He twinkled at us benevolently. "I couldn't help overhearing your discussion. Please! I am most interested in joining it."

Our new friend confided his disgust with how the business of fashion had deteriorated. Increasingly, he lamented, one saw a cavalier disregard for beauty, form, and elegance, manifested in atrocious fads perpetrated upon society by certain undisciplined anarchists with more attitude than talent, and total contempt for retail clientele.

Aided and abetted by a fatuous media, the industry was mutating into an incestuous cult of sneering personalities, with designers and models warring for headlines and air time.

Worse, he said, was the burgeoning trend toward designers surrendering control of their runway shows to stylists, who charged up to fifty thou a pop to produce S&M fantasies that were far more about titillating a jaded audience of fashion editors and jet setters, and outshocking and upstaging their own rival stylists, than about the actual clothes.

In the fashion world, it was *sewing* and reaping as stylists treated designers with the same scorn they in turn had regarded their retail customers, while everybody seemed to have completely lost sight of the fact that thousands and thousands of women besides Ivana Trump have got to buy your clothes. Despite her enormous wealth, the lovely IT can hardly be expected to support the entire industry, and the only legitimate success is a bottom line printed in yummy black ink.

Having said all that, our designer went on to admit that a whammo runway presentation was vital to the initial impact upon wholesale buyers, and he was in search of a stylist. So far though, it had been a wild goose chase.

"All the same!" he declared, waving aside the creative capitals of three continents with a manicured hand. "Threatening music, hellish lighting, demonic makeup, and all manner of androgynous kinkiness." He himself was one of the few vigorously and notoriously hetero male designers.

At the time of our meeting, he'd grown so desperate he was on the verge of knuckling under to the universal "Hurt me, punish me, androgynize me" theme, until he'd overheard Frank's and my naive burblings about fashion flowing up.

Over more cognac, he hired us to produce—and film—his winter showing in Paris!

Frank took a leave of absence, but I didn't have to.

I got fired.

Next to my thighs, the bane of my life and many others was Kitty Bitties, referred to around the agency as Shitty Bitties. One frustrated afternoon, my art director and I went temporarily insane and devised a storyboard that starred a furiously angry cat, urging cats all over America to refuse to eat Kitty Bitties because it tasted like shit. The copy read, "We're mad as hell, and we're not going to eat this shit anymore!"

There were frames of cats responding by dumping the stuff into their litter boxes, flushing it down commodes, jamming it into trash compactors. The last panel showed a long row of squatting felines shot from behind, tails twitching viciously, defecating copiously upon boxes of Kitty Bitties.

The art director secreted our mad creation carefully in his office, but my enemy, a woman who thought she should've had my job, somehow ferreted the thing out, slipped it into a stack of storyboards being presented to the client, and voila! I was on my way to France.

Since neither Frank nor I had a clue about staging fashion shows, our imagination was free to run rampant. We ended up writing a story told in modern dance, with a score composed by a French pop musician. The surrealistic choreography opened with one raggedy bag lady rooting through the trash. The motley garments she puts together are interpreted upward through stratas of society until the sudden explosion of the designer's creations onto the stage, the ultimate fulfillment of The Look.

Gleefully, the designer went along with our idea to use professional dancers instead of runway mannequins to augment those mandatory supermodels: Choreographing dancers to model clothes effectively was doable, while choreographing models to dance effectively was not. This heresy created a furor, but after the dust settled, *Fashion Flows Up* was pronounced a smash by most who mattered and many who didn't.

Then just for fun, Frank and I edited a ninety-minute piece from the show, called it *Fashion Flows Up—The Movie,* and entered it in the Cannes Film Festival where it won a prize!

Out of these earnings, plus my severance pay, B-Pix was born, and Frank soon became recognized as the director to deliver a certain glossy look to commercials and music videos. These days, while the hi-tech, musical format was no longer challenging to us as a genre, it certainly stretched our creativity to come up with something different in the same framework every time.

We produced two more shows for our designer before his death (in the arms of a new bride thirty years his junior, which is exactly how he would've chosen to go), but what Frank really wanted, and who didn't, was to direct a feature film. Directors, however, are just as vulnerable to typecasting as actors, and Frank sometimes felt sentenced to jog away his career on the commercial/music video treadmill while his biological clock ticked relentlessly on and he watched people half his age with little or no experience and/or talent get handed gazillion-dollar projects to direct.

Meanwhile, back in Encino, we had a mortgage, car payments, and two ravenous springer spaniels named Dimples and Dumpling, and Bonsai was a potential client. Who knew? We just might be able to convince Barry Lehr to invest in *Bonsai—The Movie*.

THREE

JUST AS FRANK AND I managed to squeeze close enough to grab something from the buffet—a Spartan affair consisting of flat-bread, brie, green grapes, and mineral water—the lights dimmed, leaving only a long ceiling track beaming down onto a narrow, raised platform, which stretched from one end of the room to the other. Voices grew hushed, and the sound of drills and hammers faded away, to be replaced by wailing flutes, crashing cymbals, and the muffled thud of a gong.

The Bonsai fashion show had begun.

A quartet of musicians appeared at the far end of the platform, shrouded in striped silk burnooses nipped in at the waist with tasseled white cords, designed by the Lehrs. Swaying solemnly to the music, they reached the end of the runway, dismounted, and mercifully ceased to play for a few moments.

Suddenly, all the lights went out. Darkness. A buzz of anticipation.

Then came a mighty crash from the gong, and a spotlight flashed on to illuminate a magnificent rosewood sedan chair, borne upon the shoulders of four persons of indeterminate gender wound in yards of saffron-dyed, pleated gauze bib overalls, belted in green molded rubber. Brocade turbans were wrapped around their heads to match their Aladdin slippers with upturned toes.

A collective gasp of appreciation went up, then applause, from the spectators lining both sides of the platform.

The chair was carefully lowered, the green velvet curtains were parted, and Barry Lehr, dapper in black jacquard harem pyjamas, stepped out to a thunderous ovation. As Barry bowed, the curtains were parted again and he turned to assist the person emerging.

Greater gasping, heavier applause, as Cherry Rose Lehr stood revealed in all her glory. She was dressed in elaborate traditional garb, from the intricately coiled black wig, right down to the ivory fan stuck in her obi. Her doll's face was painted pearly white, emphasizing heavily outlined eyes and bright red lips.

I would have never recognized this demure geisha as the daughter of Roy Huwei, a.k.a. the "Shushi Shogun of Manhattan," and Francesca DiMotta of Queens, New York.

As the Lehrs exchanged bows, Frank nudged me. Barry, who hadn't darkened the door of a synagogue more than half a dozen times since his bar mitzvah, was wearing a yarmulke!

To gaze upon this couple, one could've been pardoned for assuming the union had been painstakingly conjured up by Cabalists and kimonoed elders over sake and matzos. The mundane truth was, Barry and Cherry Rose met at a hockey game in Madison Square Garden, although they had in fact undergone three ritual weddings: Jewish, Shinto, and Roman Catholic. Aunt Henny succinctly summed it up after the final reception: "So! Now they're married!" She said this in a tone filled with doubt.

After the Lehrs made their triumphant exit, the pace of the show picked up. The theme—Androgynous Middle East Meets Androgynous Far East. The Bonsai clothes were light and airy, draped and artfully bagged in silk, cotton, satin. Anyone, male or female, could've conceivably worn any of them. Indeed, most of the models themselves could conceivably have been male or female.

With one stunning exception.

At intervals would appear a diminutive coolie, in the Bonsai version of traditional peasant garb, pulling a rickshaw. In the rickshaw sat the same Dragon Lady model—tall and leggy for an Asian, blue-black hair cut square and straight, eyes so slanted they were nearly vertical.

Each time, she wore a variation of the classic cheongsam, sleeveless, long-sleeved, backless, slit—all breathlessly translated into rich, heavy silks.

At a certain point on the ramp, the coolie would suddenly drop the rickshaw poles and collapse as though exhausted. The Dragon Lady, looking bored, would alight from the buggy and saunter contemptuously around the cringing coolie, feigning kicks at him in black satin, spike-heeled mules that were tipped with puffs of marabou, her husky voice growling Niponic abuse until he'd struggle wearily to his feet and assist her back into the conveyance.

Then he'd stagger offstage hauling his elegant burden, followed by wild applause.

What is it about sadomasochism and fashion shows?

We were convinced Barry and Cherry Rose had gone the limit when the quartet abruptly launched into a shrieking rendition of "March of the Siamese Children" from *The King and I,* and ten Asian youngsters, ranging from toddler to five-year-old, presented the debut of Baby Bonsai! The kids were adorable, and came in graduated sizes that intentionally called to mind those dolls whose heads unscrew to reveal a smaller doll inside, et cetera, et cetera, and so forth.

Bonsai's grand finale featured Barry and Cherry Rose, all the models, children, and musicians, with the rickshaw bringing up the rear.

There was one last encore of collapsing and kicking, but with a new twist that brought down the house. This time the coolie refused to budge, so the Dragon Lady scooped him up, plunked him into the rickshaw and pulled it offstage herself, teetering in those four-inch heels, as the coolie leered triumphantly at an audience gone wild.

Talk about drop-dead fashion.

FOUR

AT NINE-FORTY-FIVE the house lights went up, and people scattered in all directions, intent on their own agendas.

There was a general surge toward the exit, where limos idled defiantly in the red zone, ready to cart their passengers off to the next photo op, and valet parking guys prepared to swear those dings were already on the car.

Hot little actresses raced to corner Bonsai salespeople, distinguished by black jacquard harem PJ's like Barry's, staking claims on their favorite luscious Dragon Lady cheongsams.

Frank and I hung around and watched for a few minutes, then joined the hard-core fifty or so fashion groupies who were swarming up both flights of metal stairs, hoping to be allowed access to the dressing room.

Frank was already planning how the commercials would look. "A sort of a sexy Masada goes Kabuki but like from a parallel universe," he mumbled visionarily.

"Sure, baby. And don't let's forget to mention the Six-Day War or our trade conflicts with Japan, and by all means remind everybody they were allies with the Germans," I said, trying to bring him back down to earth.

Our increasingly global village has made it almost impossible to proclaim an identity, ideology, or even mention certain historical facts, without somebody charging racism or worse. The inherent problem with striving for political correctness in these uncertain times is that what counts as correct one day is subject to being declared completely incorrect—literally the next day—by the secret PC police.

For example, to qualify, distinguish or differentiate between American citizens by prefacing them with a hyphen, years ago was the height of incorrectness. In other words, to call someone African-American or Chinese-American was simply taboo among mid-twentieth-century liberals. Go figure.

Now an even trickier problem is the "correct" terminology to apply to our burgeoning multicultural couples and their offspring.

So, as to Frank's concept of the Bonsai TV spots (should we even get the account) some faction was guaranteed to take umbrage, whether it was the Japanese, the JDL, the PLO, or some pompous WASP with nothing better to do and feeling guilty about (but not enough to forfeit) their inherited wealth and lavish estates built on land their ancestors cheated the Indians out of.

But what made Bonsai so special was its very deliberate flaunting of combing two distinct and separate cultures. Otherwise, where was your marketing point? That being the case, no matter how we approached these spots, somebody was bound and determined to be offended, so why not just come out swinging?

"On second thought, let's go for it, baby!" I told Frank as we stepped onto the landing. "We'll make it a Romeo and Juliet story with a Maccabees plot twist, plus maybe we can squeeze in something about Chanukah!"

Frank looked down at me and laughed. "Ava, you're a total meshuggie."

I reached up and gave his tie a suggestive tug, which is a private little amorous signal between us. "Lucky for you, mister," I retorted.

His brown eyes kindled. "Luck had nothing whatsoever to do with it." And then he kissed me, softly at first. But it evolved into something else and for a long, sweet moment Frank and I stood there, oblivious to the foot traffic flowing around our tiny island.

Surfacing, we saw with surprise that people were now headed

back down the staircases, muttering and darting angry glances over their shoulders. "But I wanted her autograph!" one willowy young man whined to another, who grumpily replied, "Well, it's not my bloody fault, so shut up."

Similar disgruntled observations were being voiced by other would-be backstagers who had not been granted entree to personally meet and fawn over the models as they'd expected. Many, in childish retaliation, were stamping noisily as possible on their way down the metal steps.

"What's going on?" Frank asked one of the deportees, who responding by jerking a disgusted thumb backward toward a pair of swinging doors, which appeared to be guarded by a huge man in a black leather vest that made the merest gesture of covering his burly, furry chest.

At our approach, he balled giant fists. "Can't go in there," he rumbled.

Frank was exasperated. "Fine. Then you go in and tell Mr. Lehr that the Bernsteins are here. He's expecting us."

The man glared, then turned without another word. G-U-I-D-O was spelled out in silver studs across the back of his vest. He shouldered his way into the room, and a buzz of excitement accompanied the popping of champagne corks wafted out, muted as the heavy doors swung shut.

While we waited for Barry, we resumed our discussion of the commercials, confronting the inevitable problem of how to make them look like caviar on the tuna budget cheapskate Barry was sure to offer.

A jangle of keys on the stairs heralded the ascent of one last remaining security guard from a platoon hired for this show. His chocolatey brow furrowed with displeasure when he saw us, and he flexed fullback-size deltoids, which threw his badge into relief. The name tag read, "Calvin."

"You people got a problem?" he inquired in a menacing tone.

"None at all...Calvin," Frank soothed, handing him one of our business cards. "We're friends of Mr. and Mrs. Lehr. They know we're out here."

Suspicion faded from Calvin's expression as he studied the card. "That's okay, Mr. Bernstein. I just gotta make sure since I'm about to go off duty. See, I can't lock up downstairs because the fashion show people have to leave through the front door and it would trigger the alarm."

"Remind Barry we're still waiting, will you, Calvin?" Frank called after the big man, who nodded before disappearing through the swinging doors.

"So," I said, picking up where we'd left off. "Yet again, B-Pix must transform stale diet soda into champagne wishes."

"Well, I've got a great idea for the location," Frank revealed with a sly grin. "And the price is right." He paused. "Nobuo Wei's estate."

In reality, Wei-Side, Nobuo Wei's paradise domain north of Sunset Boulevard and west of Rockingham (yes, *that* Rockingham) was several locations within a location. Its high stone walls enclosed a miniature forest, lush palm groves, an authentic maze with a koi pond and waterfall in the center, and other amenities too numerous to mention. Short of Hawaii, there could be no more wonderful setting for anything that required an otherworldly yet earthy, sensual opulence.

Well, sure!" I agreed. "Wei-Side is tailor-made for a fashion spot. The only catch is, Nobuo will want to be in the commercial himself!"

Frank laughed. "I certainly hope so! Can't you just see him as the stern father, Ava? All large and looming in ceremonial robes."

In fact, Nubuo would be perfect casting, and he was a consummate professional, having been quite famous in his day.

As an aspiring actor of barely seventeen, he arrived from New York to try his luck in Hollywood after the Korean War. The studios were still cranking out WWII epics by the truckload, and running short of fierce, fanatical young Japanese naval officer and kamikaze pilot types, so Nobuo was immediately cast as one of these.

A career was born.

For the next ten years, Nobuo Wei portrayed a gallery of Japanese military villains, and when the box office for The Big One finally deflated, evil samurais and Fu Manchus in period costume dramas. After that though, about the only time you ever saw him was on *Hawaii Five-O* or *The Late Movie,* until the martial arts flick craze exploded in the seventies.

Suddenly, Nobuo Wei found himself in great demand again. But this time, he got a piece of the action by forming Snapdragon, his own production company. Through Snapdragon he went on to shoot a long string of low-budget chop-and-kick operas.

These days, though Nobuo usually confined himself to directing and producing, Snapdragon was still doing business at the old stand, which also served as the best-kept secret location within a sixty-mile radius.

Frank had connected with Nobuo Wei shortly after our marriage when he was trying to put together a cheap music video for an impoverished singer/songwriter friend who became famous because of it. Nobuo's barter with Frank had included a significant role in the video, plus Frank was to film his personal last will and testament.

Shot in strictest confidentiality (it was a will, after all) and packed with cryptic Kabuki vignettes, clips from his old movies, sumo wrestling, and an elaborate tea ceremony, this bizarre concoction was the finest work Frank's ever done. He thinks. The truth is, he never even saw so much as a daily, since Nobuo processed and edited the film himself, right there in his own studio facilities at Wei-Side.

Afterward, it was transferred to video cassette, signed and sealed in the presence of witnesses, then deposited with his lawyer, just like any ordinary will.

"I still wish I knew how it came out," Frank lamented now.

"Forget it, darling," I advised. "We'll never see the thing unless he's left us something."

"Hey!" Frank squinted at his watch in the dim overhead light. "It's after ten-fifteen. Who the hell does Barry think he is, anyhow, keeping us standing out here like loxes for twenty minutes! First, his mother gets Henny all worked up about us coming to this thing. So we're here. Then he starves us to death on grapes—and who in L.A. with a functioning artery left in their body eats brie anymore?"

As Frank's temper rose, so did his voice. When he gets like this, I've learned it's best just to let him rave on, so I tuned out. Becoming aware of a tinny, echolike quality in the air, I peered over the metal guard rail that ran around the loft down into the darkened shop, and realized we were the only people left in the building outside the dressing room.

Or were we?

A faint creak and rustling seemed to emanate from the vicinity of the staircase farthest from us, but the loft lights were so dim I couldn't see anything on this level. Then I heard another sound like a stealthy footstep on a metal stair.

Cautiously, I bent further over the rail, straining unsuccessfully to catch a glimpse of who, if anyone, was sneaking down to the shop area. Just as I was about to chalk it up to my imagination, a shadow, elongated to grotesque, house-of-mirrors proportions, slid across the wall, brief and filmy as a vapor, then was gone.

But not before I'd identified those two long things sticking up from the shadow's head like an alien's antennae. Now what in the world was Woo Kazu up to?

Frank had at last run out of steam and realized I wasn't listening. "Ava!" he called. "Hey! Be careful leaning over like that! What are you doing?"

Before I could reply, a piercing scream rang out.

A few seconds later, Barry Lehr, yarmulke askew, burst through the doors and stumbled in our direction. "Frank! Ava! Thank God!" he croaked when he saw us. As we rushed toward him he half-turned, indicating the storage room, and made clumsy gestures for us to go in. "Gotta telephone!" he wheezed, and staggered on.

Apprehensively, Frank and I entered the large, makeshift dressing area. The rickshaw had been abandoned just inside, and I would have stumbled over the bamboo poles where they rested on the cement floor if Frank hadn't caught my elbow in the nick of time.

That crisis averted, we stayed where we were, taking in the scene before us.

Dominating the room was a long, black iron clothes rack, jammed with the evening's bright garments. At the far end of it, models were clustered in various stages of undress, staring into the rosewood sedan chair, which had been parked against the wall.

Cherry Rose, wearing a lacy blue slip over a pelt of goose pimples, stood in the space between the clothes rack and the sedan chair as if rooted to the floor. She'd removed the white paint and now her face showed ashy gray, eyes glazed as a doll's. Unquestionably, it had been she who screamed.

The priceless kimono (on loan from a New York museum) lay where it had fallen around her ankles. I surmised she'd been about to enter the sedan chair, intending to finish disrobing in privacy behind the curtains, but had found the rickshaw driver's designer peasant ensemble crumpled and flung haphazardly across the seat. Definitely no way to treat such expensive threads, much less the human being who had literally been caught dead in that outfit.

It was an experience I can only describe as earthshaking, and as a Californian, I do not use that term lightly. The aftershock came when I recognized the rickshaw driver who'd gone out in style in a sedan chair.

It was Miko.

FIVE

NOBODY PAID the slightest attention to Frank and me, standing there like we'd been caught in a freeze frame, wondering what we should do.

I didn't hear weeping for the pathetically small bundle of couture that had been Miko, but the air pulsated with fear. As if in response to some inaudible signal, everyone turned away and tried to avoid looking at the sedan chair and its lone passenger.

There were a number of large wooden packing crates scattered around the room, which had been upturned to function as tables for makeup and food, as well as providing places to sit.

Davida was perched by herself on the edge of one crate, surrounded by paper napkins, plastic wineglasses, depleted liters of Evian, and recently opened bottles of Chandon Blanc de Noirs California champagne, quickly going flat. The bar, apparently. I remembered she'd mentioned something earlier about getting shots for *Vanity Fair*.

She was staring fixedly at the floor and didn't look up until Barry returned, disheveled and pasty-faced. "The police are on their way," he informed us in a choked voice. "Nobody's to leave this room."

A faint murmur of protest arose, but no one disputed his authority.

While Barry found a robe for Cherry Rose and helped her into it, Frank led me over to a vacant packing crate and we sat down. I was grateful when he put a comforting arm around my shoulders, because all at once, my insides had started to quiver.

A minute later Davida, who seemed to have just become aware of our presence, joined us. "Well, I've covered some pretty odd, strange and curious fashion shows in my day, but nobody ever ended up dead before. Not even at Gaultier's," she added, striving desperately to recapture her usual insouciance. But her eyes were strained and the stuffing appeared to have spilled out of her taut body, leaving it limp as a banana peel.

"Davida, did you know Miko personally?" I asked.

Her face closed. "In a way," she replied evasively.

We chatted desultorily for a moment. No, she hadn't noticed anything unusual, but then she was rushing to get shots of Barry and Cherry Rose together with the Baby Bonsais because the kids' parents were waiting to take them home. After that, the usual glamour stuff.

"Although right at the very beginning, I did snap a quick couple of Miko and Rikka by the rickshaw," Davida acknowledged.

"How did Miko seem?" Frank asked in a troubled voice.

Davida shrugged. "Okay, I guess," she mused, frowning. "I mean, you've got to understand when I'm in a work mode, I'm mainly concentrating on what looks potentially juicy and interesting. Sometimes I'm able to pick up on emotions, but not always.

All I can tell you, the only thing I noticed about Miko was she seemed a little quiet instead of her usual in-your-face attitude. But that's probably because she was tired from the show."

Frank shook his head. "Too weird," he remarked, and lapsed into a preoccupied silence, probably trying to recall everything Miko said to him earlier. That should make for an interesting statement.

"Who's Rikka?" I asked Davida.

In answer, she inclined her head to the right, and I turned my eyes in that direction. "Oh," I said. "Now I recognize her. She used to be on that soap. I can't remember her last name, though."

"Rikka Tring," Davida supplied.

The Dragon Lady was leaning gracefully against the wall, hands thrust casually into the pockets of toffee-colored cashmere pants that matched a turtleneck sweater. She looked even more exotic in ordinary clothes than she had in cheongsams. Her vertical eyes raked across me, then fastened onto Frank like she was having a vision examination and he was the eye chart.

Frank was too distracted to notice, but somebody else did. Guido, seething with unconcealed jealousy, clenched his big fists spasmodically.

Rikka Tring eventually grew bored with Frank's lack of response, treated me to a slitted glare, and began to study her mandarin talons thoughtfully. The other models—there where about ten, I think—had finished dressing and now slumped here and there on the bare concrete like so many melted candles.

Cherry Rose collapsed heavily onto the other end of our packing crate, while Barry, having shed his bogus *kipah,* gazed at her helplessly, running a small, nervous, nail-bitten hand over the sparse remaining growth on his head. Even at a time like this, I couldn't help but notice that, although Frank and Barry were the same age, Frank had certainly worn better.

The Beverly Hills Police Department is but a few short blocks from Bonsai's Rodeo Drive location, and though it seemed much longer, it wasn't more than five minutes before the wail of sirens invaded the depressing silence.

There was definitely something doglike about the way we all immediately tensed and pricked up our ears at the sound, which reminded me of Dimples and Dumpling, home alone in a dark house. We hadn't bothered to bring our portable phone, or I would've rung the neighbors to check on them. Hopefully, I'd be allowed to call from the office.

Barry had gone down to let the cops in, and everybody gazed with apprehension at the double doors as they flapped open to admit Lieutenant Detective Bernard Weinberg.

Weinberg, an energetic, muscular guy of forty-five or so, sported a mustache and lots of mahogany, vaguely seventies hair. He was flanked by two older, tireder men in plainclothes. The senior detective sergeant conveyed a paternal attitude toward his superior, while the face of the younger seemed permanently set in a resentful expression.

Lt. Weinberg thrust out a crumpled *kipah.* "Does this belong to any of you gentlemen?" he inquired, displaying it to the room at large.

Barry's bloodshot eyes focused on the object, and he groped at the back of his head. "Oh. It's mine," he admitted. "I...it probably fell off when I went to call the police-er—you."

Weinberg handed it to Barry, who absently stuffed it into the big pocket of his harem pyjamas and the detective regarded him with a puzzled expression.

Barry, catching the look, turned red and stammered, "I'm not...I mean, it's not...that is, it was only for show tonight...."

"Ah!" Weinberg nodded as if he understood perfectly, and was highly unimpressed with the concept.

A commotion in the hallway outside heralded the arrival of the homicide squad, and the room was suddenly overrun with noise and activity. For the second time tonight, Bonsai was charged with the flashing of cameras. But these particular pictures would be seen by very few.

After the police photographer had taken shots of Miko's body just as it was discovered, Weinberg then instructed two uniformed men to push back the curtains on either side of the sedan chair.

Only then could we see the dark bloodstain that had soaked into the pale green brocade covering the seat. It seemed to have originated from beneath Miko, somewhere around the small of her back.

A frightened gabble filled the air, and Weinberg's amber eyes narrowed. Until this moment, finding Mikko dead had been an almost surreal experience. The sight of her blood immediately translated it into stark, ugly reality.

Instantly, the photographer sprang into action again, whirring and clicking like some demented insect.

When he was done, the two uniformed men returned to lift Miko out of the sedan chair and lower her gently to the floor. The flashing resumed and Cherry Rose squeezed her eyes tightly shut, but most of us couldn't seem to look away. A couple of times I saw Davida's hand stray automatically toward her own cameras, then halt in belated recollection of the circumstances.

Finally, the grisly photo session ended. The coroner's investigator came forward with his entourage and they surrounded Miko's body, screening it from our view.

We seemed to hang suspended in a cocoon. The room was utterly still, except for Barry picking nervously at his cuticles and the low murmur of conversation among the officials.

Presently, the CI straightened up, looked around for Weinberg, and the two spoke inaudibly. When the CI rejoined the group around Miko's body, Weinberg turned to face us.

Surveying the room with an ironic glance that seemed to take in the entire subculture of fashion he said, "Ladies and gentlemen. I'm sure it will come as no shock to any of you—especially not to one or more of you—that a young woman has been murdered here tonight."

He watched us closely as a communal gasp denied his assumption. To have hideous suspicion confirmed as immutable fact is always shocking.

Weinberg went on. "Now. Here is the procedure in cases like this. First, you will at no time leave the room until you have been questioned. Following that, each and every one of you will be searched."

He indicated the fatherly man. "Sergeant Meacham will search the males, and a policewoman will be arriving shortly to conduct a search of the females."

Weinberg's eyes glinted dangerously as an indignant buzz circled the room. "Yes, I know it's a form of violation, and so are the fingerprints we are also going to take. Just remember, while you're feeling sorry for yourselves, that a person who was alive earlier tonight was violated to the point where she is no longer alive.

"And"—again that ironic glance that seemed to absorb so much—"don't let the fact that this murder took place in Beverly Hills lead you to suppose that our investigation will be conducted along the lines of any movie you might have seen."

Somebody gave a nervous titter, which was immediately squelched. Weinberg let a heavy silence linger, then remarked casually, "Pending further investigation by the coroner's office, the cause of death appears to be from internal bleeding as a result of two puncture wounds inflicted to the right lumbar region."

It was unbelievable! At some point soon after the fashion show, Miko had been stabbed twice in the back, and nobody noticed a thing!

But Weinberg wasn't done yet.

"I said that's what *appears* to be the cause of death," he continued in a low growl. "Because her neck's been snapped like a pencil, as well, which doesn't really require a lot of brute strength, believe it or not. No, a little martial arts know-how, plus the element of surprise, and—" The sudden pop of his fingers conjured up a nasty graphic. Weinberg favored us with a grim smile. "Looks like our killer meant to make damn sure he'd finished the job. Or maybe she. No glass ceiling here, folks.

"Meacham! Take that side of the room," he ordered abruptly, waving the fatherly man to the left with a powerful hand. "You take the other side, Forrester," he added, to the bitter-looking type.

Forrester hesitated, obviously preferring the center of the room where Barry, Cherry Rose, Davida, Frank, and I shared the packing crate, and Rikka Tring stood like a jade statute, with Guido hovering around her. Just as obviously, Weinberg was saving us for himself, and directed an anxious rookie to list our names.

Forrester gave us a hungry look, then stalked off to his allotted territory.

"All right!" Weinberg pushed up the sleeves of his herringbone jacket in a gesture that indicated he was ready for action. "I'm going to talk to you one at a time. Beginning with"—he frowned at the list as if the rookie's handwriting was illegible—"Mrs. Lehr."

Barry had visibly relaxed as some of Cherry Rose's exquisite color seeped back into her face. She managed a weak smile at him, then said to Weinberg, "I want Barry with me."

If Weinberg was startled at the strident New York whinny that issued from those perfect geisha lips, he didn't reveal it by so much as a twitch of his mustache. Frank and I exchanged glances that awarded the lieutenant ten points for a poker face. Even we, often as we'd heard it, were still jarred by the phenomenon at times.

Before a discussion could ensue (and I knew it would because Barry has a tendency to wax positively Talmudic on any subject, often supplying three opinions all by himself), I jumped in.

"Lieutenant Weinberg, I know what you said about leaving the room, but may I just make a fast phone call to my neighbor? Our dogs..."

He beamed a benevolent dog lover's look upon me. "What kind of dogs do you have, Miss—er— " He consulted his list again. "I'm sorry, *Mrs.* Bernstein?" He enunciated the "Mrs." in a flattering tone of disappointment.

"Two springer spaniels, Lieutenant," Frank put in, with a knowing grin at Weinberg. He takes it as a personal compliment when other men like me. "I don't dare let my wife answer because you'd have to arrest her for obstructing justice or something, she'd take so long to describe them."

Like he didn't make a total fool of himself over those hounds.

"Black and white, or liver and white?" inquired Weinberg, seeming completely oblivious to Barry furiously grinding his teeth.

"One of each," Frank answered. Any minute he'd be pulling out his wallet to show photos.

Weinberg chuckled. "I had a springer when I was a kid. Liver and white. His name was—"

I cut this delightful interlude short when I noticed that Barry himself was turning liver and white.

"Telephone?" I begged sweetly.

The lieutenant nodded. "Yes, but you'll have to make it fast and—I've got to send someone along with you, Mrs. Bernstein."

He was apologetic but firm, and it gave me a shock.

That I, Ava Bernstein, should have lived to become a murder suspect!

SIX

A UNIFORMED OFFICER escorted me down the hall to Barry's and Cherry Rose's office, once and for all dispelling the myth that Beverly Hills police blues have Gucci stripes running down the sides of their pants legs.

No furniture had been moved into the office yet, but a charcoal and red contraption that looked capable of going into orbit sat on the floor. Surprisingly, the phone wasn't cordless, which meant I had to assume the position so as to enter Lillian Meyers' number, while the cop in generic trousers watched over my shoulder and made a careful note of it. Very cozy.

I almost chuckled when I thought of the earful somebody was sure to get when they called to verify that number and ask questions about Frank and me. The Meyers have a lot to say.

Frank and I met Russ and Lillian Meyers the day we moved into the house next door to theirs, and were arguing about at how much of an angle to nail the mezuzah. The four of us have been so close ever since, our other friends call us "the Riccardos and the Mertzes."

Lil, a small, sleek blonde who was once a standard-issue sit-com bimbo, is now a popular interior designer and set decorator. Her big and woolly husband, Russ, happens to be one of the best directors of photography in Hollywood.

The phone rang several times and I remembered Russ was still in Tahoe on a shoot, and this was Lil's late night in the kitchen of Challah Dolly, the catering service she co-owns. Lil is the only woman I know personally who can approach a stack of filo dough without hyperventilating.

I was about to hang up when I heard her voice in my ear. She sounded slightly out of breath. "Ava!" she exclaimed. "I just came from your house. I was so worried when I drove up and didn't see any lights.

"Thank God you're okay," she added. The Meyers, who incidentally are very spiritual, are always thanking God for something, which is understandable, considering how they met. Their first encounter occurred on the evening Russ literally saved Lil's life.

Among the many jokes about Los Angeles is that everybody here has got a screenplay and a backstory, and Russ and Lil are no exception.

Lil's backstory starts off sounding sadly familiar and trite. Her father is a famous television producer who gave her far too much of his money, and far too little of his time, when she was growing up to be a spoiled, rich, Beverly Hills princess.

Although nepotism opened many doors for her, Lil actually had a valid talent for comedy, and dabbled with surprising success at an acting career between her tabloid blurb escapades featuring wild nightclubbing, madcap limo antics, and drugs. Finally, one of her sprees ended in arrest and she was fired from her hit TV show by none other than her own father.

Right on the heels of that disgrace, her live-in lover moved out of the fabulous Malibu beach house she owned, then immediately moved in with her so-called best friend. When, to add insult to injury, the schmuck sued her for palimony, she decided, with more reason than some, that life wasn't worth living.

One night, she snorted a massive amount of cocaine, washed down a handful of 'ludes with a bottle of vintage champagne, then wandered out onto her own private strip of moonlit beach. Not surprisingly, she doesn't remember anything after that until she opened her eyes to see a huge man straddled across her soaking wet body, bearded mouth covering hers, his big hands pressing her lungs.

He somehow managed to convince the panic-stricken Lil it wasn't rape but mouth-to-mouth resuscitation, then carried her indoors and held her head while she threw up. After that he called a doctor, got her into a flannel nightie and wrapped in a down comforter, then built a blazing fire.

Lil's mysterious rescuer had an even more mysterious tale to tell.

He was a cinematographer-turned-rabbinical student who had been preparing for his final thesis. His subject was the Prophecies of Daniel as seen in the light of twentieth-century events, specifically concerning the Jewish people and the nation of Israel.

This project had required much research into ancient Hebrew manuscripts as well as the theories of modern-day students of biblical prophecy, and somewhere along the line, without realizing quite how it happened, Russ had vaulted from laid-back California Reformed straight to ardent Messianic, without even touching down at Conservative.

Inevitably, emotions, doubts, and fears began to assail his new convictions, and it was to work through the dilemma he found himself in that Russ rented an isolated house in Malibu to slug it out with *YAWEH*. After much agonizing, he had fallen back on the venerable Jewish tradition of demanding that God give him a Sign.

Almost instantly, he found himself descending the steps leading from his deck down to the beach. While totally aware of his actions, he was without the slightest logical explanation for them.

When he'd gone about a mile, he saw a tiny figure stumbling across the sand, pale moon lighting her curly hair like a halo.

The surf had been exceptionally high that night and to his horror, she was swept off a rock and into the sea before his very eyes.

Russ rescued Lillian, fell in love with her, returned to films, and they were married in a hot air balloon by a Messianic rabbi with a yarmulke anchored to the top of his crash helmet with Lil's nail glue.

With skeptics like Frank and me living next door to true believers like the Meyers, there's bound to be some fairly interesting and rather loud theological fireworks going off periodically, not to mention the creative sparks that naturally fly between a producer/director, writer, DP, and actress/set decorator/caterer who work together whenever possible because we all think each of the others is the greatest.

Now Lil listened intently while I gave her a brief synopsis of what had happened at Bonsai and finished with, "And so will you be a darling and see if Dimples and Dumpling—?"

Lil interrupted calmly. "When I went over, they were each eating one of your pink satin slippers so I gave them some of those cheese things instead. And in a minute, I'm going to take them for a moonlight stroll."

"Bless you, my child," I told her. "How are my baby girls?"

She giggled. "They hate you! They want to come live with us."

The cop who'd escorted me to the phone tapped my shoulder and cleared his throat portentously, cutting short Lil's description of the dog's guilty expressions when she'd caught them dining on my new Natori slippers.

Back in the storeroom, the scene had shifted slightly during my absence.

Looking sullen and remote, Davida now stood propped against the wall, cameras and leather satchel heaped in a pile at her feet; Weinberg was huddled in a corner with Barry and Cherry Rose; and Rikka Tring had claimed the Lehrs' spot on our packing case, while Guido glowered murderously at Frank, who remained innocently oblivious.

Without apology to Rikka, I wedged myself into the narrow gap she'd left between herself and Frank. "The babies are in capable Meyers' hands," I reported in a whisper.

Frank expressed his relief then muttered, "Why is Weinberg keeping us in here with the body? And don't they always question witnesses separately? This way, you can't help overhearing what somebody else says. I can see this getting nerve-racking before long."

I shrugged. "Well, he's the boss and I guess he can do it however he likes. Maybe that's just what he wants—somebody's nerves to start screaming bloody murder."

"No talking!" Forrester barked at us suddenly from across the room.

Frank waited until Forrester's attention was diverted elsewhere, then, barely moving his lips he said, "Do you realize I was probably the last non-Bonsai person to speak to Miko?"

I shrank closer to him as two men in white wheeled by a stretcher, its flat surface scarcely rippled by the tiny, blanket-covered form it bore. The room itself seemed to breathe a sigh of relief when they were gone.

Frank's words had set me to thinking. I knew somebody else who'd spoken to Miko not long before she'd cornered Frank, the same somebody whose shadow I was almost positive I'd seen sneaking downstairs just before Cherry Rose screamed. A mere shadow, however, was not evidence, and I couldn't decide whether to mention it to Weinberg or not.

Something else had altered while I was telephoning to Lil. At the far end of the room a screen of sorts had been rigged by tacking a couple of the large, unbleached muslin sheets used to protect the clothing from dust, to the fiberboard ceiling. They hung awkwardly, but provided adequate privacy for the physical search.

Sergeant Meacham, with a skill honed over many years, made short work of his assignment. Frank took his turn like a trooper and after a tall, dark-haired boy emerged, fiery-red of face, Barry was the only man left who hadn't been searched.

Meacham motioned with his pipe stem to a bouncy woman in

uniform who took over his post at the sheets. Before I could look away, she caught my eye and summoned me to approach.

It wasn't a strip search; there are limits, after all, to where one can conceal a presumably bloodstained knife upon one's body—but it was sufficiently humiliating. The only person who didn't seem fazed by the procedure was Rikka Tring. She approached the partition with slithery grace, observed by a passel of Beverly Hills' Finest who were not bothering to hide their willingness to conduct the operation themselves.

Meacham and Forrester had quickly weeded out the irrelevant witnesses, who faded thankfully away as soon as they were dismissed and let out the front door by the uniformed cop guarding it. Only two models beside Rikka Tring remained behind, waiting to give their statements.

Meanwhile, Frank was right. Barry and Cherry Rose's joint narrative was audible to anyone who cared to listen.

The gist of it was that after the Grand Finale, led by the four eunuchs bearing the sedan chair containing Barry and Cherry Rose, with Miko and Rikka's rickshaw bringing up the rear, everyone had crowded into the storeroom.

Cherry Rose then rounded up the kids to pose for a few fast pictures with herself and Barry, then marched them through the side door that opened onto a short passageway leading to the fire exit, where they were distributed among their respective parents. The parents themselves never entered the building again at any time after seeing the show, but simply came around back, collected their little ones, and returned to their cars via the fire stairs, which led down to the Bonsai parking lot. These logistics had all been worked out beforehand.

It was unnecessary for the kids to change because they'd been awarded their individual outfits by Barry—an act of largesse that was really the only practical thing to do since the clothing had already been specifically altered to fit each child. Additionally it was the cheapest, most effective advertising possible for Baby Bonsai, because the well-heeled parents would undoubtedly flaunt the goods before other well-heeled parents.

I gathered the possibility that someone could've entered unnoticed through the fire exit was quickly eliminated by previous statements from two models who'd helped Cherry Rose with the children. They both witnessed Calvin, the security guard, unlocking it. After they'd matched up the fledglings and their families, a process which took less than ten minutes, they'd heard Calvin lock the door behind him. Since he was going off duty, he'd also exited down the fire escape because his car was parked in the Bonsai lot. One of the models had even tested the door, just to make certain it was secure.

They didn't think anyone else left or reentered through that door during the time it was open, but the police were trying to contact Calvin, who had vanished Cinderella-like into the night when his work was done, to corroborate.

And of course, back inside the storage dressing room, pandemonium reigned, as models scrambled to undress, make sure what they'd worn was properly hung by either themselves or Guido, and fight through the crowd to get to their street clothes, which hung on a section of the rack designated specifically for that purpose.

Privacy? Kiss it good-bye. One of the shyer models wanted to use the sedan chair as a dressing room, but was informed that privilege was reserved exclusively for Cherry Rose.

Both Cherry Rose and Barry claimed they never saw Miko after the fashion show since they were heading the procession, while the rickshaw was at the end—until Cherry Rose parted the velvet curtains of the sedan chair and found her lying dead inside.

Cherry Rose's voice grew harsh and loud as she recounted the horror of that discovery to Weinberg, who made her repeat the sequence of her movements several times, ignoring Barry's protests.

Weinberg was not being gratuitously sadistic, as Barry charged. Cherry Rose's story was vital, for it narrowed the time frame of Miko's death and concealment in the sedan chair down to the few minutes when she was last seen alive—shortly after Rikka pulled the rickshaw with Miko as passenger into the storeroom—to when Cherry Rose returned to the dressing area after getting the kids off.

When he questioned her delay of several minutes in following the other two models, Cherry Rose retorted, "I stopped in the bathroom to get all that paint off my face, among other more personal things. I had a big jar of Noxema ready by the sink, because Clown White makes me break out and I didn't want to wear it one second longer that I had to."

"Approximately what time was that, Mrs. Lehr?" asked Weinberg.

Cherry Rose shook her head. "I can't say, exactly. I do know it was about ten o'clock when we got the kids outside. And since their parents were already waiting for them, I'm sure it didn't take more than ten minutes. So right after that."

Weinberg nodded. "And then?"

Cherry Rose sighed dismally. "I came out here and got Perla"— she indicated one of the models, a sultry Latina with slicked-back hair and flashing eyes—"to help me undo the obi, which took a couple of minutes, probably. I was going to finish dressing inside the sedan chair, but..." Her voice trailed off.

Weinberg nodded again. "So you discovered Miko Hayashi's body at ten-fifteen?"

She shrugged. "I guess."

If Frank's watch was correct, it would've been more like ten-seventeen, because he had first noticed how long we'd been waiting for Barry to let us into the dressing room at ten-fifteen, and Cherry Rose's scream erupted shortly afterward.

"Okay, I think I understand the sequence pretty well," Weinberg told Cherry Rose. "And what were you doing all this time?" he suddenly asked Barry.

Caught off guard, Barry sputtered, "Why—uh...I was all over the place, Lieutenant. You know, congratulating everybody on the show, making sure none of the clothes were left lying around or had fallen off the hangers onto the floor. Like that."

"So you can't confirm your wife's story," Weinberg remarked.

Barry scowled. "Now see here, Lieutenant—"

"Yes or no?" Weinberg interrupted.

"No, not really," Barry admitted reluctantly, "but—"

"And you never saw or spoke to Miss Hayashi subsequent to your return to the dressing room?"

"I did not!" Barry snapped.

"Miss Hayashi wasn't one of the people you thought it necessary to congratulate on a show well done, then. Thank you, Mr. Lehr," Weinberg said dismissively before Barry could remonstrate, then addressed Cherry Rose.

"One more thing, Mrs. Lehr. You say you removed your makeup in the bathroom with Kleenex and Noxema?"

Cherry Rose gave a puzzled nod, and he went on. "So there should be ample evidence to that effect?"

"Well, the wastebasket's full of mushy Kleenex, if that's what you mean."

"Forrester, go check out the bathroom," Weinberg ordered, then turned back to Barry and Cherry Rose. "Mr. and Mrs. Lehr, thank you for your cooperation thus far. However, you will be required to make an official statement sometime within the next forty-eight hours. Do you understand?"

Irritably, Barry acknowledged they understood.

Weinberg was on the verge of releasing the Lehrs when Forrester returned. "Lieutenant! The bathroom door's locked, and there has been no response to repeated requests to open!" he announced, his nostrils twitching with feral anticipation.

Barry jumped up. "But you can't lock it from the outside without a key and I've got the only one. That means somebody's locked it from the inside, because I didn't use that key tonight."

Weinberg was already on his feet. "Do you have the key on your person, sir?" he demanded.

"Right here," Barry said, pulling a brass ring from his pyjama pocket. "This is every key to the shop. There's only one other set, which is what the security guards used, because we haven't had time to make multiple copies." He flipped along the ring and singled out a key. "Here."

Putting Meacham in charge, Weinberg and Forrester left the

room through a side door which I assumed led to the back hall-way.

A few minutes later, Weinberg returned, an unreadable expression on his face. "Mr. Lehr, are you positive that ring of keys was in your possession at all times this evening?"

Barry looked alarmed. "Of course I'm positive. Why? What's going on?" Weinberg didn't answer.

When Forrester reappeared, he was carrying a red metal wastepaper basket by its rim, protected from his fingerprints by a handkerchief. With barely suppressed excitement, he tilted the wastebasket so we could all see inside.

As Cherry Rose had stated, the can was about three-fourths full of scrunched-up Kleenex, gooey smears of lipstick, eyeshadow, and mascara all bearing silent witness to her story.

Except for the wad right on top, which seemed to be screaming with bloodstains.

SEVEN

WHILE THE FORENSICS TEAM dashed for the bathroom, Weinberg, who in car terms had portrayed himself as a Volvo—substantial, reliable and proceeding at a stately pace toward his goal—now revealed there was a powerful Porsche engine lurking beneath the utilitarian hood.

After ordering Barry and Cherry Rose to be searched, he questioned Davida, Rikka, and Guido in rapid succession.

Davida, who also denied seeing Miko after taking a couple of shots of her with Rikka, basically confirmed what everybody else had already said about the time frame. She was royally pissed when Weinberg confiscated the film from the camera she'd used in here after the show, but had to be satisfied with his assurances she'd receive an entire set of prints plus the negatives back—that is, if they didn't turn out to be evidence.

There was one lighter moment when, while gathering up her paraphernalia, Davida directed a few choice Hebrew phrases at Weinberg. To her consternation, he shot back a few of his own. A slight smile twitched beneath his mustache as he watched her stomp out in a huff.

Next, Rikka Tring, who identified herself as a model and an actress, asserted she hadn't seen or spoken to Miko after Davida took their pictures together. She had immediately started getting dressed, and didn't notice where Miko went, she said, crossing long cashmere legs and twirling a slender ankle, causing one of the black satin mules to dangle lazily from her toes.

Weinberg was appreciative, but invulnerable to such wiles. Rikka gazed meltingly up at him from beneath her bangs as he told her formally she could go, but to remain available.

Then came Guido's turn. As he and Rikka passed he hesitated, seeming about to speak, but she snarled something at him out of the corner of her mouth and kept going.

Guido momentarily appeared to dwindle, as if he'd been an annoying dangling thread Rikka had simply snipped off and let drop to the floor, but his macho quickly reasserted itself. With a bit of a swagger, he continued across the large room to the two packing cases now serving as Weinberg's office.

Cherry Rose observed Rikka Tring's approach to where she and Barry were standing, with an enigmatic expression. When Rikka reached them, she automatically glanced over at Frank and tossed her inky hair, but her real attention was on Barry.

"Who's going to manage the store now, Barry?" she demanded bluntly.

Barry, who'd clearly not considered Miko's death in terms of an employee shortage, gaped at her, then mumbled, "I can't believe you're asking me this right now."

But even as he protested, I could almost hear his brain clicking. Miko was dead, murdered—a terrible thing. But every bit as terrible for the Lehrs was the possibility of losing several million bucks—not to mention their hot reputation—if Bonsai was uprooted before it even got started. It was going to take his and Cherry Rose's every waking moment and all of their energy, plus a clever PR campaign (hmm, I could almost smell that mortgage payment) to, let's face it, make Miko's murder work for Bonsai rather than against it.

Meanwhile, there was still the actual business to run, which required a competent manager who'd be able to focus completely on operations and the bottom line. There was simply no time to launch an executive headhunt. Barry and Cherry Rose engaged in a silent struggle over the obvious, immediate solution, then surrendered.

"Perhaps you'd like to be manager, Rikka?" Cherry Rose inquired dryly.

Rikka lowered her slanted eyelids in false gratitude, which looked like a quick reverse tug on the vertical blinds. "Thank you, Cherry Rose," she murmured throatily. "I will begin on Monday morning at ten o'clock."

She started to sashay out the doors, but Cherry Rose's Manhattan honk stopped her in mid-stride. "Wrong, Rikka! You will begin *tomorrow* morning, at *eight* o'clock. If the police even allow us back in here that soon."

Rikka swung in protest toward Barry, who wisely kept his mouth shut while Cherry Rose continued to lay down the law. "There's a lot to be done before Monday, and I damn well don't intend to do it by myself."

"Whatever." Rikka lifted a scornful shoulder. "You know where to reach me," she added with peculiar emphasis and another twist of the blinds, then sauntered through the double doors, which the police had propped open, without even a backward glance for her worshipful Guido.

"Frank!" Barry hissed furtively, keeping a lookout for Meacham or Forrester. "We want you and Ava to have a late dinner with us when we get out of here."

Frank raised inquiring brows at me and I shrugged, indicating it was his call. As bizarre as it was to imagine they wanted to discuss advertising at a time like this, with Barry you never knew. At any rate, we were naturally consumed with curiosity.

"C.R. and I know a fantastic new Mexican place," Barry added, clinching it. Obviously, he was well acquainted with one of Frank's major weaknesses.

"Please come, Ava," Cherry Rose whispered, adjusting the hem of the plain, longish dress of golden raw silk she'd changed into.

"Okay. But we probably won't be finished until after midnight," Frank warned, pointing to his watch.

"I don't see why," Barry countered. "You guys just stumbled into this by accident."

"Even so, we know the chef," Cherry Rose assured us, like the bicoastal foodie she was.

"More importantly, the chef knows us," said Barry complacently.

EIGHT

As BEFITTED THE MOST unimportant witnesses, Frank and I were the last to face Lieutenant Weinberg.

Innocent lamb that I was, I suddenly felt guilty and confused because I had overheard Weinberg ask every single witness if there'd been anyone else in this room not connected with the show. Without exception, they'd all answered no. Which meant either everybody was lying, or my eyes were playing tricks on me and I hadn't seen Woo Kazu's shadow on the wall, after all.

Even in such a flashy crowd, Woo would've stood out and it's highly unlikely a famous designer could've passed unnoticed among a bunch of freelance models who always need work. Besides, there was no way to exit the storeroom except down the fire escape, which according to all witnesses he did not, or through the swinging doors, which he couldn't have without Frank and me seeing him in the flesh.

Or else...Woo really had been here, only not in the storeroom! But where? And why? The floor plan was simply Barry's empty office at one end, a smaller empty office at the other, with the storeroom and that badly lit ladies' I'd visited between. I'd have to ask Cherry Rose why they'd put the female facilities upstairs where it was less convenient, but had the men's downstairs. Did it help prevent shoplifting?

Anyway, back to my problem. What, if anything, had I actually seen? Maybe it was Woo's shadow, but maybe it wasn't his, or anybody else's for the matter. Assuming Weinberg didn't laugh in my face if I mentioned such a sighting, was it fair to involve Woo Kazu at this point? I thought not. My conscience only nibbled at me briefly for this decision before subsiding.

Weinberg's first question to us was completely unexpected. "How are the dogs?"

"Angry, but in good hands," Frank informed him with a grin.

"And I'm out another pair of slippers," I remembered.

To our surprise, Weinberg threw back his head and laughed hugely. "Our springer, Desmond, was also very fond of slippers," he explained. "My mother always used to buy Macy's cheapest for everybody in the family."

Of course that was the signal for an exchange of what-side-of-town-do-you-know? between two former New Yorkers. As one Angelino to another, Meacham gave me a paternal smile of commiseration.

Frank was exclaiming, "Sure, I remember Bonnie Nustein! Did she ever marry Jake what's-his-name?"

"For a while," Weinberg said quietly. "Then she married me for a while. Our divorce should be final next month."

"I'm sorry," Frank murmured, feeling awkward.

Without warning, Weinberg shifted into cop mode.

Why were we there tonight?

For old times' sake. (Requiring an explanation of Henny, Sonia and Morrie, Barry and Frank in high school.)

How did we happen to be at the scene of the crime?

Barry had invited us backstage after the show, plus we hoped he'd hire us to do his commercials. (Requiring an explanation of B-Pix.)

Our relationship to the Deceased? "None," I assured him confidently. "We never laid eyes on her before tonight."

Frank looked uncomfortable. "Wait, Ava. That's not exactly true." He addressed Weinberg. "Miko was, uh, talking to me before my wife joined us. And she reminded me she had worked on a job we shot a few months ago."

"What job?" Weinberg and I demanded simultaneously.

"Nobuo Wei's," Frank replied. "She said she did some of the Kabuki wardrobe and makeup."

I still didn't remember Miko, but then Wei had hired the crew himself. (Requiring an explanation of Nobuo Wei's video will.) Weinberg remarked that the actor had always been one of his favorites.

"What exactly did Miss Hayashi say to you tonight?" Weinberg inquired. "Did she seem to be fearful or anxious?"

Frank shook his head. "Not that I noticed. Basically, we discussed our company creating a couple of Bonsai commercials, and she said she'd set up a lunch meeting tomorrow with Barry." The tips of his ears reddened. "And then she propositioned me," he muttered. "Fortunately, Ava showed up and Miko left in a hurry."

Weinberg confirmed our address and telephone numbers, and told us we needed his permission to leave town. "Sorry about that," he said, "but you guys just happened to be at the wrong place at the wrong time." I suppressed a guilty wince when he added, "You never know. There might be something you saw or heard without realizing it that could turn out to be vital."

Outside, we found Barry in a snit because Weinberg had not only confiscated the designs that were modeled by the adults in

the show, but was also going to contact all the parents of the priv-
ileged youngsters who'd worn theirs home.

"Evidence, he says!" fumed Barry. "He thinks there could be
bloodstains where somebody concealed the weapon!" He threw up
his nail-bitten hands to the unjust night sky. "As if anybody would
plant a knife on a little kid!"

Nobody felt particularly compelled to point out that anyone
who would commit murder was likely to stoop to just about anything else. Besides, we knew his anger rose from a fear of being
made to look bad in front of his customers.

As we walked toward our cars, Barry subsided and gave us a
curious glance. "What the hell took you so long?"

"Because we had to wait for Weinberg to finish with your
goony friend Guido," Frank retorted. "If I hadn't been starving to
death, I could've taken a refreshing nap."

Cherry Rose remarked absently that she guessed they always
spent more time with the next-of-kin.

"Next-of-kin?" I echoed. "Don't tell me they're—"

"Brother and sister," Barry finished.

"Half!" Cherry Rose corrected him sharply.

Frank protested. "But, he doesn't look..."

"Doesn't look what, Frank?" Cherry Rose challenged, with the
ghost of her old playfulness.

"He really doesn't look Japanese, so don't act like some little
PC prig, which we all know you're not, Cherry Rose," I said. "For
starters, how do you explain that chest hair?"

"Same mother, different fathers," Cherry Rose answered, embarrassed for some reason I couldn't imagine, while Barry seemed to be
struggling to conceal the first smile he'd had since the fashion show.

Intrigue with the juicier aspects of Guido's genealogy faded in
relation to the immediate need for food. Barry instructed us to follow their car, and Frank laughed.

"Maybe you'd better follow us, Barry. We're not the ones who
live in Puerto Rico and New York."

I paused in the act of getting into the car. "Speaking of New
York, Barry. It turns out Frank knows Weinberg's future ex-wife."

"Remember Bonnie Nustein, Barry?" asked Frank.

"Bonnie? No kidding!" Barry exclaimed, in a flash of fond re-
membrance of golden high school days when the world was a few
years younger, a lot less convoluted, and murder never happened
to people you knew.

NINE

THE DISTANCE BETWEEN Bonsaii's Rodeo Drive address and Beverly Glen wasn't far, but the Saturday night traffic made it slow
going.

Frank and I used the time attempting to reduce the insane mess
we suddenly found ourselves in, to something relatively manage-
able. From force of habit, we approached this the same as we
would a challenging work situation.

By the overhead light, I jotted down a rough timetable on the
pad Frank keeps on the dashboard to note the license plates of offensive drivers.

9:45	Fashion show ends.
9:45-9:50	Bonsai people go upstairs and into dressing room; Rikka drops rickshaw right inside doors; she and Mikko are last ones in except Davida.
9:51	Davida immediately begins taking pics of Rikka and Miko posed with rickshaw; starts snapping Barry, Cherry Rose and kids about one minute later.
Landing:	
9:54-9:55	Fashion groupies turned away by Guido; also Frank and Ava.
9:59	Security guard Calvin comes upstairs to Frank and Ava re: not locking front door; enters dressing room.
10:00-10:10	Cherry Rose, two models, Calvin, take kids down hallway to fire escape to meet parents.

10:11   Calvin locks door behind him and with the only other known set of Bonsai keys and leaves by fire escape to parking lot.

10:12   Cherry Rose goes to employee bathroom and removes makeup.

10:15   Frank notices time; Ava thinks she hears somebody going down far staircase; sees Woo's shadow?

10:16   Cherry Rose asks Perla to help her undo obi.

10:17   Cherry Rose starts to enter sedan chair, sees Miko, screams.

Though this was fairly accurate, it was by no means perfect and might well prove meaningless in the end, because while the police were collecting evidence from the staff bathroom, the diligent Forrester had discovered a way to leave it when locked from the inside.

The shelves of the large linen closet, not yet stacked with cleaning supplies and toilet paper, were found to be attached to one side of a door which had never been sealed. This door opened into another linen closet with the identical shelf/door treatment, which in turn opened into the public women's restroom accessed from the landing.

Barry, Cherry Rose, and Guido all insisted they were unaware of this rather unique remodeling feature. Then one of the younger cops, a studley blond guy with incredible pecs, told Weinberg this building was formerly a very hot gym, of which he had been a member until it went bust. The two connecting baths, he said, used to be his and hers saunas.

He continued to wax nostalgic about the running track—now the loft—which originally went all the way around the building, the rare European equipment, the stylish workout wear sold exclusively in the downstairs boutique and nowhere else, until Weinberg managed to cut him off.

At least the discovery of the connecting door solved the problem of how someone could've left the building without using the fire escape or being seen by anyone in the storeroom, but it created several more for Weinberg. Now, instead of having a short list of suspects, it was fairly wide open again, though the time frame still applied.

Barry and Cherry Rose had to be breathing a lot easier though, because after the gym closed, the premises were remodeled to suit the next tenant, which soon followed in the bankrupt footsteps of its predecessor. The Lehrs could prove they'd leased the building "as is," seeing no need to renovate beyond the current relatively minor cosmetic flourishes. So it was quite conceivable they'd known nothing about those back-to-back restrooms, as they claimed.

Also, Cherry Rose's story was verified by the last two models to be questioned. Perla confirmed she'd seen Cherry Rose come out of the bathroom with her makeup off, just prior to her request for assistance in unwinding the obi.

The other said he'd noticed Perla helping Cherry Rose right before he tried to get into the bathroom and found the door locked.

My conscience started to prod me again. This new factor meant Woo Kazu was back in the running, always assuming he knew the riddle of the doors. Except nobody inside the storeroom acknowledged seeing him, or anyone else not directly involved with the fashion show except Davida.

Although...if Woo (or some other person) could've gotten out of the storeroom without being seen, didn't that also mean they could've gotten into the storeroom with equal invisibility?

Frank was unaware of the note I'd scribbled on our timetable about maybe seeing Woo's shadow, and I decided to tell him about it. But just then the traffic cleared and we were turning north onto Beverly Glen. Since we'd be at the restaurant before I could finish explaining, I put it on hold.

Pintoz was one of those places that every time Frank and I drove past, we would say it looked interesting and we should try it, but so far never had.

The restaurant was set well back from the busy street behind a low stone wall, in a pink stucco hacienda with a red tile roof which had once been a private home. As we angled left onto the circular driveway, Frank surmised the owners had been able to convert it for commercial use because of the same zoning which allowed the neighborhood market to be built just around the bend.

Barry and Cherry Rose pulled up behind us in their rented

Range Rover, full of assurances they'd phoned from the car and our arrival was eagerly awaited.

The first clue as to what lay ahead was the nine-by-twelve-foot replica of the Wailing Wall in the courtyard. A sign in English, Spanish, and Hebrew invited patrons to write out their prayer requests and place them between the authentic Holy Land stones before entering the dining room.

Matter-of-factly, the Lehrs paused to do just that, using tablets and ballpoints attached by chains at intervals along the wall. Frank and I followed their example, but I found it difficult to decide what to ask for.

Much as I'd like to believe that world peace is at the forefront of my consciousness, in all honesty I must confess I'm more concerned about cellulite. Was it selfish to petition for thinner thighs, fuller lips, and an indefinite postponement of that impending triceps crisis? How many requests were allowed per person? Surely God didn't limit you to three, like Aladdin's genie.

"Well, now we definitely know where to bring Russ for his birthday!" Frank chuckled, as we wedged our folded papers among the other slips fluttering in the night breeze. I didn't have to ask what his said. More than anything else, Frank wanted to direct something besides commercials and music videos.

We followed Barry and Cherry Rose around the Wall, past a fountain depicting Moses holding the rock from which streams of water gushed forth for our recalcitrant ancestors in the wilderness, into the tile and stucco interior of Pintoz.

I can truthfully say, even in this city of my birth where excess is the norm, I'd never seen anything quite like it.

The walls were painted with murals of Middle Eastern scenes—white stone houses clinging to terraced hillsides, olive groves, vineyards, palm trees, sheep, camels, and moonlight on the Sea of Galilee—all done with a distinctly Latin flair.

Stained-glass windows, angels, Stars of David, Spanish communion cups, crucifixes, tallit, mezuzahs, and much, much more, mingled ecumenically on the shelves of tall open pine hutches adorned with Mexican religious carvings.

Burning votives in a wrought-iron stand flickered shadows on another case filled entirely with candles for sale—yorzheit, altar, and raffia-tied bundles of slim tapers labeled as being made from pure olive oil by a Greek Orthodox settlement near Mobile, Alabama.

Frank nudged me to point out a wall where an enormous velvet painting of *The Last Supper* brushed its fringes across the top of a charcoal portrait of Golda Meir.

It was as if we'd wandered into a Judeo-Christian Hard Rock Cafe.

The piped-in music was harder to define, but only in the sense of whether it was Israeli being played by a salsa band, or just the reverse.

We watched as Barry and Cherry Rose were swept into the embrace of a large, swarthy man with a ponytail and payos.

"Frank and Ava, meet our friend Yossi Tozer," Barry said.

"Delighted," Yossi murmured in that strangely musky voice bestowed upon some Israeli men, his bushy mustache tickling my knuckles as he kissed my hand. I was just thinking, hey, he'd be great for Davida, when a tall, slender woman dressed in red, with long black hair and Goyaesque features, appeared beside our host.

Yossi grinned fatuously as she twined one arm possessively around his, while the other reached out to shake hands with the Lehrs. Yossi introduced her to Frank and me as his beautiful wife, Maria. So much for the Davida idea.

After insisting they were only too pleased to accommodate their dear friends, Yossi went off to his kitchen to chef, while Maria led us to one of the tables with bases of plaster cast to resemble boulders, topped by rounds of stainless steel to match the chairs.

"Boy, I'm starved!" Frank announced to Maria. "Could we see some menus right away, please?"

Maria frowned. "There is no need," she said reproachfully, then vanished into the shadows of a Gothic altar.

Frank was bewildered. "What'd I say, what'd I say?" he demanded.

Barry shook his head at Frank's obtuseness. "Frank, Yossi is the one who's going to decide on the menu. Don't you get it? He's cooking a dinner especially for us. *Himself!*"

"Himself," Cherry Rose echoed in reverent, foodie tones. Any minute now they'd be genuflecting.

We might've guessed the Lehrs' concept of a Mexican restaurant would differ radically from ours. Just how radically, we discovered when the corn chips and guacamole we were craving arrived in the form of crisp little toasted triangles of Pintoz' unique chickpea and stone-ground corn pita bread, served with jalapeno hummus. Nachos were more pita points topped with a blend of melted Monterey Jack and feta cheeses, with siftings of cayenne and cumin.

The Holy Frijoles, which augmented the usual pinto beans with chickpeas and lentils, were deliciously startling, but a tray of deceptively ordinary-looking burritos, quesadillas, enchiladas, shwarma, dolmas, and falafel billed as Mexaraeli Manna, sent us into total tongue shock. For a moment there, I felt like I was on the verge of Divine Revelation.

A platter of charred veggies (which the Lehrs promised had been grilled over imported Hawaiian kiawe wood and not passé mesquite) was plunked down on our table by a sullen Hispanic waiter whose nametag identified him as Jesus.

Frank grinned. "Well, it isn't every restaurant where you'll find Jesus, Yossi, and Maria at your beck and call."

Barry, unwilling to be diverted from the roasted ear of corn he was gnawing, didn't get it, but Cherry Rose snorted with laughter.

While Barry and Frank quizzed each other on the whereabouts of old neighborhood cronies, Cherry Rose and I discussed the pluses and minuses of androgynous fashion. Of course, the only truly important plus was the dollar sign.

"Because," Cherry Rose explained, "the people we design for have a lot of money to spend on clothes, but they're not into tradition. No, they go out a great deal, specifically to see and be seen, and they want to make a bold, definite statement of identity with their clothing."

This struck me as hilarious. "C'mon, C.R. A definite statement of identity through androgynous garments! What are they saying? 'Hey, look at me folks! I am definitely stating I am neither male nor female.'"

Cherry Rose chuckled but insisted, "It makes a crazy kind of sense, though, Ava. Because so many people—even successful people with lots of money—don't know who they are, so they find their identity and glamour in wearing the same clothes as a certain group."

I considered. "I remember my father saying that during World War II a lot of young guys enlisted, not even waiting to get drafted, because the pictures of other young men in uniform looked so glamorous. The idea was, the uniform would make them glamorous, as well."

"Ava, you've just put your finger on the exact element that propels every successful fashion trend," Cherry Rose informed me, spooning up the last of her flan, the only thing at Pintoz that was actually what it appeared to be.

Over Turkish coffee in lieu of espresso, she and I wondered why nobody seemed interested in designing really hip clothes for aging baby boomers who, despite spartan nutrition plans and religious workouts were losing the battle with gravity, but still wanted to look good when they showed some skin.

I recalled years back reading a quote from Bob Mackie, who'd raved about Cher having the most beautiful armpits in the world and how he'd designed all her costumes around them.

"In my opinion, the real challenge would be to create something bold and bare for women whose armpits could not tolerate close scrutiny," I declared. "I think Edith Head was probably the only designer on earth who knew how to camouflage a less than appetizing upper arm without shrouding it in six yards of fabric. But she obviously died without passing her mantle to someone else."

Cherry Rose agreed. "Triceps and thighs, the terrible twosome." Then lapsed into thoughtful silence.

Frank and Barry's conversation had run out of steam as well. Frank caught my eye and made slight movements with his head toward the door. Either we had been wrong about them having a motive for dragging us along to their midnight supper, or they'd since changed their minds. In any case, my reflection in the stainless steel tabletop (presumably distorted) made the lines around my mouth, always more pronounced when I'm tired, look like the San Andreas Fault.

The sense of relief I felt at managing to get through this dinner without discussing Miko's murder turned out to be premature. Just as Frank and I were preparing to make parting comments, Cherry Rose suddenly said:

"Listen, you two. What happened back at Bonsai tonight is a lot more complicated than you could possibly imagine."

Frank darted an alarmed glance at me. "How so?" he inquired cautiously.

"Because there's something very crucial C.R. didn't tell the police," Barry sighed. "You see, Miko Hayashi was her first cousin."

"And you're telling it to us instead because...?" Frank prompted.

Cherry Rose intervened. "Let me explain, Barry. It's like this, guys. Miko is...was...the daughter of my dad's younger brother who left Toshiko—that's Miko's mother—soon after their daughter was born. Miko used 'Hayashi' because it was her mother's maiden name."

"So where does Guido come in, then?" I asked.

Cherry Rose colored slightly. "Oh, it's all so silly! Guido is the son of Toshi...and my mother's brother-in-law, Vitello."

"Vitello!" Frank and I chorused in amazement.

Frank demanded, "You mean the big bald man with the little mustache and—"

"The hairy chest!" I concluded. I must confess to a purely aesthetic fascination with Vitello's chest, ever since he took off his shirt to play bocci at a Huwei/Lehr/DiMotta picnic one hot July the Fourth at Sonia and Morrie's summer place in Long Beach.

"Ah, that explains Guido's chest..." I murmured.

"But I thought he was married to that, um, rather large lady." Frank was starting to sound whiney.

"Dear Aunt Octavia," Cherry Rose drawled. "Yes, he is. For better or worse. But look. You've been to a couple of our family things. You know how crazy they can get."

"Only this particular craziness was before the Jews ever got into the act," Barry interjected, with an unexpected spark of humor.

A faint smile flickered across Cherry Rose's face as she continued. "Here's what happened that fateful day. Our family and Toshiko had never hit it off, for a lot of reasons. But like all Italians, mama thought we should stick together, especially after my uncle bailed out on her. Somehow, she managed to persuade Toshiko to come to a party at our house.

"Aunt Octavia wasn't feeling well, so she stayed home. Since Uncle Vitello was alone, he was assigned to make Toshiko feel welcome. She was very old-line Japanese and insular, you know—hardly even spoke English.

"Well, Uncle Vitello kept pouring the wine, to show Italian hospitality, and Toshiko kept drinking it, to show Japanese courtesy. I'm sure Uncle Vitello didn't start off with a seduction in mind. But when a healthy Italian man has been ordered to entertain a beautiful girl who can't even carry on a conversation, the least he can do is get drunk.

"However, Toshiko wasn't used to drinking anything at all. The wine hit her like an aphrodisiac, and one thing led to another. And finally, to Guido!"

The story had a certain dark streak of humor, which quickly faded in light of the fact that Toshiko had eventually ended up in a mental institution.

"And how did Aunt Octavia take all this?" I inquired.

Cherry Rose hesitated, then said, "Oh, she decided to pretend it never happened." Her voice softened. "Poor Guido. He started off with so many strikes against him."

"But I still don't understand what you want from us," Frank protested. Obviously, advertising had nothing to do with this.

"We want you to get in touch with Cherry Rose's uncle—Miko's father," Barry answered.

"It's urgent, " Cherry Rose added. "Toshiko needs expensive

surgery. Our family has been paying all the bills until now, and the least he can do is help out."

We were confused.

"I don't understand," Frank complained. "If you can't contact your own uncle, how do you expect us to?"

Cherry Rose's reply was oblique. "You're already in contact with him, Frank."

Just then we spotted Yossi and Maria bearing purposefully down upon our table. Having learned from experience just how adroit Barry can be at sticking other people with the check, Frank and I pushed back our chairs in perfect synch and stood, making it clear to the Tozers this wasn't going on our plastic.

"You seemed cursed in your selection of uncles, Cherry Rose," Frank observed from his vantage point. "Who is this one?"

She smiled oddly. "Oh, he calls himself 'Nubuo Wei.'"

TEN

TO UNDERSTAND ENCINO, where we live, one must first be aware there's a luscious prime rib of real estate tucked between Cahuenga Pass running into Ventura Boulevard to the north, and Mulholland Drive to the south. Marbled with tasty canyons, hills, and vistas at nearly any given point from east to west, this section of the San Fernando Valley offers relatively easy access to almost anywhere in Los Angeles County. Encino is as far northwest along the rib as one can reside and still retain the accessibility factor.

For many generations, Encino's cliffs were inhabited exclusively by Indians. Now it seems to have become a magnet for Middle Eastern immigrants of every stripe. Thankfully, they all get along much better here than they do in the Golan Heights.

In earlier days, the main restriction imposed upon developers was that their houses must exceed a certain dollar amount; architectural harmony was obviously of little concern. Unimaginative seventies tracts may suddenly give way to a cluster of custom-designed monuments to bad taste, and the very same street might dead-end abruptly at a pair of massive wrought-iron gates marking the entrance to a lavish estate.

Our house is the middle of three Hollywood Spanish bungalows built by the same contractor, and were originally the only homes on Cactus Terrace. Russ and Lil are on our right, and a sweet older couple named Kirschner have lived in the left house since the fifties. From our deck, we have a mountain/canyon view dusted with nighttime city lights.

It was after two in the morning when we finally pulled into our garage. "Brace yourself!" Frank warned, as he unlocked the door.

Two spotted bundles of floppy ears, feathery paws, and stumpy tails flew out at us, scolding loudly. Once we were inside, they broke off long enough to sniff at the Pintoz doggie bag I waved enticingly.

Dimples sat down abruptly, breaking into a wide pink grin. The large black dots on either side of her soft mouth showed how she got her name. Dumpling froze, then stared fixedly at the bag as if she could levitate it to herself. She did this a lot and sometimes I almost believed she succeeded since, though we feed both dogs the same, her brown-and-white waistline inexplicably takes on a spare tire from time to time. Dumpling, who can hear a banana peeling in her sleep, had also named herself.

Frank rumpled their ears, offering to play, but they were entirely focused on the treats they knew were coming. "Fine. Just see if I care," he told them huffily, and went off to check the message machine.

Dimples adopts the gourmet approach to her food, chewing leisurely, savoring every bite. Dumpling simply inhales hers. I doubt more than one mouthful in three ever touches her taste buds, and she will eat—or at least try to eat—anything. The one time I ever saw her defeated was by a kumquat, and only after a valiant struggle. We have pictures.

Now, Dimples sniffed curiously at her exotic treat, but Dumpling bolted hers in two gulps, then cast envious eyes upon Dimples' full dish.

"You'd just better not, Miss Piggy!" I scolded.

Frank came into the kitchen, wearing a funny expression on his face. He looked exhausted, I thought. "Poor baby. Let me make you some hot cocoa with that Mexican chocolate stuff I bought— real Mexican, this time!"

"Okay, thanks," he said absently, and leaned against the work island.

Dumpling, my assistant chef, bustled importantly from refrigerator to cabinet to stove as I got the cocoa things together.

"Any juicy work offers on the machine?" I asked idly.

"Just one." He sounded strange.

"Frank! What is it?"

"I don't know but it sure smells like gefilte to me," Frank grunted. "A little after midnight, Nobuo Wei left a message saying he wanted me to come over tomorrow afternoon. Well, this afternoon, now."

"What! Why?"

"Get this. He wants to tape a codicil to his will."

I caught the milk precisely one second before it scorched.

ELEVEN

IN BED WITH second cups of cocoa, a springer on either side, we tried to make some sense out of the last eight hours or so.

"Frank, what do you think Barry and Cherry Rose were up to tonight?" I asked.

He shook his head tiredly, and I saw with a little shock that he almost looked his real age. This murder had taken more of a toll on him than I'd realized. "Beats me, darling. For that matter, how did they know we had any connection with Nobuo Wei in the first place? I know I never mentioned him to Barry. And Barry sure as hell never mentioned to us he was married to Nobuo's niece."

I had been pondering that one. "Did you ever say anything— even the tiniest thing—about Nobuo's crazy will to Henny?"

Frank groaned. "Oh, no!"

"Oh, yes!" I countered. "And you know how she can't resist bragging on you to all her alte cocka friends at—"

"—bridge," he finished ruefully. "Sonia and Morrie."

"Who else?"

"But," he protested weakly, "I'm positive I never so much as breathed his name..."

"Baby, how many Japanese film stars are there in this country? I mean, do you think it took Henny five minutes to figure it out? I'll bet she didn't even wait for bridge night. She was probably back on the phone to Sonia the minute you hung up."

Frank shifted his position, nearly dislodging a snoring Dimples from the bed. "And about two months ago, we started getting the big push to go to the opening."

I saw where he was headed with this. Barry and Cherry Rose had returned to the States from Puerto Rico nearly three months back to finalize all the Bonsai details. We'd had just one quick call from them during which Cherry Rose complained they were spending so much time flying between New York and Los Angeles, they were meeting themselves in mid-air.

About the only break they took was for Cherry Rose's dad's birthday party, which would coincide with when Henny's every phone call would contain a reminder of the Bonsai opening.

At least we'd figured out the who and when, if not the why. But we were still uneasy. That message from Nobuo Wei coming right on the heels of our dinner with Barry and Cherry Rose was too coincidental.

I wondered how on earth Sonia had been able to keep the secret of Nobuo Wei being Cherry Rose's uncle for so long. Because for sure if Henny had known, Frank and I would've known it five minutes later. Those two yakkety old biddies were always trying to top each other, and I couldn't imagine how Sonia managed to resist playing such a trump, so to speak. Too bad her bridge lacked such finesse.

I smiled in the dark. When Henny heard about this, any other secrets Sonia might be keeping from her now had less chance than a snowball in Palm Springs in August.

When at last I closed my eyes, I saw a picture of Henny and her bridge club cronies gathered around the kitchen table of her Westside apartment with its superior view of Barney Greengrass, the Sturgeon King. How often I'd enjoyed watching and listening to "The Survivors" as they called their team, bickering over cards and gossiping in five languages, while Henny in her green eye-shade double-checked the scores with a cigarette dangling from her wrinkled bottom lip. "I'll never die young from smoking," she'd snap when I tried to get her to quit.

I needed to videotape them before it was too late. They wouldn't be survivors forever.

TWELVE

UNDERSTANDABLY, we slept very late the morning after Miko's murder. When I finally shuffled into the kitchen, it was practically time for lunch.

I got Frank installed with coffee and toast in the den. Since there was sadly nothing happening at the B-Pix Hollywood office today,

he decided to study a storyboard for a commercial we were bid-
ding, and catch up on some phone calls.

Of course the dogs were ravenous. Even Dimples ate faster than
usual, then joined Dumpling in schnorring for more. I knew how
they felt. When I get off my schedule, I tend to try to readjust the
mechanism with food I wouldn't ordinarily touch, and plenty of
it. That's why, when Lil came in the back door carrying the *Times,*
she caught me plunging into a carton of Häagen-Dazs Swiss Almond.

"Why don't you save some time and rub it directly into your
thighs, Ava!" she teased.

"I'm just digging out the almonds," I said defensively, hurriedly
restoring it to its rightful place in the rear of the freezer.

"Anyway," she went on, "you'll want to be especially careful
of your image, now you've made the paper."

"What are you talking about?"

"I didn't think you'd seen it yet!" Ll handed me the *Los Angeles Times,* which had been folded open to page three.

GLITZY OPENING AT TRENDY BH BOUTIQUE SCENE OF FATAL
STABBING! it proclaimed, above a mass of celebrity snapshots
from Bonsai.

Sure enough, somehow a really terrificpicture of me had been
included, though I was billed as the former Mrs. Big Star. Fortunately, Frank doesn't take umbrage, knowing that unless I write a
hit screenplay, or he directs one, Hollywood, should it acknowledge me at all, would forever do so as the former Mrs. Big Star. I
checked the photographer's credit. Davida, naturally. I was glad
she'd been able to salvage something from whatever hadn't been
confiscated by Weinberg.

The hard news story was on the front page and contained no
revelations as far as the investigation was concerned. I did learn,
however, that Miko had graduated from the prestigious New York
Institute of Design and Photography, and was involved in the production of the Coty Awards for several years preceding her move
to Los Angeles eight months ago. Evidently, nobody had yet con-

nected her with Nobuo Wei or Cherry Rose Lehr, since the only surviving relative listed was her half-brother, Guido.

Lil's small sensitive face was thoughtful as she sipped coffee and listened to my firsthand account of the events. "Who's shooting this thing today, Ava?" she asked, when I'd finished.

"Oh, Frank's just going to do it himself with the minicam. After all, it's no big production number this time—a few minutes of straight on-camera stuff, I imagine."

"Are you going along?"

I stared. "After all this? You'd better believe it!"

Lil stood up. "What time?"

"He said around two-thirty. Why?"

"Because we're coming with you!" she informed me.

"What on earth for? There's nothing artistic to do, and Frank can handle the taping himself."

"Ava, Russ got back from Tahoe this morning. You know he'd never forgive Frank for shooting something himself when he's been waiting a month for Paramount to decide if they're ever going to make that feature in New Orleans. The only reason he took the Tahoe commercial was because he can't commit to anything longer and he's bored stiff."

Halfway out the door she turned, blonde curls glinting in the sun. "We'll use our wagon because it can hold all of us and the equipment. See you around two."

Russ Meyers is the old-fashioned kind of DP who likes the feel of a camera in his hands. Since both feature films and television movies adhere to the union guidelines that there must be an actual camera operator who is a separate entity from the director of photography on the set, Russ's physical contact with the equipment has to occur within rigid guidelines, and he complains that it's like trying to have sex within the boundaries of the rhythm system while being forced to use a condom anyway. This rule does not apply to commercials or music videos, however, so he shoots as many as he can. In fact he shoots *anything* he can.

Consequently, at two-thirty that afternoon the Meyers's black Mercedes wagon, containing four adults, two dogs, and some expensive equipment, turned into the private road that marked the beginning of Nobuo Wei's estate, Wei-Side.

There must have been some interesting wildlife about, for Dumpling suddenly raised her head alertly from my lap, while Dimples leaned out the window to sniff, long ears streaming in the breeze.

The main house was huge—a wonderful example of Old Tinseltown Tudor. Scattered in the distance to one side were some nondescript buildings, which I recalled were a sound stage and production facilities.

There was a black limousine parked in the drive when we pulled up. A large Hawaiian-looking man in a chauffeur's uniform was leaning against the hood. After a disinterested glance in our direction, he returned his attention to the lurid magazine he was reading.

We'd planned to leave the dogs in the car with the tailgate open, but it seemed terribly unfair when they were literally quivering to get at the gopher holes. "All right! But you'd better not make us have to organize a search party to comb the grounds for you!" Frank shook a warning finger at the two pleading, upturned faces.

Lil chuckled. "I love how you talk to them!"

Dimples and Dumpling bounded off, yelping joyously, while we unloaded the equipment.

The door was opened by a short Japanese maid dressed in a uniform of black silk mandarin pyjamas, not nearly so dramatic as those to be purchased from Bonsai at no doubt four times the price. Her glossy black hair was pulled straight back from a very high forehead, and she had the thickest, longest pigtail I'd ever seen, hanging to just below her hips. Still-smooth skin stretched over a finely boned face caused me to judge her age as a well-preserved fifty-something, but as Henny says on the subject, "With them you can never tell, Ava. They look fantastic until they're about a hundred. Then suddenly, they shrivel up and blow away."

I quickly dismissed any thought she looked familiar; after last night, I didn't trust myself to recognize Connie Chung.

Silently, she turned and beckoned us to follow, her tiny feet sliding along the bleached oak floor in brocade slippers, pigtail swinging heavily. When we reached the double mahogany panels at the end of the hallway, she slid them apart for us and we filed into a spacious library. I was last in line, and had barely cleared the threshold before she snicked them shut behind me.

Nobuo Wei possessed the bold kind of masculine appeal that transcends any age or racial barriers. Vitality radiated from his large, muscular body, richly upholstered in a sleek Italian suit. Not much of the traditionalist about Nobuo, except the livery of his household staff.

He rose to greet us with a cordial handshake for Frank and charming compliments for me. "Ah! I feel most important, Frank, to rate a full crew!" he boomed, when introduced to Russ and Lil.

Nobuo Wei continued. "May I present my attorney, Mr. Masumo?"

A fragile little bird of a gentleman, whose skin was the color of old ivory, arose with some difficulty from a large, soft chair that had practically devoured him in its depths.

He bowed politely. "It is an honor," he fluted in a high, thin voice.

"And now!" exclaimed Wei, rubbing his large hands together in anticipation, as enthusiastic about filming this strange little scene that would have a very limited viewing audience indeed, as he would have been a feature film.

Lil and I had nothing to do but lounge around and look pretty. Frank was setting up the audio, and Russ was already stalking the room with a light meter.

Mr. Masumo observed the preparations intently with beady little avian eyes. Despite his wispy appearance, I got the impression he didn't miss much.

While Frank, Russ, and Wei huddled over the exact camera angle—our client wanted to be sitting on the right edge of his beautiful rosewood desk and Russ was explaining why that was impossible—Lil wandered around the lovely room, making little cooing sounds.

The decor was a very successful mixture of English and Japanese—a classic combination, but done from the Japanese perspective instead of the English—which made all the difference.

Svelte rosewood sofa and chair frames swelled voluptuously in all the right places with cushions covered in green, cream, and mauve chintz. The walls were washed in a color that reminded me of fragrant green tea, trimmed in ivory. An exquisite jade silk rug woven with fantasy birds, their feathers the color of ripe plums, shimmered across the parquet. It must have been worth a fortune.

The marble fireplace was flanked by floor-to-ceiling windows that overlooked a seemingly endless stretch of lawn, making it difficult to remember that busy Sunset Boulevard was three minutes away.

At last, the setup had been agreed upon and Russ was fussily adjusting the pale green silk balloon window shades. A compromise had been reached—Nobuo could sit on the edge of his desk, but the opposite side from where he first wanted.

"Another great moment in film-making." Frank muttered as he passed us.

Nobuo politely inquired if either of us had any face powder and Lil produced a compact of Cornsilk.

"It has no color so we don't have to worry about matching the shade," commented Lil, not too tactfully, I thought, but Nobuo seemed to find it hilarious.

As he applied the powder with swift, expert strokes, I said, "Mr. Wei, we're sorry about Miko. You see, we were there last night—"

The big man froze, and his eyes grew hard. He snapped the compact shut, thrust it at Lil, then turned to me. All traces of geniality had vanished. "You are referring, I presume, to the opening of Bonsai?" he demanded harshly.

Taken aback, I stammered an affirmation. I certainly hadn't expected this reaction.

Nobuo called to Frank, "I understand you were present when my daughter was murdered."

"Unfortunately, yes," Frank said quietly.

Nobuo waved a hand abruptly. "We will talk later." Turning, he took up his position on the edge of the deck. With supreme effort, Masumo hitched himself from the clutches of the chair to upright attention. Russ made one final adjustment to a light, then hoisted the minicam to his shoulder. Frank pointed at Nobuo. "Last night, my daughter Yamiko Hayashi was murdered," he stated flatly, gazing steadily into the camera lens. "It has therefore become necessary for me to make this addition to my previous will in the presence of these witnesses.

"First, my attorney, the honorable Mr. Luk Masumo." He gestured to the little man, who nodded serenely when Russ angled to get a two-shot.

Nobuo certainly knew what he was doing, making it clear that others were present at these unorthodox proceedings, doubly ensuring credibility by appearing in the same shot.

Then Nobuo suddenly rose and crossed to stand behind the sofa where Lil and I were sitting. Startled, Russ looked at Frank, who shrugged and motioned for him to follow.

"And these two lovely and impartial ladies," Nobuo continued, "who will now identify themselves for the record."

"Lillian Beth Meyers," replied Lil with enviable composure.

"Ava Bernstein," I said, trying not to worry about whether my eyeliner was smudged, as if anybody would care. Back on his desk corner, Nobuo was saying, "It is my decision that the entire portion of my estate, which was to have gone to my daughter, Yamiko Hayashi..." He named a sum that caused Lil to dig an elbow into my ribs. Martial arts had been good to Nobuo Wei. Miko, had she survived her dad, would've been one very rich little critter.

"... will now be divided equally between..." Nobuo's theatrical pause at this point was clearly the cue for: ENTER WOMAN THROUGH SIDE DOOR.

Lil stared at me in astonishment as I caught her wrist in a death grip. Now I understood that little byplay I'd observed last night, the oddly taunting tone used to tell Cherry Rose, "... you know where to reach me." It also explained how Nobuo knew as early as midnight his daughter was murdered, though neither police nor press had made the connection between them.

The woman stood beside Nobuo as he repeated, "...will now be divided equally between this woman, whom I herewith acknowledge as my mistress, and the child to be born in approximately six months, whom I herein acknowledge to be my child.

"I now identify her for the record as Rikka Tring."

THIRTEEN

RIKKA'S VERTICAL EYES slid shut demurely.

She certainly wasn't doing any mental undressing of Frank today. In fact, he might not have even been there for all the notice she took of him.

Nobuo resumed his narrative. "In the event said child predeceases Miss Tring, said child's portion of the estate will revert to Miss Tring. Conversely, in the event that Miss Tring predeceases said child, Miss Tring's portion of the estate will revert to said child."

It all sounded portentous and professional. Little Mr. Masumo had served as script advisor, no doubt.

"In the event..."

He wasn't through yet. What other event was left?

"...that both Miss Tring and said child predecease my niece Cherry Rose Huwei Lehr, their joint portion will revert and become a part of said Cherry Rose Huwei Lehr's existing portion of my estate."

The echo of his words hung in the air, and Rikka gave a slight start, as did we all. Rikka Tring obviously hadn't realized Cherry

Rose was already provided for in her uncle's will. But had Cherry Rose?

I saw a reflection of my own suspicion in Frank's eyes as they met mine. Suddenly, it was all over.

Flashing plenty of golden thigh through the slit in her saffron cheongsam, Rikka undulated back through the side door where she had staged her entrance.

Wondering if it were really possible she had ensnared a man like Nobuo Wei to such a degree he couldn't see straight, I glanced over at him and got my answer. He was observing her exit with a sardonic twist to his full, rather sensual, lips. Clearly the man harbored no illusions about his lover. Why then, had he placed such a lethal weapon into her taloned hands?

I was still pondering their strange alliance about twenty minutes later, after our equipment was loaded and Mr. Masumo had been borne away in his black limo by the giant Hawaiian.

At Nobuo's request, the four of us remained behind in the library with him, curious as to the nature of the "important matter" he said he wanted to discuss. Whatever it was, he didn't plan to do it on an empty stomach, for the pigtailed maid entered, followed by two black-pyjamaed menservants pushing a laden tea cart.

Dumpling appeared immediately, pressing her chocolate nose against the French window, stumpy tail gyrating hopefully. Amid our laughter, Russ exclaimed, "How does she do it? I mean, every time!"

Dimples turned up a moment later, grinning as Dumpling informed her of the tea cart. They gazed imploringly through the window, long ears stringy and muddy from their adventures. It looked like they'd gone fishing in one of the koi ponds. Nobuo chuckled. "They've been working very hard, I see. And bound to be hungry."

"Oh, bound to be," drawled Russ.

Nobuo snapped his fingers at the maid without looking at her. "Naki! Fix plates and take them to our guests outside."

Lil raised her eyebrows at me. Nobuo's autocratic tone might not sit well with American girls like us, but the maid's smooth face was impassive as she removed domes from several dishes. Heavenly odors arose like incense as the steam escaped.

Nobuo spoke to me. "Please choose what is okay to give them."

I selected some fat rumaki, several spareribs, and two egg rolls apiece, while outside the dogs dashed about in a frenzy of anticipation.

Naki took the plates from me and left.

"Just don't let them notice your slippers!" Russ called after her, and Nobuo joined in the laughter when Frank explained the joke to him. Hopefully Naki didn't think we were making fun of her. If she had cooked this gorgeous food, I definitely wanted to stay on her good side. Nobuo's large hands were surprisingly graceful as he poured tea one shade of green paler than the walls and divinely flower-scented, into frail ivory china cups. Meanwhile, we were served generous portions of everything by the two men in black. I wondered if the older one was Naki's husband.

Dimples and Dumpling had made short work of their goodies, and were settling down with a pile of rib bones for some serious gnawing. We did the same.

After Naki and her helpers wheeled the tea cart away, Nobuo rose swiftly from the same chair which had held Mr. Masumo captive like a Venus flytrap, and went to his desk. Unlocking a drawer, he removed a script bound in blue and silver.

At the sight of this object, we sat up like little soldiers, despite our full tummies. Nobuo smiled at us. "This"— he tapped the script with a strong forefinger—"is the business I wanted to discuss with you."

Frank and I gripped hands tightly, scarcely daring to breathe. Russ and Lil were looking cautiously intrigued.

"It is the pilot episode for a type of martial arts series that"— he mentioned the network—"has bought as of this morning with an option for four more scripts." His big teeth flashed in satisfaction, then he frowned.

"It is not, however, yet another reincarnation of *Kung Fu*—I want that clearly understood!" Nobuo paused until he had extracted a nod of comprehension from each us, then went on to explain the concept.

The hero was a magician of generic Asian origin (I knew who would play that role) who combined a stunning and elegant repertoire of illusions with an equally stunning and elegant display of martial arts.

"He is a master of every form," Nobuo explained, "but shuns karate, except in emergencies. He has become an international sensation, and travels the world—first class, of course.

"Not surprisingly, because he is so good at so many things and somewhat arrogant as well, he makes enemies. The stories will feature conflict of two natures: against him personally—for example, challenges from other masters; and the situations he becomes involved in on behalf of others. Sometimes his motives are pure; other times, purely selfish. Occasionally, enlightened policemen welcome his assistance; more often they dismiss him as a kook.

"In most of the stories, he will have a romantic interest, and, oh, yes! He travels with his assistant, a beautiful and mysterious woman named Lotus, also skilled in illusions and combat. And we are never quite certain exactly what they are to each other."

He paused and I thought it was certainly no great mystery who would play Lotus.

"And so, there it is!" Nobuo addressed Frank. "What do you think, my friend?"

Frank leaned forward excitedly. "How long is the piece?"

"Two hours, cut for commercials," Nobuo said.

Frank grinned and squeezed my hand so hard my fingers were crushed painfully against the diamond ring, a memento of our last juicy job. But it was worth a diamond bite if Frank was about to get the big project he'd been yearning for. We'd have to slip God a thank-you note in the Pintoz Wailing Wall. Sure enough, Nobuo wanted Frank to direct, me to write additional dialogue, and Russ to DP. He offered Lil an associate producer's credit to oversee the art direction, set design, and wardrobe.

Since Nobuo had already preproduced most of the piece in order to project a typical budget, the lion's share of tedious, time-consuming work had been done, and we were to begin shooting in about three weeks! Russ declared that even if the Paramount feature happened, he'd have his agent get him out of it and to count him in.

"Mrs. Meyers's area is the only one that might pose a time problem," Nobuo observed.

My friend Lil, who has single-handedly decorated a seven-bedroom mansion and catered the housewarming party a week later, smiled languidly. "Why don't you call me Lil?" she invited.

A rapping at the window caught our attention, and there stood Dimples and Dumpling, faces smeared with barbecue sauce.

"Mommy! Daddy!" whined Russ in his "doggy voice."

Shortly thereafter we departed, armed with four blue and silver copies of *Dr. Upharsin and the Flying Cloak of Death*.

FOURTEEN

WE WERE SITTING around the big pine table in Lil's kitchen. It was nearly midnight before we finished the read-through of Nobuo Wei's script, because Lil had to keep getting up to check on the test recipe she was planning to debut at a studio wrap party. The memory of those exotic delicacies we'd feasted on had faded long ago, and by the time Lil's masterpiece emerged from the oven, we were more than ready to serve as guinea pigs. Or just plain pigs.

Lil is truly a creative genius. Her jalapeno cheesecake was to die for. Toasted corn chip crumbs formed the crust, the filling was cream cheese, crispy onions, and finely chopped jalapenos. The sour cream topping was spiked with more jalapenos, plus the liquid they'd been packed in, and Lil thought she could pull off a tasty low-fat version as well.

Between mouthfuls, we bestowed rave reviews upon Lil, while Russ beamed proudly. "I think you should add this to Challah Dolly's menu, honey," he told her as she sliced him another chunk.

"It did turn out pretty good, didn't it?" Lil smiled. "Actually, Ava, it was your description of the dishes at Pintoz that inspired me. I loved the idea of food that tastes entirely different from what it appears to be."

Which brought us back to the subject we'd had to shelve in order to concentrate upon *Dr. Upharsin*—the Bonsai murder.

We finished off the cheesecake in silence, and I remembered the shock I'd gotten when I timidly broached the subject of money for Miko's mother to Nobuo.

His attractive face had darkened with anger, and he'd made me repeat every word the Lehrs had said. Afterward, he didn't speak for a minute or two, simply continued to stare suspiciously from Frank to me.

I felt like a fool. What had Barry and Cherry Rose gotten us into? At last, Nobuo's face cleared and he said softly, "I see." Then he smiled at us. "I'm sorry to have reacted so strongly, because I realize you spoke in ignorance—as well as innocence.

"But"—he leaned forward and his black eyes were glittering with malicious amusement—"I'm afraid you have been shall we say, misinformed? My niece is certainly aware that my unfortunate wife was never left unprovided for, nor is she in need of anything now."

Then he'd frowned as if at a sudden unpleasant thought, and dropped the subject. But the fact remained, the Lehrs had told us exactly the opposite, and we now felt ourselves to be in a very awkward position.

On the drive back to the Bernstein/Meyers compound, Russ had come up with an intriguing angle. "How are the Lehrs for money?" he asked.

Frank said he thought they were doing fine, since Bonsai was so hot, and pre-Bonsai, Barry had been an architect. Plus, his wife was heiress to the Sushi estate.

"That only makes them slightly better off than some," Russ pointed out. "How many buildings did Barry design before launching his career as fashion guru? Was he a happening architect?"

Despite Sonia and Morrie's paeans of praise to their son, Frank and I were inclined to believe that Barry had not caused many uncomfortable moments for Michael Graves or Aldo Rossi. If so, Henny would've heard about it, which meant Frank and I would have heard about it. And heard about it.

Russ reminded us that the sushi boom had long since peaked and probably the only people still eating the stuff with any gusto at all were the same people who had been doing so millenniums before it became a fad—namely, the Japanese.

Roy Huwei may have made a comfortable living prior to sushi's American popularity, and even racked up a good profit when he took advantage of the fad and sold Sushi Shogun franchises. But even so, there weren't that many of them—fewer than ten in Manhattan and New Jersey combined.

He had waited too late to try a West Coast expansion—the beaches from Baja to Eugene were littered with sushi bars. In fact, the trend had probably swept from west to east in the first place.

Anyway, Cherry Rose had two brothers and two sisters, not to mention that Francesca DiMotta Huwei liked shopping. So, while the Sushi Shogun may have contributed in a few fins as an investment in Bonsai, it could've hardly been something major.

Frank and I had always assumed the Lehrs were extremely well off, but one question from an objective observer like Russ caused us to look at them in a whole new light, seeing little facts we hadn't bothered to add up.

Like Barry and Cherry Rose leasing out their tres glam SoHo loft and taking up residence in Puerto Rico. How often had Frank and I endured Henny's accounts of Sonia's moanings about her son being so far away from his mother, which were invariably concluded with the pointed phrase, "Although I tell Sonia she should only be glad he doesn't live Out There." Out There is Henny's little way of saying California.

Russ knew quite a bit about Puerto Rico, having shot two features there. Its commonwealth status offers some seductive fringe benefits to resident business owners, the best of which is no federal income tax upon on-island earnings. Additionally, the Puerto Rican native garment workers have the reputation of being more skilled and diligent than others elsewhere. And, of course, there were the lower wages.

Russ's theory was that Barry and Cherry Rose had seen the advantages of residency as outweighing the disadvantages, and probably as high a percentage as they dared of worldwide Bonsai sales went on the books as having taken place in Puerto Rico. There were legal ways of accomplishing this.

Now Russ said, "What this all boils down to is that the Lehrs may be very hard up for cash."

Lil glanced up from the ideas she was jotting down for the presentation of her jalapeno cheesecake—such as piping guacamole rosettes around the rim, and asked suddenly, "Did Cherry Rose know she's a beneficiary of Nobuo's will, I wonder?"

"Well, after today, she'll eventually be a millionaire. If enough other people die first, that is!" Frank tossed off the careless cliché before he realized what he'd said.

Across the table, our eyes met in consternation.

One other person had already died.

FIFTEEN

THE FOLLOWING AFTERNOON was warm and bright, so we were working on the script out by the Meyers's pool.

During the winter we alternate months running our pool heaters, which Frank says is exactly like throwing twenty dollar bills into the fireplace. Nevertheless, he's usually the first one up at the crack of dawn on the day of an early call, ready to do his laps.

And I find something stirringly primeval about the sight of steam rising from a pool in the chill morning air which beckons me to plunge in, though barely awake.

It was Russ and Lil's turn to heat their pool, but the day was still a little too cold to allow Dimples and Dumpling to go in. Our dogs had other ideas however, and Frank and I spent a lot of energy trying to keep them from sneaking a swim. Dumpling even tried the tactic of bringing her ball along when we came over— her favorite game in the world is to have someone throw it into the pool so she can swim to retrieve it. She made the rounds several times, offering the ball to each of us in turn, batting her eyelashes and growling throatily.

"She sounds just like Lauren Bacall," Lil commented.

Dimples, on the other hand, kept creeping around to the diving board when we weren't looking, and the last time, Frank barely managed to grab her stumpy tail just before she went into her unique version of the belly flop.

"Try that one more time and I'll put you inside the house!" he threatened, and Dimples knew daddy meant business.

Though the dogs' antics were entertaining, their willful behavior alerted Frank and me to the immediate need for some serious pool obedience training. It wouldn't be funny to come home and find a tragic accident had occurred.

Moreover, they'd been covered with pond scum after their outing at Wei-Side, which meant they had indeed been after the koi. If the dogs were going to run free on the estate while we were shooting, we didn't want to have to worry about that happening again. Yes, springer spaniel bootcamp was about to go into session.

We had no idea what a vital decision this was.

After the girls had been bribed into submission with gigantic rawhide chew bones, we were at last able to concentrate on the job at hand.

My eye was caught by the silver lettering on the script cover, glinting in the sunlight.

"'Dr. Upharsin,'" I read aloud. "That name sounds portentous."

Russ's green eyes gleamed, and he reached for his Bible, never far away. "Shall I tell them, baby?" he asked Lil, rhetorically.

Frank groaned. "I should've figured it would be something biblical."

So that explained it! We'd been wondering why Russ had so readily agreed to participate in the birthing of *Dr. Upharsin,* though that character's spiritual credentials were dubious, to say the least.

Russ was flipping pages confidently. "Ah, here we are," he announced. "Daniel, Chapter Five."

"Oy. Daniel again!" Frank winked at me.

Russ began reading us the story about King Belshazzar's last feast, which sounded like your typical Babylonian drunken orgy. That is, until a giant hand appeared out of nowhere and wrote on the wall—an event guaranteed to put a damper on any party.

Naturally, nobody could interpret the writing but Daniel.

"Who else?" That was Frank.

"Verse twenty-five!" Russ said sternly. "'And this is the inscription that was written: Mene, Mene, Tekel, Upharsin—numbered, numbered, weighted, divisions.'" He looked up. "'Upharsin' means 'divisions.'"

"Of course. I recognized the word right away," Frank said pompously.

Russ ignored him and scratched his reddish beard thoughtfully. "The thing that intrigued me was why a guy like Nobuo Wei would go to the Bible, of all places, for his character's name—especially this particular character.

"I began to wonder if he just liked how the word looked and sounded, or whether he actually knew what it meant. Because not every Bible translation includes the literal root meanings of those words."

Lil chimed in, "You see, scripturally, any time a word like 'divided' or 'division' is used, it indicates demonic activity that causes structural spiritual weakness and eventual collapse."

Russ amplified, "As in '*A house divided against itself cannot stand,'* which is equally applicable to a nation, a family, or an individual."

In spite of ourselves, Frank and I were becoming fascinated by this extrapolation.

Russ continued. "Naturally, I was curious to know if this was the point of vulnerability Wei wanted to bring out in Dr. Upharsin—is he supposed to be a brilliant man, tormented by all his strange and terrible knowledge? Will it finally prove to be his undoing, thereby providing a graceful ending for the series?"

Frank was frowning. "But—does it have to mean anything at all Russ? Maybe it's what you said earlier—maybe he simply liked the sound of it."

Russ nodded. "That's entirely possible."

"But you don't believe it for one minute." Frank grinned at his friend.

"Dr. Upharsin's first name is 'Tek' isn't it?" I remembered. "Wasn't one of those other words you read us 'tek' something or other?"

"Tekel," said Lil.

"What's the interpretation of that one?"

"Verse twenty-seven. 'Tekel—you are weighed in the balances and found wanting,'" Russ read.

"Whew!" Frank exclaimed. "That's heavy."

"So then," I said, feeling excited, "the translation of Dr. Tek Upharsin's name means roughly, 'one who has been weighed, found wanting, and divided.'"

"Omigod!" Frank's sudden exclamation startled us all.

"Weighed!" he shouted, and we stared at him uncomprehendingly.

"Don't you get it?" he demanded. "Weighed, weigh—Wei. As in Nobuo Wei!" We all pondered that one for a moment.

Finally, Russ shook his head. "I don't know," he said, it's getting pretty convoluted."

Frank said stiffly, "Excuse me. I know I'm not a spiritual giant like yourself, but—"

Lil protested. "That's not what Russ meant at all, Frank."

"No, of course I didn't." Russ hastened to assure him. "It's just the type of pun that would appeal to Wei. I freely admit, I have no idea what it all means."

Frank was mollified. "Well," he said. "At least one thing came out of this weird discussion. I know exactly how to direct the character. Dr. Tek Upharsin is wealthy, handsome, brilliant—and doomed."

When the smoke cleared, we had decided that "doom" would be the unspoken but palpable feeling woven throughout the pilot— a sense of vulnerability and uncertainty mixed in with the man's near-omnipotence. Has his time almost run out?

Somehow, I thought Nobuo Wei would be pleased.

SIXTEEN

DESPITE ITS SLIGHTLY seedy aura—or perhaps because of it— Chez Mouche above Sunset Strip does a brisk year-round trade in wealthy eccentrics.

It had been the scene of many curious events, the most celebrated of which was the rather dicey death of a famous comedian on its premises. Yet for some reason, the stories merely served to enhance the Mouche's macabre cachet.

The Wednesday after Miko's murder, as we crossed the courtyard toward the bungalows, Frank reminded me of the actor who used to pee upon the heads of unwary pedestrians from his balcony. Involuntarily, I glanced upward and Frank chuckled. But he wasn't laughing when Barry Lehr opened the door. Barry was astonished to find us on his doorstep.

"What—?" he began, but Frank cut him right off.

"We'll ask the questions, Barry!" he decreed. "Like, what the hell are you and Cherry Rose playing at, anyway?"

Barry made a shushing motion and glanced back over his shoulder, then stepped outside, pulling the door to behind him. "Frank, for God's sake—"

Again, Frank sliced off the end of Barry's sentence like it was salami.

"All that bullshit about Nobuo Wei and Toshiko. You bastard! We nearly lost a major gig because we bought that sob story."

Barry stared at him. "Frank, I have no idea what you're raving about."

Frank exploded. "Raving! You think this is raving? I'll show you raving!"

Just then the door opened. "Why, Mr. and Mrs. Bernstein. What a nice surprise. How are the dogs?"

Bernard Weinberg was smiling, but his eyes were watchful. "They're waiting in the car, Lieutenant." Frank had regained his cool. "Would you like an introduction?"

The eyes warmed for an instant. "Now, what do you think?"

"Hello!" I gave him my own best Bette Davis eyes. "Whatever brings you to the House of Flies?"

Weinberg looked faintly startled, since I had taken the words out of his mouth, but he gave me an appreciative glance and parried swiftly. "A spot of business, as I'm sure I don't need to remind you, Mrs. Bernstein. And yourselves? But then, you and Mr. and Mrs. Lehr are old friends, as I recall."

Frank looked at Barry, who appeared decidedly moth-eaten in the lamplight, then at Cherry Rose, impassive and unfamiliar behind big Italian sunglasses, and agreed with an ironic grin. "More or less."

Barry scrambled around doing host duties, and when we'd been distributed among the strange collection of furniture in the sitting room—that fifties salt-and-pepper-covered sofa Frank and I drew would've gone for a bundle to an aficionado—Weinberg asked, "Mr. Bernstein, did I hear you mention Nobuo Wei's name?"

Barry and Cherry Rose stirred in protest, but Frank merely gave Weinberg a brief account of our unexpected meeting with Wei (omitting only the fact that the Lehrs had asked us to put the bite on him for whatever reason) and that coincidentally, Wei had engaged us to film a TV pilot.

The detective was silent, observing us through those red-brown eyes, then remarked, "And at no point in your years of association with Mr. and Mrs. Lehr did you ever learn of Mrs. Lehr's relationship to Nobuo Wei?"

"No way!" Frank retorted decisively, then added quickly, "No pun intended."

Cherry Rose uttered an involuntary croak, the first sound I'd heard out of her since we showed up, then offered in a surly tone, "Of course Frank and Ava didn't know. We never mentioned his name to outsiders. He brought dishonor to his family."

Weinberg caught her up on that last statement, "Now that's very interesting, Mrs. Lehr. Just how did he do that? You see, I've always been a big fan of Nobuo Wei's so I would've thought his own family would be very proud of him..."

"Oh, it wasn't his movie career that was a dishonor." Cherry Rose's voice had grown more strident than usual. "It was the disgusting way he abandoned his wife and baby daughter. The one who was killed, Lieutenant.

"What's more, his wife—whom he never divorced, incidentally—is very ill and hard up for money—he's never bothered to help."

"But—" I began, only to break off at the warning pressure of Frank's hand on my arm.

Weinberg turned alertly. "Yes, Mrs. Bernstein?"

"Why, uh, just that—he doesn't seem like that type of man," I finished lamely.

Weinberg had several other questions for us about the night of the murder such as, what had we noticed before we entered the changing room, that sort of thing—but he was really preoccupied with the revelation that Miko had been Nobuo Wei's daughter, and I knew we weren't going to get off the hook so easily this time, dogs or not.

My foreboding was confirmed when he finally announced, "Okay, folks. That's it for tonight. But I'll be checking in with you sometime tomorrow."

"Oh? Well, you'll simply have to reach us long distance, Lieutenant. We're flying to New York in the morning for a business meeting," Barry replied.

Weinberg's eyes frosted over. "You won't be on that flight, Mr. Lehr," he contradicted. "You see, I'm sorry to remind you that you're both material witnesses in a murder case, and those kinds of witnesses don't leave town until they're completely cleared of suspicion!"

"But then how about Passover?" protested Barry. "We always go to New York for Passover."

"Well, so do I, for that matter!" Weinberg returned crossly, preparing to leave. "But, guess what? Murder has a nasty way of disrupting plans."

Cherry Rose spoke up. "Listen, Frank, as long as you and Ava are here, why don't you stay and have a drink?" I could see the bubble-shaded lamp reflected in her sunglasses.

But Weinberg stated firmly that he had a couple more questions for the Bernsteins, as a matter of fact. "So, we'll just talk as I walk them out to their car." Then he gave Frank and me a real smile. "Besides, I was offered an introduction to their dogs!" He closed the door of Bungalow 3 upon Barry's ineffectual detaining gestures.

"Look," Weinberg said companionably as we strolled toward the parking lot. "I'm sure you people don't intend to tell me that you just popped in for a short little visit tonight with your old friends. From what I heard, things didn't sound so friendly."

We had paused under an old-fashioned lamppost a few feet from the car, and I saw indecision pass over my husband's handsome face. After all, he'd known Barry years before I'd met him, which was just prior to his marriage—or marriages—to Cherry Rose.

"Honey, no matter what, we'd better explain," I advised. Between us, we filled Weinberg in, from our late apres murder supper with the Lehrs, to the impromptu codicil benefiting Rikka Tring and progeny, and that Cherry Rose was a major beneficiary under Nobuo's will.

Weinberg whistled. He hadn't expected anything like this.

Frank described Wei's angry reaction to the charge of nonsupport to his wife and child. "And that's why we drove over here tonight, Lieutenant," he finished. "We were furious because we did as they asked and it backfired right in our faces. It's a miracle we didn't lose the job."

Weinberg rubbed his chin. "I'd like to know why the Lehrs set you up," he mused.

"That's what we were trying to find out, Lieutenant," I reproached him gently.

He smiled at me and said, "Then you should ask them directly. In fact, you don't even have to mention you told me about this. Know what I mean?"

Frank studied him. "You mean, we are to find out and report back to you, right?"

"Got a problem with that?" Weinberg challenged. I was flattered and excited. "Like Mr. and Mrs. North and Bill Wiegand?"

Weinberg laughed. "Except the Norths kept cats, instead of dogs, as I recall."

Frank, who had never read the Pam and Jerry books, looked at us like we were crazy.

"And speaking of dogs"— Weinberg gestured at the car where Dimples and Dumpling had begun leapfrogging over the seats at the sight of us—"How about that introduction?"

SEVENTEEN

ONE OF THE REASONS Nobuo Wei had been able to sell *Dr. Upharsin* to the network was because of a deal they made in a rash of enthusiasm with a British actor named Manfred Walter.

In exchange for his guest-starring on a miniseries, he'd extracted their commitment to give him leading roles in three American television movies over the subsequent five years, or pay him a tremendous amount of money. Of the two films he'd been in so far, one was a flat-out ratings stinkeroo, the other only a mediocre success.

Despite the fact that several episodes of *Dr. Upharsin* were ordered, it had filtered through the grapevine that the honchos expected the series to fail, using it as an expensive but effective means of getting rid of Manfred Walter, plus a handful of other pay-or-play deals, in one fell swoop.

Whether the rumor was true or not, the outcome was beyond our control and we were still obligated to deliver the goods. Which is why I spent every waking moment of the following week watching martial arts films in preparation for the project, as if I'd never heard a discouraging word.

Initially, the plots were confusing, but little by little, I began to make some sense of them. The storylines were basically similar—either the Koreans or the Chinese were fighting off the Japanese; the students of one Kung Fu teacher were competing with those of an evil rival; or lone, mysterious masters would appear from nowhere to defeat the Japanese Mafia trying to take over a mama and papa-san restaurant.

There was an entire subgenre devoted to African-American black belts, living for obscure reasons in Hong Kong. Most of these were relics from Superfly days—clunky three-inch heels, bell-bottoms, psychedelic shirts, afros exploding into atomic shapes.

I found the action sequences especially fascinating—fights with wooden staffs wielded in poetic symmetry; strange, deadly weapons devised by archfiends; daring escapes through labyrinths filled with diabolical booby-traps.

Then there was the one-to-one faceoff, wherein two opposing masters, recognizing and respecting each other's gifts, nevertheless set about to systematically destroy each other in the most painful ways. One image that may never leave me is that of Bruce Lee ripping out a thick patch of an unflinching Chuck Norris's chest hair.

But even the higher-end productions were liable to take on an inappropriately comic aspect when uncompromisingly Oriental faces exchanged dubbed English dialogue with equally uncompromising cockney, German, and Italian accents, while their lips continued to move well after the audible speeches had ended.

Yet in some inexplicable way, that very overt foreign funkiness actually served to enhance the appeal of these films; perhaps it even defined them. All my creative instincts told me to find a way to weave the same coarse thread through *Dr. Upharsin,* without unraveling its essential elegance. But how?

The solution came from Marty and Sam, a team of rambunctious young network producers also slated for pay-or-play death row. Their idea was to have characters occasionally speak their lines in other languages, and use English subtitles whenever they did. Retaining the flavor of a speech while condensing it into a number of words that would not obscure the screen was hard at first, but I'd quickly gotten the hang of it, thanks to my advertising background. More importantly, this technique was creating exactly the effect I'd hoped.

Marty and Sam had been told they had a free hand, then shoved like Uriah onto the front lines for extermination. They, however, saw this as a rare opportunity to have all the fun they never got to have while they were worried about keeping their jobs.

Far from twitching with fear and making conservative decisions and wimpy second guesses trying to get back into grace, Marty and Sam plunged into the project like condemned men who were by golly going to eat hearty meals, and what's more, have a big dessert.

Under their eager and skillful hands, *Dr. Upharsin* was emerging much as the Bernstein/Meyers team had envisioned—a moody, textured piece with just a whiff of *The Avengers* classy camp.

I could understand why the network had seized upon *Dr. Upharsin and the Flying Cloak of Death* for Manfred Walter, who was the larger-than-life type; a big, bluff character with a thick shock of white hair and matching mustache, bushy black eyebrows over narrow blue eyes, and a desert tan. His forte was the wealthy, jovial, and slightly sinister white man you just knew made his money from bilking the natives. The problem was, American television had very little use for such a character.

Roughly, the plot of *The Flying Cloak of Death* concerned a wealthy, slightly sinister white man who loves to throw English house parties in classic Christie style, and has a fetish for collecting an assortment of guests to deliberately create an atmosphere of tension. He has invited, along with others, Dr. Upharsin and Lotus, and one of Upharsin's sworn enemies, "the Baron." The Baron is a Viennese magician who also fancies himself a martial arts expert, and travels with his assistant, an enormous Amazon Indian named Fero, who, for the Baron's performances, dresses in a loincloth, but for everyday, in decadent designer outfits. I was especially proud of the subtitle I'd done between the Baron and the Major speaking of a World War II incident in High German.

No matter what the final ratings verdict on *Dr. Upharsin* turned out to be, everyone involved was determined it would be a quality production, never to be forgotten. Mercifully, we didn't fully comprehend the impossible odds we were up against, including a killer who would turn our fantasy fiction into true crime.

EIGHTEEN

DURING THE NEXT WEEK, Frank and I practically lived at Wei-Side, leaving our house at around six every morning, and rarely getting home before midnight. Since Russ and Lil were on a similar schedule, Mike and Molly Kirschner were foster-parenting Dimples and Dumpling.

But no matter how late we came home, unless we were paralyzed with fatigue, we drilled the dogs in pool obedience for at least fifteen minutes every night, in preparation for being able to keep them with us at Wei-Side throughout the shoot. Since Dimples and Dumpling were water dogs, it was hardly fair to expect them to exercise discretion over their primeval instincts when, in addition to the koi ponds scattered over the grounds, Nobuo also had an enormous swimming pool and another very deep ornamental fish pond set into one of the terraces. However, once they were completely trained, we could let them roam free on the estate with no anxieties.

I was discovering there are some advantages to crewing a ship the network expects to sink, the main one being they rarely want to come aboard. The only real concern in cases like this is that cost time overruns will give the bean counters an excuse to pull the plug.

Nobuo, an old hand on the *S.S. Hollywood* lines, knew where the dangerous reefs were and how to steer clear of them. For instance, he could completely control the major expenses of location fees and production office leasing because the location was his estate, and we were using the Snapdragon production offices, also on his estate. If he chose not to pay himself for either, who could object?

The few network representatives actually involved in the day-to-day production chores had every reason to suspect their heads were also on the block, and they quickly adapted to Marty and Sam's eat, drink, and be merry policy.

As to the time factor, we were having to proceed at breakneck speed to make our start date, and if various union reps hadn't chosen to turn a blind eye at certain points, we would never have made it. For some reason, everybody seemed to be rooting for this stepchild.

The first real glitch we encountered was the defection of Lil's costume designer, Tex Wing, a gay Asian with a penchant for very large ethnic men. In a fit of jealous hysteria, he'd phoned Lil to notify her he was off to pursue a lover who'd escaped his clutches to rendezvous with another guy in Baja.

To Lil's objections he'd shrieked, "Oh, God! You couldn't *pos-*

sibly understand what a *turmoil* my life is in! I mean, what is a TV *movie,* compared to my *life!*"

Tex was exceptionally talented, but reveled in his well-deserved reputation for creating trite—but nonetheless terrible—scenes. Lil hired him in the first place only because of his extensive martial arts film credits and there was no leisure to shop around.

But before Marty and Sam could push the panic button, she'd already signed a trio of replacements for Tex and his two assistants—Barry and Cherry Rose Lehr, and Woo Kazu. "They've agreed to bury the hatchet," Lil assured us soothingly, when we expressed dismay.

"Yeah, but did they specify exactly where they intend to bury it?" Frank inquired pessimistically.

"How does Nobuo feel about this?" I wondered.

"Actually, the Lehrs were his own suggestion," was Lil's surprising answer. "I only wish I'd thought of them myself two weeks ago. Did you know they designed all of Tori Spelling's wardrobe for *Beverly Hills Tai Kwon Do?* It's just that same little zing of satire without getting spoofy we need for *Dr. U.*"

Frank's and my first reaction to this news was disbelief. Why would Nobuo recommend his niece and her husband to work on his precious project after the lies they'd told about him? Their motive in doing so was still unclear since we hadn't seen or heard a word from them after the night of our encounter at Chez Mouche.

For that matter, Weinberg hadn't exactly been panting after us for inside information either, not that we had any to impart. Apparently, our role as sleuths was to be a mere walk-on, if at all.

"Don't tell me Nobuo also proposed Woo Kazu," I said to Lil. She shook her head. "No, that came from Barry and Cherry Rose."

I gave up trying to figure it out. After all, television is known to make for strange bedfellows. Just a coincidence that Cherry Rose had been in bed with both fellows.

The next problem to arise was relatively minor. The still photographer Russ preferred to work with was suddenly unavailable, due to having been invited to join the world tour of a mega rock band.

"Obviously Delbert couldn't afford to turn down a gig like that," Russ conceded. "But I hadn't counted on needing a backup."

"I'm getting a lightbulb about this," I told him. "My friend Davida Yedvab would be perfect. I just don't know whether she'd be interested or not."

But Davida was interested, although there'd been a longish pause after I explained the situation. "Well..." she finally replied, with a strange note in her voice.

"Oh, just say yes, Davida," I urged. "It'll be almost like old times, us doing a project together after all these years. And Nobuo Wei's estate is gorgeous. Think of it as a working vacation. Plus you'll have a great chance to get lots of that dark, moody stuff you like so much. It's a *Ninja/Magician/Equalizer* kind of guy in a *Murder, She Wrote* format."

Davida chuckled. "You'd better repeat that, Ava. I'm going to write it down in those exact words. Uh, is Nobuo Wei also going to be in the movie?"

"Only the star, is all. And he deserves it. Nobuo is really a wonderful actor, I don't care what anybody says."

"Well, you won't get any argument from me about that," she said, with a little laugh. "Okay, Ava. I'm in."

NINETEEN

RUSS, FRANK, AND I were working—along with the production staff and some technical people—in Snapdragon's main office

building, while Props, Wardrobe, and the other services had set up
shop in a row of cinderblocks behind us.

As associate producer in charge of costumes and sets, Lil spent
most of her time in the workshops, but kept her database in the
main office building. Consequently, when she came in to down-
load status reports into her computer, we'd also pump her for the
latest gossip.

Without leaving our desks, we learned that Presley Shores,
Frank's AD, was hot to trot for a pretty wardrobe assistant; that
the seemingly self-effacing Naki privately queened over Nobuo's
other servants like they were dirt; and that Rikka Tring and Davida
Yedvab had taken an instant dislike to each other. And more ominously, that the Lehrs and Woo Kazu were having "creative dif-
ferences."

The bone of contention was the Baron's cloak, for which *The
Flying Cloak of Death* was named. Without question, the garment
had to be something ultimate, a thing of beauty which concealed
its deadly secret. Whenever the Baron flung the cloak at an enemy,
a network of tiny barbs protruded and caused disfiguring wounds—
the loss of an eye or ear, perhaps—to his opponent. Often the
barbs were coated with a powerful contact poison which brought
a rapid, but particularly agonizing, demise. Depending on how it
was thrown, the cloak was also capable of slitting a person's throat.

The clash came when Barry, whose task it was to engineer the
mechanism that would trigger the barbs, insisted Woo and Cherry
Rose alter their cloak design, which had already been approved
by Nobuo.

The sketch we'd seen was fabulous—a triumph of deep plum
iridescent silk embroidered with metallic silver thread and lined
with dull apricot silk. I suspected Barry's main problem with the
design was jealousy that his wife and her former lover had so
quickly fallen back into their co-creative mode and produced such
a wonderful costume, while he was expected to act as a mechanic.

Fortunately, Lil was able to negotiate a successful compromise
and Barry went back to the drawing board where he conceived a
truly ingenious device—a pulley system of thin, flexible wires upon

which were mounted hundreds of tiny barbs made from rubber, but looking exactly like lethal steel as far as the camera was concerned.

This web of wires was suspended between the cloak's two layers of silk, and Cherry Rose and Woo added silver tassels at the throat and other strategic spots that allowed the wearer to control the mechanism.

After this crucial hurdle had been cleared, the Lehr-Kazu menage hunkered down to work, with only an occasional snit or flare of temperament.

From our windows, Frank and I could see the overworked wardrobe assistants dashing frantically about with bolts of fabric, and various actors trudging to the workshop for fittings. Obviously, the Lehrs had every excuse not to pop in and say hi, but Frank and I believed they were deliberately avoiding us.

This was confirmed when I unexpectedly encountered Cherry Rose in the ladies' room and she'd muttered, "Oh. Hello, Ava," brushing past me.

"Hold it right there, girlfriend!" I ordered, blocking her path to the door. "In the words of a great American, 'Lucy, you got some s'plainin' to do.'"

Cherry Rose's shoulders sagged. "You're right," she sighed. "And I will. I promise. I just don't have time right now."

Up this close, I was shocked to see her usually beautiful skin had taken on an ochre tinge, her eyes were dull and bloodshot, and her shiny black hair was lank and oily.

"Honey, what's wrong?" I asked in concern.

Sudden tears sprang to her eyes. "Oh God, Ava. I'm so tired. But it's not just the movie. We've got Bonsai to run, as well."

"But I thought Rikka was supposed to be managing Bonsai," I said. "She practically forced you guys to give her the job."

Cherry Rose smiled grimly. "Ah, but that was before Big Daddy's network deal came through."

"Well, I don't see how on earth you're coping with both things," I said.

"Oh, we've got it all worked out, Ava. At least Bonsai's less than ten minutes away, so that's one bright spot. During lunch break either Barry or I, sometimes both of us, rush over to put in a guest appearance to make sure our celebrity clientele is getting stroked, because poor Guido just doesn't have what it takes in that department. We check the salespeople, return phone calls, handle whatever problems, then rush back here.

"At night, no matter how late, we compare receipts to inventory, write up orders, and on and on."

I was aghast. "Nobody can keep up a pace like that, C.R. Do you want to kill yourself?"

The wraith of a smile played on her lips. "I'm working on it, Ava."

TWENTY

SEVERAL DAYS PASSED without Cherry Rose making good on her promise to explain those lies about Nobuo, but now that I knew what a treadmill she and Barry were on, I didn't hold it against her.

Bernard Weinberg had no such compunctions, however, about disrupting their painstakingly calculated schedule; he showed up at Wei-Side very early one morning, looking like a hanging judge, demanding to see the Lehrs.

He questioned Barry and Cherry Rose separately, then together, and remained closeted with them for what seemed like hours while Marty and Sam paced and worried.

Later on, we found out why.

The forensics examination of the garments worn during the fashion show had finally been completed, and the antique ivory fan nestled in Cherry Rose's obi had turned out to be a charming little gadget that converted into a dagger. This discovery, however historically fascinating, wouldn't have meant a thing if the dagger hadn't also proven to show traces of dried blood the same type as Miko's.

Weinberg had been nonplused by Lehrs' calm admission that

the blood on the fan dagger was indeed Miko's. Try as he might, he couldn't shake their story, which was that the incident occurred during the unpacking of the geisha outfit, which had arrived only one day before the show from the museum via UPS.

According to Barry, Miko and Cherry Rose had been so enchanted with the lovely old things they were like little girls playing in mommy's clothes, taking turns trying on the wig and kimono. Miko, attempting a geisha flourish with the fan, unwittingly triggered the switchblade mechanism, slicing the skin between her right thumb and forefinger.

Outraged, Barry had called the museum's curator, who was horrified to hear of the mistake. That ivory fan was one of a pair owned by a famous courtesan in eighteenth century Japan, who had put it to excellent use upon the throat of a cruel warlord. The matching fan—which was the one to have been shipped—was as pure as, well, ivory.

The curator had demanded the relic's immediate return, whereupon Barry predictably became stubborn and insisted he had to have an authentic piece for the show the next night. The curator reluctantly agreed, on the condition that Cherry Rose would not open the fan at any time.

I remembered wondering why she hadn't been fluttering it around. When the autopsy report on Miko turned out to list a half-inch diagonal cut between her right thumb and forefinger, Weinberg grudgingly let Barry and Cherry Rose get back to work.

Miko's wound was a prophecy of what lay ahead, had anyone been around to interpret it. As Frank commented to Russ, where was Daniel when you really needed him?

TWENTY-ONE

"SO WHAT IS THIS about nobody coming here for Passover? I can't tell you how upset Sonia and Morrie are. Oy, the kvetching I have endured. Something, it's always something, to keep you Out There, Frankala. Why did you have to go and get yourself involved in this?"

Frankala, who was listening in on the den extension (because that's mainly what one did when Henny called) managed to insert, "But, Henny, it was you who insisted Ava and I go to the Bonsai opening."

"And why shouldn't you go, please tell me, when here is Barry doing so well and one of your oldest friends?" she demanded. "So let the police find out who killed that girl, why should it have anything to do with you?"

When I explained that Frank and I had been on the premises when the body was discovered and the Lehrs were material witnesses not allowed to leave town without permission, she proclaimed triumphantly, "Now you see why I worry that you live Out There? And they say New York is bad. So what are you doing for Passover?"

When Frank replied we were invited to a seder at the Meyers's, Henny sniffed and observed that of course it wouldn't be as good as in New York—Cousin Grescha was giving it this year—but we were lucky to have such nice people living right next door.

Actually, Russ and Lil's seders were a far cry from rotund Grescha capering in his apron that read, "Why is this night different from all other nights? Don't ask!" Russ read the service from a highly unorthodox Haggadah that identified Jesus as the Pesach lamb prophesied in Isaiah. The matzoh was said to be a symbol of His body—pierced, striped, and without the leaven of sin.

When Henny temporarily paused for breath, I asked if she'd ever met Toshiko.

"Oh, you mean the Japanese woman who was married to that movie star which my dear friend Sonia conveniently forgot to mention was Barry's uncle-in-law?"

I smothered a laugh. As I'd predicted, Henny wasn't about to forgive Sonia so easily.

"Suddenly I should know everybody in New York?" Henny asked. "You forget, Ava, I never met any of those people until Barry got mixed up with that Huwei girl. Forty years ago, which is when

Sonia tells me they had to lock up that Toshiko person after she tried to kill one of those Italian women whose names I can never keep straight because they all end in 'a,' I had better things to do." Her voice cracked suddenly. "It was the year of Simca's and my twenty-fifth anniversary."

Her words conjured up the photographs of that occasion I'd pored over many times, finished in that strange process unique to the fifties which seemed to combine the best of black-and-white and color. They'd managed to fit little round tables into that roomy New York apartment, so many it looked almost like a nightclub. There were flowers, and food, the irreplaceable hydrangea wallpaper, Uncle Simca bartending, people playing the piano, the men exuding prosperity and the women looking like gorgeous movie stars in their fabulous short haircuts and strapless semiformals. You'd never have guessed that nearly all of them had been in concentration camps less than ten years before. I thought of the shot of beautiful Rosl, clearly shikker, dress hiked up to her garters and vamping naughtily at the camera. She'd died last year at the age of eighty-two, still nearly as beautiful.

"Huh?" Frank's voice faded in and I knew he'd dozed off somewhere along the line. "Who killed an Italian?"

"Oh, so there you are, Frankala," Henny observed caustically. "So nice of you to rejoin the conversation. If you had been here you would have known the Japanese woman failed to kill the Italian woman, don't ask me what her name is."

Light dawned. "Henny, was the name Octavia?"

"I can still hear myself telling you don't ask me, Ava, but yes, I think that's her. It sounds like something that should've happened Out There," Henny added resentfully, and hung up.

A moment later, Frank wandered back into the living room. There was a little chill in the air, so he began to build a fire. Dimples and Dumpling helped by promptly snatching out the balls of crumpled newspaper he put in the grate and throwing them into the air.

"Well, at least now we know why Toshiko was committed to a

mental institution," Frank said. "Obviously to prevent the DiMottas from pressing charges of attempted murder."

"But Uncle Vitello and Aunt Octavia seemed to have gone along with it readily enough," I pointed out. "Maybe there was a little gelt involved?"

Frank added pinecones for kindling to the newspaper retrieved from the dogs and lightly swatted Dimples's nose as she tried to thrust it back into the fireplace. "Maybe. Although I bet the biggest price was paid by Uncle Vitello himself to Aunt Octavia."

"We still don't know why Cherry Rose accused Nobuo of nonsupport for Toshiko," I reminded him as the fire sprang into a crackling blaze.

"At this rate we never will, and I'm not sure I care anymore," Frank growled, flopping down beside me on the sofa. "Why do I feel like somebody put that old Japanese curse on us? You know the one. 'May you live in interesting times.'"

"That's Chinese, darling."

"Whatever. Come here..."

Of course the phone would ring at just that moment. Sighing, Frank groped among the sofa cushions for the handset. Like doctors, self-employed show biz types cannot afford to ignore a ringing telephone.

"Henny!" he exclaimed. "What's the matter?"

"Right away something's the matter," she said indignantly. "What, I can't call twice in one night? Anyway, I was thinking more about that old incident with the Japanese and Italian women, so I have just finished discussing it with Marta, who as you know is very discreet."

Frank groaned.

"What is that noise?" Henny's voice bristled. "Does it mean you don't want to know what Marta found out from the Italian woman who came in for a manicure today?"

Henny's bosom friend Marta is a fabulous creature of eighty-plus, who looks like a deposed Hungarian countess of fifty-five. She escaped to America from Belgium in 1939 by the skin of her teeth, beginning as a lowly manicurist in a famous salon and rising to become a legend. Though now mostly retired, Marta still has her own special domain in the salon where she caters to a small, select clientele, most of whom have been with her for decades.

"Just which Italian woman are you referring to this time, Henny?" I inquired.

"It is Francesca, the mother of Barry's wife which I only remember her name because I met her at all those weddings. Why must Italians end all their women with 'a'?" she complained, blithely ignoring the fact that the names of her own closest cronies—besides Marta—were Manya, Frieda, Anya, Rena, and Sonia.

Until Marta reminded her tonight, Henny had forgotten ("Am I a computer?") that Francesca was one of Marta's longtime clients. A status, Henny added in a an aside, highly coveted by Sonia, who mistakenly assumed Barry's marrying Francesca's daughter would automatically grant her fingernails access into Marta's inner sanctum.

Anyway, it was only natural Francesca should confide in Marta about what happened to poor Miko, which inevitably led into a rehashing of the old tragedy surrounding Miko's mother. For years Marta always felt Francesca was keeping something back, but maybe it was only because she was embarrassed about having an in-law go loony-toons.

"But everybody already knew that, Henny," Frank said through a huge yawn.

Henny was insulted. "Excuse me if I'm boring you, Mr. Bernstein-who-already-knows-everything. I'll tell your wife, who doesn't. Ava, did your brilliant husband also know that everybody was killed when that mental home or whatever it was, burned down a few years ago, because of a fire they said was arson?"

Frank, suitably chastened, apologized profusely until Henny said with extreme satisfaction, "Don't grovel, schmekel!" and hung up again.

Henny had certainly given us a lot to chew on. Now Cherry Rose also had to explain why she'd claimed her aunt Toshiko was seriously ill when she was in fact dead. Surely, she knew Nobuo would contradict that story when it got back to him.

Only the story had gotten back to him, via Frank and me.

So why hadn't he contradicted it?

TWENTY-TWO

DURING THE LAST frantic week of prep for *Dr. Upharsin and the Flying Cloak of Death,* we hit more high and low notes than an opera. Mostly because the unique, barn-raising approach to this project meant all victories and disappointments were experienced more feverishly in a communal way than would normally be the case, but there was also an indefinable undercurrent of personal tension and conflict adding to the already high stress factor.

By Wednesday my script doctoring was nearly complete, except for a few miscellaneous incisions and stitches, and two very critical subtitles which were pivotal to the plot. In order to get a better feel for the mood, I decided to walk over to the maze, where one of them would be shot.

In the business of art and entertainment—or any other business for that matter—perspective can mean the difference between success and failure. The more people who respond favorably to your specific angle on a vision, the more visions you'll be paid to interpret.

Since we'd begun working at Wei-Side, I'd never varied my route between car and office, and the change of pace was refreshing.

It was a pleasure to encounter such well-maintained beauty as

I crossed the red wooden bridge arching across a decorative but deep stream—yet another body of water for Dimples and Dumpling to resist—which led to the garden maze.

Classic British horticulture had been approached from an eastern direction, and nowhere more so than in the topiary art form known as a maze, where traditional yew hedges were translated into severely disciplined eight-foot bamboo stands with sudden small groves of fragrant mimosa, persimmon, Japanese plum, and oleanders marking the dead ends.

The goal was a clearing in the center, shaped like a crescent moon, where one of Nobuo's koi ponds boasted a waterfall and was ringed with flowering ginger, vermilion, orchids, and birds-of-paradise.

In addition to the gardener's scene, to be played against one of the oleander groves, there would also be a dramatic stalking sequence through the maze which Frank and Russ had storyboarded to cover helicopter, stalker, and victim POVs.

At the maze's entrance I hesitated. Though the true path to its heart was clearly marked with Malibu lights, the false trails were not, and I had no way of knowing which led to the oleander bushes. To perhaps get lost and wander through a half-acre of jungle until somebody realized I'd disappeared was not my idea of how to spend a couple of hours, but the day was beautiful and it felt so good to be away from my computer screen, I turned onto the path leading to the center.

Immediately, I was enveloped in tall bamboo shadows, surrounded by a loud rustle of leaves and the tinkling of invisible windchimes. It was deliciously spooky and sexy, and I had half a mind to go back and lure Frank into the maze for something that would truly amaze him.

The bamboo was so thick you could barely glimpse a crack of light between the poles, its angles and curves so incredibly precise as to look artificial. Nobuo had told me that this effect required an unrelenting, arduous, and complex process of cutting each unwanted reed down to a certain ring joint, then pouring poison into the resulting hollow to destroy its root system, or the stuff would run rampant practically overnight, choking everything in its path.

Which makes it perplexing as to how the virtually extinct panda population in China could possibly be devouring bamboo forests at a rate beyond regrowth capacity as has been reported.

The breeze picked up, setting the reeds to creaking and sighing, sounding almost like voices echoing mournfully along the narrow corridors. At one point I stopped, certain that I did indeed hear people talking, but given the acoustics of the maze it was impossible to determine from what direction they emanated.

As I continued on the path, the maze worked its magic and I began to visualize the encounter between the two men. In fact, I was so caught up in the scene that for several moments after turning a sharp corner, it didn't register I was really looking at two flesh-and-blood women, standing about fifty yards away.

When I recognized Davida and Rikka, some impulse urged me to duck out of sight before they spotted me. Inexplicably, I obeyed, wedging uncomfortably between the bamboo and a huge boulder arranged artistically on the trail, praying there were no cobras lurking in this bamboo like the terrible movie that had given me nightmares as a child.

Although now I couldn't see Davida and Rikka, the change of position enabled me to hear them better. Maybe the boulder acted as a transmitter.

"... why you're still hanging around," Rikka's voice faded in. "Doesn't it torment you to watch the great Nobuo Wei being putty in my hands?"

Davida laughed. "Let me define torment for you. Torment is when something sweet and good suddenly ends and you don't know why. Now that I've seen the situation with my own eyes, I'm frankly relieved."

"What do you mean?" demanded Rikka.

"Oh, come now." Davida sounded impatient. "You're definitely not in love with Nobuo, which means you're using him to fulfill some private agenda. And by the way, if you think he hasn't picked up on that vibe already, then you are the naive putty person in this scenario."

Rikka's tone contained a shrug. "I doubt that very much, since I am the woman he moved into his home and you are not."

"Then maybe you should ask yourself why," suggested Davida. "Could it be that Nobuo also has an agenda and he's just using you while he's got you where he can keep his eye on you?"

Swift as a snake, Rikka struck back. "His eye isn't what he's been keeping on me," she gloated. "When I said Nobuo is putty in my hands, what I really meant was—"

"Shut up! Just shut up!" Davida shouted hoarsely.

The dry bamboo leaves carpeting the path crackled beneath her running feet as she fled from Rikka's jeering laughter.

I'd come to the maze for atmosphere, but this was ridiculous.

TWENTY-THREE

I STAYED WHERE I WAS, waiting for Rikka to leave, shocked because my friend Davida, who'd engaged in vicious, kill-or-be-killed knife combat beneath the scorching Sinai sun, had turned tail and retreated from a mere Rikka Tring.

But I was even more stunned by the revelation that Nobuo Wei had been Davida's "inscrutable" Asian lover, the one who'd pleaded with her to marry him and then abruptly abandoned her. Among Cherry Rose's accusations against Nobuo was that he'd abandoned his wife and daughter—maybe he was one of those men who simply bail out of their responsibilities. And yet he seemed like such a mensch. There had to be another explanation.

I knew Davida's heart, so newly mended, was breaking again. Why wasn't Rikka leaving? I'd been crouched in this deep-knee bend for nearly two minutes, and my thighs were killing me. Maybe holding the same position for so long would break up some cellulite.

At last I heard feet crunching on the path. I figured I'd slowly count to thirty before I stood up so Rikka would be far enough ahead not to notice I was behind her. I'd gotten to three when I realized the steps were arriving, not departing.

"You're late," Rikka greeted the new arrival. What was she doing, using the maze as her office?

"Some of us have actual labor to do as opposed to slinking around looking like Kwan Yin," whined Woo Kazu. "Don't confuse me with one of your big Nip studs who'll come galloping to your service whenever you whistle."

Rikka made a derogatory noise. "As if."

"Now is that any way to talk when I come bearing a lovely gift?" Woo huffed. "Remember, this clandestine little rendezvous here in the jungle was your idea, I can't help but wonder why."

"Well, I thought it was time we got to know each other better, Woo. But for that we need privacy, and what better place than this? Or what better way to get to know somebody than to open that nice present you promised me?"

"Just call me Santa Claus," Woo invited archly, "and watch me make it snow. Shall we get ourselves comfy on that great big rock over there? It's got a flat spot in the middle where I can lay out some lines."

Oh, no. They were heading right for my hiding place! At least I was able to use the noise of their approach to shift the crouch to a kneel.

"I was kinda surprised when you hit me up for some blow," Woo confided, tapping a glass container against the boulder. "Miko said she'd never seen you use anything but a little grass now and then." He tapped the glass several more times. "There. Now that's what I call coke on the rocks!"

A bit later Rikka said dreamily, "Miko doesn't...didn't know everything about me."

Woo sounded doubtful. "Well, maybe not. But I'll tell you one thing. She figured you're running some kind of scam on her father."

"She did? How so?" Rikka drawled lazily.

"Frankly, I didn't pay much attention," admitted Woo. "Except she mentioned something about New York and we should all start looking for a star in the east, whatever that means. Oh, yeah. And that her brother was such a moron he'd believe anything. Hey, this is good stuff. Let's do a few more lines."

"So what do you think happened to Miko?" Rikka asked Woo.

"Beats the hell outta me," he muttered, absorbed with the careful tapping of glass against rock. "All I know is when I saw blood, I—" He broke off abruptly. "Here, you go first."

While they went another round, I fantasized about what would happen if one of them sucked a couple of ants up their nasal passages.

Eventually, Rikka said, "Woo, you know that hot-looking, red-haired cop?"

"Weinberg, you mean? Not my type, honey!" Woo camped.

Rikka laughed. "Oh, but you could be his type, Woo. See, I heard him tell Nobuo something nobody else knows. Nobody but me. They got back the toxicologist's report on Miko this morning and guess what? There was almost a whole gram of coke in her bloodstream. Seems like she'd just done some right before she died. Now where on earth do you suppose she got it?"

"Miko always had coke." Woo's words seemed to travel from a distance.

"Not that night, Woo. I specifically threatened her if she got high before the show because it could ruin our act, and she told me to chill out, she didn't even have any but she'd made a date to fly kites after the show. Because Miko knew she could always count on her kite-flying buddy to score her some, didn't she?"

Woo tapped the glass container suggestively. "Does that interest you?"

"I'm a woman of many interests," Rikka replied obliquely. "Beverly Hills real estate, for example. I got to wondering about certain things, so I looked up the title to the building where Bonsai is now and you know something? One of the former owners was also a partner in that gym. Seems like he financed the boutique as a showcase for an exclusive edition of his famous workout wear."

"Then you must also know he went bust and sold out," Woo said grumpily.

"Yes, but not before he personally approved the remodeling plans of the next tenant," Rikka countered. "So this guy would have to know all about that weird door arrangement, don't you think?"

"There must be a point to this story," Woo observed sourly.

"See how well we're getting to know each other?" Rikka purred. "The point, my dear little Woo, is that from now on I really do expect you to come running to my service when I whistle. Like right now." She whistled softly. "Make it snow again for Rikka, Santa Claus."

TWENTY-FOUR

TWENTY MINUTES LATER, I limped into the production office, looking for my husband, but no one knew where he was.

After instructing the secretary to send the next available GoGo Gofer (the independent bicycle messenger service we were using) out to search for him, I got a liter of Evian from the fridge and dragged my aching self to the haven of my office. Flopping onto the sofa, I pressed the cool plastic bottle against my forehead as if it could still the thoughts tumbling around my skull like a heavy load of laundry in the dryer.

What I'd unintentionally overhead was far more than I ever wanted to know, but not nearly enough.

To recap, Davida and Nobuo had been lovers, the relationship so serious he'd proposed to her several times. At the Bonsai opening she told me her then-unidentified boyfriend suddenly dropped her about two months ago. This roughly coincided with when Miko would've been recruiting models for Bonsai's grand-opening fashion show. How could Miko have guessed she was also providing Rikka Tring with her own personal grand opening to (quite literally) a cushy berth in her father's house?

Somehow their affair tied in with what Woo said about Miko figuring out Rikka was running a scam on Nobuo.

Prior to moving in with Nobuo, Rikka had obviously been physically intimate with Guido; just as obviously, she'd cut him off. Whatever story Rikka told Guido, he'd been gullible enough to buy it, but Miko knew it wasn't true.

However, that didn't necessarily have anything to do with her murder. It wouldn't be the first time a gold-digger had gotten her hooks into a rich older man while keeping her big dumb stud on the back burner.

More sinister was Rikka's frank admission to Woo that she'd deliberately set out to get something on him, and succeeded. So he had known how to sneak into the storeroom unnoticed, and virtually admitted he'd seen Miko's body. Most likely touched her, too. Which would explain those bloody tissues in the wastebasket.

Since the show had been rehearsed many times, Miko knew exactly where the sedan chair would be and arranged to meet Woo there to "fly kites." Though why she'd chosen that particular spot when there were two empty offices available, I couldn't imagine. But if Miko was already dead when he got there, where did she score all that coke, when she'd previously told Rikka she was completely out? Of course, she could've just been lying to get Rikka off her back.

Unless Woo was lying and killed Miko himself after they'd done a big load, though it didn't seem like there would've been enough time for Woo and Miko to snort such a large amount of coke, then for him to stab her and break her neck.

As to what his motive might have been, apparently they had a history together, however coke-addled. And unless I told Weinberg about this, I would be history, too.

I am not, however, famous for confronting issues and this time was no exception. To avoid taking immediate action, I returned to my desk and escaped into the fantasy world of Dr. Upharsin, where I could control the characters to some extent. I managed to lose myself so completely in hammering out the subtitle involving Dr. Upharsin and the Major's enigmatic Japanese gardener at the oleander grove, that when my phone rang I experienced the same heart-pounding sensation as being awakened by the sudden clang of an alarm clock.

It was the production secretary, calling to say Frank had been with Russ at a special effects house in Santa Monica, but Russ had just called from his car to say they were on their way back.

As I hung up the phone, Nobuo gave a cursory knock on the door frame, then entered, filling my office like an air bag.

"How are things going, Ava?" he asked.

"I think I'm about to hit the home stretch," I told him. "Just a little more to do on this piece, then comes the gardener voyeur scene and finally, the biggie with Dr. Upharsin and the Baron before their showdown."

He smiled. "Very good. Which are you doing right now? Mind if I take a look?"

"The one about how leaves of poison protect delicate flowers," I said, turning the paper I'd been scribbling on to face him. "And of course, I don't mind. *Dr. U* is your baby, after all."

Nobuo made a face. "I find that particular expression distasteful in the extreme, Ava."

I was taken aback. "I'm sorry."

"No, it is I who should apologize for reacting in such a boorish way," he said contritely, patting my hand. "I think I must be more stressed out than I realized."

I studied him as he leaned forward over my desk to read the

subtitle, strong face close to mine, catching a breath of his cologne—something French and dry and seductive—and thanked God I was at last happily married to the most wonderful man on earth and no longer vulnerable to being swept away by a muscular, volatile being with looks, creative genius, and oodles of money.

Been there, done that.

Nevertheless, I was relieved when he jotted down a couple of suggestions, then straightened up and walked over to the window. Staring out, he said abruptly, "Tell me, Ava. You know my niece fairly well. Do you think she is capable of murder?"

"No, I don't," I said honestly. "But for every murderer that's ever killed, there are family and friends swearing it's not possible the person they've known and loved could have done such a terrible thing. I'm sure Adam and Eve felt that way when Cain killed Abel, and that's when they were the only four people on the planet!"

He was gazing out the window once more, so I addressed his broad back, straining against the fine white cotton shirt. "Anyway, how is this relevant? Cherry Rose is in the clear. Barry, too, for that matter."

Nobuo looked at me over his shoulder. "As you just said, Ava, things are not always as they appear to be."

I began to feel angry. "If you're going to paraphrase me, Nobuo, have the goodness to do it as accurately and honestly as I'm trying to do with these subtitles," I retorted, pounding my fist on a copy of the script. "And given the timetable, just how do you suppose your niece managed to kill her cousin, your daughter? But more importantly, why?"

Nobuo turned and crossed to sit on the edge of my desk. "Since we are hypothesizing, I will admit I have formed no opinion on the method," he said harshly. "But the motive is a time-tested one, Ava. Money." He shifted his weight and leaned toward me again, fixing bottomless black eyes upon mine compellingly. "I am worth a few million dollars and change. And as you know, Cherry Rose now stands to inherit more sizably than before."

I shrugged. "Cherry Rose and who else?"

He looked confused. "I beg your pardon?"

"Who else besides Cherry Rose might have had reason to hope to inherit a larger share than before Miko died?"

"Why—well, but that's not the point," he blustered.

"Oh, yes it is, Nobuo," I argued. "Technically, any of your major legatees—not just Cherry Rose—would've been one up in line for a bigger piece of the pie, should you have chosen to give it to them. But you're overlooking a couple of pivotal things, in my humble opinion."

Nobuo gave me a challenging look. "Do tell," he said icily.

"First of all, forget Cherry Rose getting more. Did she even know she was down for anything in the first place?"

"That is most unlikely, since for years I had virtually no contact with any of my family until comparatively recently. Naturally Miko, as principal heiress, was aware of her own position and some of the generalities. Beyond that, only I and Mr. Masumo know the exact contents of my will. The exception being the codicil you witnessed concerning...Miss Tring."

I nodded. "Fine. Just hold that thought, Nobuo. Because if Cherry Rose had no certainty, only a vague hope that someday her rich uncle might remember her in his will with a few bucks, then the money motive doesn't wash. And even if she somehow got wind of your intentions, killing Miko did her no good at all because your lady friend came along and scooped the entire pot."

By now Nobuo was regarding me with grim amusement.

"Please continue," he invited, in a silky, dangerous voice.

"Obviously, Cherry Rose couldn't have anticipated that. So, what are we left with? If Cherry Rose knew she would inherit, but didn't know that Rikka would walk off with Miko's share, and if she indeed did kill Miko..." I paused delicately.

"Go on!" he thundered, no longer amused.

I stood and leaned forward until my face was very close to his, bracing myself against that enticing cologne. "...that means she's totally desperate to get her hands on your money. But, of course, she can't get it until you die, so Cherry Rose must've been planning all along to kill you, Honorable Uncle!"

TWENTY-FIVE

FRANK WALKED INTO the supercharged silence and grinned knowingly.

If he thinks every man in the world is after me, who am I to disillusion him? Besides, this confrontation with Nobuo, coming right on the heels of my eavesdropping session, left me too wrung out to try to explain the real reason why an incredibly sexy actor and I were standing with our faces mere inches apart.

Grateful for the interruption, I slumped back down into my chair and left Nobuo to fend for himself.

"Your wife would've made an excellent defense attorney, Frank," Nobuo observed. "If we had been in court just now, and I were the prosecutor, I would have lost the case."

Frank winked at me, not getting it. "That's my girl."

"Speaking of lawyers," I said. "Did Miko make a will of her own?"

Nobuo and Frank looked surprised. For some reason, this question had never been raised before.

I was thinking out loud. "If she did, then of course she must've left everything to Guido—" When I heard the echo of my words I could've cheerfully bitten my tongue. In his present mood, Nobuo wouldn't take kindly to the mention of his estranged wife's child born of adultery. Who also happened to be the former lover of his current mistress. Guido Hayashi certainly qualified as a thorn in Nubuo's flesh from every angle.

However, Nobuo merely gave his broad shoulders an impatient twitch and said he'd check on it with Mr. Masumo.

"What if she made a will through someone other than Masumo?" Frank asked.

Nobuo smiled briefly. "Miko had recently become obsessed with 'exploring her Asian roots,' as she put it. Apparently, she felt I wasn't sufficiently Japanese to be of much help, and insisted on moving out and buying a condo in Little Tokyo. If Miko consulted a lawyer other than Mr. Masumo, you can be certain it would have been a member of the Asian community, and he will easily be able to discover the person's identity. There's not much that goes on in Little Tokyo he doesn't know about."

Or Little Saigon or Chinatown either, I'd be willing to bet.

"You know, I found Miko's sudden Asianization rather odd," Nobuo confided frankly. "Prior to that, she had lived at Wei-Side since relocating from New York as daughter of the house. A novel experience for both of us, and one too long postponed for...various reasons. I had every indication she was enjoying our reunion and her position of honor in my home as much as I.

"For instance, when my cook of many years mysteriously failed to return from her weekend off, abandoning her quarters here without notice or a word of explanation, Miko, on her own initiative, undertook to arrange for an immediate replacement. Naki has proven quite satisfactory."

Which was a highly conservative assessment of Naki's delectable culinary skills, in my opinion.

He rose to go. "Right after she'd seen Naki established, Miko moved out, despite my efforts to persuade her to stay. It was all very puzzling.

"Incidentally, Frank"—Nobuo paused in the doorway—"I wanted to ask you about that still photographer you hired. I understand she's causing trouble on the set."

Frank looked baffled. "Somebody's got their wires crossed, Nobuo. In fact, the actors Davida's worked with so far are wild about her because she gives them any pictures she doesn't plan to use for free. And Russ says she's even better than Delbert, which is high praise indeed."

Knowing what I did, I was so angry with Nobuo I literally couldn't speak for a moment. But when I found my voice again, I said, "Nobuo, Davida Yedvab is a dear friend of mine, and a woman of high personal and professional integrity. Rest assured, she did not ask for this job, nor did she ever reveal to me she was previously acquainted with you, something which I learned only today.

"Therefore, her being here at this nanosecond in time and space was clearly arranged by a Higher Authority, which perhaps should cause you to stop and ponder the great Why."

Both Frank and Nobuo were watching me as if I were a strange exhibit on display.

Gazing directly into Nobuo's eyes, I added quietly, "You know, it really wasn't worthy of you to try to get Davida fired in such a roundabout way. She doesn't deserve that. If you want her gone, tell her yourself. But by all means, tell her why."

A wave of anger and pain surged over his face, then he said softly, "But, of course, she will stay. It was indeed...foolish of me to be influenced by...rumors." He cast an ironic glance at Frank. "You see what I mean? Perhaps we should seriously consider enrolling Ava in law school." And with that, he hurried away.

Frank gazed after him in confusion, then turned to me. "What was that all about? I felt like I was watching a tennis game being played with an invisible ball."

I rose from my desk chair and closed the door. "Just remember you asked," I warned, taking his hand and pulling him down beside me on the sofa. Then I gave it to him straight, from the shadow of Woo Kazu on the wall, to Rikka taunting Davida about usurping her place with Nobuo, to Woo and Rikka doing coke in the maze, to Rikka's implicit blackmailing of Woo.

When I'd finished, Frank sat in stunned silence for a few beats, then said, "Remember that one tennis ball I couldn't see? Well, now I see them bouncing all over the place."

I sighed. "Because a lot of people are playing the games."

"Yeah. And I'm sorry to point this out, Ava, but maybe Davida's got her own inner tennis thing going on."

"What do you mean?" I demanded, childishly wanting to stick my fingers in my ears so as not to hear what I knew he was going to say.

That because of Davida's affair with Nobuo, she could've had a motive to murder Miko that didn't involve money at all.

Davida, whose Israeli army training had taught her how to kill with guns, knives, and her bare hands...

TWENTY-SIX

BLAME IT ON THE SWITCH from Evian to Pinot Grigio, but I was beginning to get cranky. "I don't care what you say, Davida would never kill anybody!" I proclaimed loudly to Frank, who was sprawled on the brown leather sofa in my office, plastic wineglass balanced on his chest. A half-empty bottle rested on the floor within easy reach.

He responded to this announcement with a grin, which caused me to halt in mid-diatribe and consider what I'd just said. "Well, okay. So Saul has slain his thousands and Davida her ten thousands. But you know what I mean. Davida would never attack an unarmed civilian, it wouldn't be kosher. So, ha!" I drained my own shatterproof goblet. If there'd been a fireplace, I'd have hurled it. Instead, I held it out for a refill.

Frank hoisted the bottle from the floor and motioned me over. "Murder's not kosher," he observed, splashing wine first into my glass, then his. "Thou shalt not kill. Very basic Torah stuff."

"Oh, shut up. you're beginning to sound just like Russ!" I snapped, then we both started laughing.

"All right," Frank conceded. "We don't talk about your pal anymore for now. Where does that leave us?"

I sat down on the floor across the coffee table from him. "I guess right back to where we were. Frank, there's so much we don't know, and probably never will.

"For instance, did Miko ever brag to anybody about how much she was going to inherit? I bet you anything she at least told Woo during one of their coke parties. And if she went that far, what would stop her from mentioning those 'generalities' Nobuo had apprised her of?"

Frank sipped thoughtfully before replying. "But even if she did blab everything to Woo, so what? I mean, how could he benefit by killing Miko? It's not as if he's in the will or anything."

I acknowledged his logic.

"However," he continued, "if Miko told one person, she probably told others. Like Cherry Rose and Barry."

I sighed. "Who do benefit from Miko being out of the way. No, I don't like that either, Frank. Because, as I pointed out to Nobuo, nobody benefits until he dies anyhow, no matter if every heir on the list goes down like a row of dominoes."

"Maybe that's the ultimate goal," Frank suggested. "Getting rid of Nobuo."

"Somehow, I can't see Mr. Wei allowing himself to be gotten rid of. Certainly not by a couple of pishers like Barry and Cherry Rose Lehr." But then I recalled Nobuo's expression when I'd said if Cherry Rose—or anybody else—had killed out of greed to inherit a bigger slice, he himself was their ultimate target—and realized something. He'd already thought of that and was taking it very seriously, however he might dismiss the notion as ridiculous.

"I'll tell you what I'm suddenly wondering about," Frank mused. "Nobuo said he and the rest of his family were estranged until recently. That includes Miko, as well as his brother Roy, Cherry Rose, and her siblings. I'd sure like to know what caused the thaw, and when it happened."

"Good point," I said. "Let's see. Right now, the farthest we can backdate it is before the Bonsai store plans were finalized, because when Miko came to L.A., she moved right in with Nobuo."

What could have happened that was powerful enough to dissolve forty years of ill will? Especially between Nobuo and the daughter he deserted, leaving her at the mercy of a mentally disturbed mother.

Finally, we were all talked out. The wine bottle was empty and shadows were filling the room. Frank caught my eye and patted the sofa seductively. "If you close the blinds, I'll lock the door," he offered.

I crossed to the window, but paused to admire the sunset. It was positively breathtaking, with purple and orange muted by a pearly haze of pink and gray. Frank stole up behind me and put his arms around my waist.

"Zee smog eez gorgeous tonight, my leetle pigeon," he Charles Boyered, "but not zo gorgeous as you. Come weeth me to zee zofa..."

Things got sillier from there. I was trying to remember one of Hedy Lamarr's sultrier lines when something outside caught our attention. We weren't the only couple taking this opportunity to enjoy the sunset, among other things. Though twilight was now falling rapidly, it was impossible to mistake the forms of Nobuo Wei and Rikka Tring.

As Frank and I watched, Nobuo took Rikka in his arms and kissed her, his hands roaming repeatedly from shoulders to derriere to back in a manner that impressed me as more of a gesture of possession—even ownership—than passion.

Frank nudged me, and motioned with his head toward a big pine tree outside our window. A woman was standing there staring at Nobuo and Rikka. Even in the dusk there was something clearly malevolent about her posture. It was Naki. As if suddenly aware of our presence, she started to turn around, and I twisted the wand just in time to click the mini-blinds tightly closed before she caught us looking.

There was no point trying to pick up where we left off. The promising moment had fizzled out, and I felt the initial stirrings of a post-vino headache. Anyway, we both had a couple more things to finish up before we went home.

Frank switched on the desk lamp. "Baby, will it bother you if I make my calls from here?" he asked.

"Not at all," I assured him. "In fact, after that creepy little scene, I'd be more bothered if you didn't."

Frank extracted a massive Filofax from his briefcase and sat down at my desk. "If people who spy on other people making love are called voyeurs, what does that make people who watch people spy on other people making love? Trois-yeurs?"

I shrugged. "I'm sure whatever it is sounds much better in French than it does in English. But listen, Frank. Do you think we've stumbled into that old standby gothic plot? Attractive servant girl living for years in hope of marriage to the master, only to watch him hook up with Dragon Lady instead?"

"Great storyline, Ava, but it won't fly." Frank laughed. "Remember? Nobuo said Miko just hired her two months ago."

"That's right, I was forgetting. Still, love can strike hard and fast. And so can jealousy."

"Uh-huh," Frank muttered absently, as he focused on punching up a phone number.

Since he had taken over my desk, I curled up on the sofa to study the last subtitle. It featured Dr. Upharsin and Lotus, pretending to be unaware of the Japanese gardener's presence as he spies on them. Using the gardener's tortured lust for Lotus, they fake a hot and heavy love clinch, trying to goad him into jealousy strong enough to show her where the maze's secret treasure is buried.

I pondered the curious parallel between this scene and what we'd actually witnessed a few moments before and decided things were getting just a little too déjà vu around here.

TWENTY-SEVEN

IT WAS SURPRISING that Barry or Cherry Rose eventually left a copy of the *Dr. Upharsin* script behind at Bonsai during one of their frantic lunchtime excursions. To me, the surprise was that Guido Hayashi could even read—much less comprehend—anything beyond simple words and phrases contained in balloons over the heads of unpleasant comic book characters like *Spawn*.

Nevertheless, two days before we had to break for Passover, Guido showed up on the set, wanting to be in the film. Marty and Sam hailed his arrival as serendipitous, since they were having a hard time rounding up enough young male Asian extras who could do karate to augment the scene where Lotus and Dr. Upharsin stage a sexy combat demonstration for the pleasure of the Major's houseguests.

Guido, however, had his sites set on auditioning for the Japanese gardener, understandably identifying with that character's unrequited Lotus-lust. But not only was he too physically large for the part, this particular gardener was a difficult, sensitive role requiring the finesse of a seasoned character actor. Marty and Sam were waiting for a final decision from Robert Ito, the guy who played Jack Klugman's assistant on *Quincy*.

When Guido realized it was combat arts extra or nothing, he grudgingly adjourned to Wardrobe, where he was issued a wide red-and-black-printed headband, and red drawstring sweat pants designed by Woo Kazu.

A couple of hours later, Guido and the others were drilling out on the east lawn, directed by Presley Shores, who stood on a tall ladder, yelling commands at them through a bullhorn in his North Florida twang. Guido was easily the best of the bunch, no doubt working out his frustrations in the strenuous routine. And showing off as well, for among the admiring audience observing from the sidelines was Rikka Tring.

Davida, dodging here and there, snapping pictures of the action, accidentally backed into Nobuo. When she realized who it was, she jumped like a scalded cat and raced away. But I noticed his eyes followed her.

Woo Kazu was also darting back and forth, trying to gauge the visual effect of his "Combat Stud Wear" as he'd named it. At one point, he even swarmed up the ladder behind Presley, impervious to even the rawest Floridian epithets the AD hurled down at him.

Finally Presley called for a break. Clambering down the ladder, he headed toward the drinks table, where I was standing with Marty and Sam. "Gotta tell ya, that big ol' boy out there is damned good," he announced, reaching for a cold bottle of Fat Weasel ale. "Better'n the others. Except for his you-know-what."

Guido was posing a technical problem. The Combat Studs were working shirtless. And shirtless Asians are supposed to be hairless, or very nearly so. But Guido came equipped with that Italian shag carpet on his chest, plus matching runners on the forearms.

The makeup man was summoned, and recommended waxing since shaving or depilatories would not only not produce that smooth Niponic sheen, but would probably make Guido's chest and arms break out in unattractive little red bumps. "But the waxing can cause ingrown hairs," the makeup man cautioned. "Anyway, where is it written they all have to have baby-butt chests? Besides, I think the fur looks good on him. Don't you?"

"Oh, yeth! Thimply fetching!" Presley lisped, drooping his wrist.

"Shut up, you redneck bigot!" the makeup man snarled.

"Ooh! You're so beautiful when you're angry!" squealed Presley, and swept the makeup man into a tango. Then the two clowns stomped off cheek-to-cheek.

A moment later, Naki and her houseboys arrived with the afternoon's load of dim sum. While everybody else scrambled to get in line, Guido opted to lean picturesquely against a tree, and I had to admit, that chest looked positively ab fab, as was.

Naki evidently thought so too, because the minute she got a look at him, her face lit up. I couldn't believe it when, with her very own hands, she filled a plate and, wearing a dazzling smile, trotted it over to Guido. While Guido devoured the food, her eyes frankly devoured him from head to toe. It looked like our Naki had found a new love interest to take her mind off Nobuo for a while.

Marty and Sam were equally stunned. "If she-who-never-laughs responds like that to Guido, just think of the reaction of more normal women all over America!" Sam gloated.

Marty chewed one end of his wispy mustache. "We're going to get mail about that chest," he predicted. Sam replied cheerfully, "Then let's go for great big sacks of it!"

Whereupon they upgraded Guido to Lead Stud, which meant plenty of full-on frontal torso shots. "He'll be a star!" they crowed.

Despite his promotion, during the next two days it was all too evident Guido yearned to resume his former real-life role as Rikka's pet poodle, but she never gave him the chance. If, however, she thought she was fooling Nobuo by ignoring the poodle, she was kidding herself, because I caught him wearing that cynical expression as he observed Guido staring forlornly after her.

It got right down to the wire, but by sundown Thursday, the casting was complete (minus Robert Ito, who became unavailable but fortunately Marty's and Sam's second choice signed on) the scenes were blocked, and the costumes finished.

Davida, Woo, and the Lehrs were among the first to leave, all politely declining Lil's invitation to seder. By now, Cherry Rose's skin looked like a nicotine-stained filter tip.

A limo had delivered Manfred Walter from the airport to Wei-Side, where he was now ensconced as Nobuo's houseguest.

When Lil got a look at Jose, the mahogany giant of an authentic Amazon Indian who was to play Fero, the Baron's loinclothed assistant, she clutched her forehead and uttered a fervent prayer of thanksgiving that Tex Wing had reneged.

Marty and Sam departed to their separate family gatherings, uncharacteristically subdued as the gates of Wei-Side swung shut behind their cars.

After so much intensive preparation, it was difficult to realize that, come Monday morning, the actual shooting of *Dr. Upharsin and the Flying Cloak of Death* would begin at last.

TWENTY-EIGHT

MY BODY CLOCK was still set to 5:00 a.m., the hour we'd become accustomed to leaping from bed to shower to the 405 freeway. The bliss of recalling I didn't have to do that today was tempered with an accompanying awareness of a mild hangover.

It had been a night of matzohs and madness, beginning with the Meyers's traditional seder for forty—one guest for every year our forebears wandered in the Wilderness of Sin. Really, that's what it was called.

Table talk featured a lively and colorful debate about whether the Ark of the Covenant (as in *Raiders of the Lost*) would be unearthed in Ethiopia or from beneath the Temple Mount, with excellent cases presented by both factions; a messianic rabbi who was recruiting support for an expedition to find the Ark (as in Noah's) a potentially dangerous mission because of the former Soviet Union Army's tendency to shoot impartially at anyone getting near the believed site. Frank thought the venture would make for a fantastic documentary. Yes, it's been done, but what hasn't?

There was also some angst I didn't quite understand about the prophetic significance of the ten toes on the iron and clay feet of the statue in King Nebuchadnezzar's weird dream as recounted in Daniel, Chapter 2; and an unlikely rapport between Lieutenant Bernard Weinberg and an earnest, bespectacled young man regarding the latter's thesis on the Dead Sea Scrolls. It didn't seem quite the moment to bring up what I'd overheard in the maze, cluck, cluck, cluck.

Afterward, Frank and I had merely rolled about twenty feet into our own living room, where we'd made some serious inroads on that barely touched bottle of Remy XO, and he'd presented me with a surprise gift—a beautiful emerald silk kimono purchased at a shop recommended by Nobuo Wei.

And, of course, I was expected to model it...

When I woke the second time, it was nearly noon and I was feeling lethargic. In the distance, I heard the faint click of computer keys, which meant Frank was putting in some last-minute work on *Dr. U.* My heart skittered with excitement at actually standing on the brink of our first real film together. No matter how many times you've been burned in Hollywood, it only takes the tiniest flicker of hope to get you to stick your hand back in the fire.

I lay in bed for a few minutes, entertaining visions involving Emmys, a large boat awaiting our pleasure at Marina del Rey, and his 'n hers Land Rovers nestled in the garage of our small but jewel-like Bel Air estate. New wardrobes filled our his 'n hers walk-in closets: It would be nice to buy Escada on the second markdown instead of waiting for the third.

Oh, well. At least I didn't have to fantasize about that rich aroma of freshly brewed coffee wafting into the bedroom. I got up and slid on the kimono, tying the sash as I entered the kitchen. It looked great, but I was having problems with the sleeves, which billowed out of control with my every move like sails flapping uselessly in the unskilled hands of a landlubber. Finally, I just gave up and draped them back over my shoulders so I could pour a cup of coffee.

Hearing kitchen noises, Dumpling galloped in, followed by Dimples at a more sedate pace. I figured they hadn't been fed yet, and they made no effort to dissuade me from the notion. I was just getting out their bowls when Frank walked in, wearing a terry robe and a yummy sliver of Speedo trunks.

"Ava, I just fed them ten minutes ago," he informed me. "Bad girls!" he scolded the dogs, trying not to laugh at Dumpling's effort to look innocent. It wasn't the first time she'd played the double-breakfast scam, getting Dimples to go along with her.

When the dogs spotted Frank's bathing suit, they promptly abandoned their plans to embezzle more food and bounced enthusiastically. I'd forgotten today was to be the final exam for their pool obedience certificates.

Promising to join them outside in a few minutes, I'd just gotten the sleeves arranged for another coffee-pouring maneuver when the doorbell rang. I shoved the carafe back onto its Teflon warmer, wondering who could be so thoughtless as to just turn up on our front porch this early, when I remembered it wasn't that early.

Squinting through the peephole, I was astonished to see Cherry Rose Lehr, wearing those big sunglasses that made her look like an insect.

"Hi, Ava," she greeted me as she entered, giving my kimono a professional glance of appraisal. "Very nice, good color," Cherry Rose commented, and uttered a brief cackle because when I closed the door behind her, one of my sleeves got caught on the knob.

"Ava, you're wearing the sleeves all wrong!"

"Excuse me?" I retorted haughtily, knowing she had to be right and hating it because I couldn't see how. "There's some esoteric Japanese thing I'm missing here?"

"Yeah, there is." She raised my arm and pointed to a slit. "Look. And there's one under the other arm, too. See, when you are doing non-glam things, you put your arms through those slits. But when you are doing a glam thing, like raising a glass of champagne to your lips, you put your arms all the way into the sleeves."

Although I'd noticed the slits, I hadn't understood their purpose and last night, when I'd made my debut in it for Frank, it hadn't stayed on long enough for me to get the technique of the thing. With poor grace, I inserted my arms through the slits and proceeded to pour coffee for us both with the greatest of ease.

"Frank's outside giving the dogs lessons in pool etiquette," I told her. "Shall we join them?"

"No!" she rasped quickly, then gave a deep sigh and stared down into her cup. On the surface, Cherry Rose was a gritty, direct New Yorker, but she occasionally reverted to Oriental obliqueness and there was nothing to do but go along with it. While I waited for her to say whatever she'd come here to say, I experimented with the sleeves some more until I could smoothly transit from "glam" to "non-glam."

Finally, Cherry Rose spoke. "That robe looks good on you, Ava, but I always think a kimono seems a bit foreign and forlorn on Caucasian women in general."

"I expect it's the same with a cheongsam," I said, with some regret. If a simple kimono had inspired Frank to such an extent, logically, the next step would've been one of those luscious cheongsams. From Bonsai, of course. At a deep discount, of course.

"That's right." Cherry Rose was growing more animated and relaxed. "There has to be just the right ... attitude."

"Ah, like 'Hey, Joe! You got cigarette?' kind of thing?" I struck what I fondly imagined to be a World War II Shanghai B-girl pose.

She gave a faint smile of amusement. "Yes, but more like, 'Hey Joe! You got cigarette, nylons, and French perfume but don't count your eggs before they're laid, Roundeyes!'"

I thought I might be able to pull it off, at that. Maybe set the scene with some Andrews Sisters music and a bottle of sake ... even a black wig ...

"Ava." Cherry Rose's voice broke abruptly into my fantasy. "I need to talk to somebody. I'm really messed up."

I thought about warning her not to tell me anything she didn't want Lieutenant Weinberg to know, but I didn't. My curiosity was too overwhelming. However, I wasn't in the least prepared for what she told me.

"Ava, I...want a divorce."

I sat down suddenly. "But—Barry—Bonsai-all those weddings!"

Cherry Rose went on as if I hadn't spoken. "When I met Barry,

I was at a very low point in my life and my career. I had spent several years working for Miyake, Kenzo—all the big Asian designers. They incorporated a lot of my ideas, and a few times even bought a whole design. But my name was never on them—part of the deal. Those guys were getting all the press, all the glory, and all the glam. And then there was that two-year nightmare with Woo, which almost finished me off forever. I just couldn't see a way to break out of the pattern, so to speak. And then, Barry came along."

I refilled her cup and she sipped pensively. "Barry had the energy I needed," Cherry Rose explained. "The perspective and the drive. He loved my work and saw how we could get something going together." She glanced up at me ruefully. "No, Barry isn't such a great architect or designer," she admitted. "He is a fantastic engineer, though. You'd be amazed how important that can be in a garment. Also, he had very good concepts, even if he couldn't execute them properly. That's where I came in."

To Cherry Rose, floundering for an anchor both creatively and personally, a total partnership with Barry Lehr seemed like the perfect solution. And so they were married, and at some length.

Cherry Rose caught my expression. "Believe it or not, Ava, all those ceremonies really meant something to me."

And presumably to Barry as well, who hadn't exactly distinguished himself on his two previous trips to the altar. The first time was (Frank's eyewitness account) to an archetypical Jewish princess by the name of Roberta, who took Barry to the cleaners. Then there was Sandy, the potter, with her unshaven legs and armpits, who dragged Barry to Israel to live in an art kibbutz for what was supposed to have been six months. While Sandy soaked up the local clay, Barry was arbitrarily assigned to shepherd a flock of particularly ornery goats. Shepherd's and flock's hatred of each other was immediate and mutual, and quickly became the um, butt, of jokes around the old kibbutz.

Sandy, who had fallen in love with the land of her fathers, wanted to make aliyah, but Barry the shepherd adamantly refused. The last anyone heard, she had adopted the Hebrew name of

Sascha and was happily throwing pots as bride of one Shlomo Levinson.

At first, the union of Barry and Cherry Rose seemed made in hype-heaven. As they began to gain acclaim with their Bonsai label designs for various manufacturers, they also received plenty of press for their diverse family backgrounds, plus lots of attention from the paparazzi at international trendy spots. Cherry Rose's dream of nonstop glam seemed to be coming true.

The Puerto Rico plant was their next logical step, and eventually a Bonsai flagship store became a practically mandatory risk. But it was in Puerto Rico that fundamental flaws in the Huwei/Lehr liaison were exposed. Extended isolation from the pace of New York and other fun places made it clear that just getting along fine, working well together, and a love of exotic food, while important elements, did not necessarily make for a stable marriage.

Early on, they vowed never to discuss their relationship to death like many of their friends had, so an unverbalized estrangement developed, inevitably resulting in fear and insecurity. Barry began to demonstrate an unpleasing tendency to react to Cherry Rose as if she were his mother, a double blow when one remembered that his mother was Sonia.

But just when Cherry Rose was ready to pull the plug, things with Bonsai began to move at warp speed. This momentum carried them to the mainland, where the Lehrs found their former role as a moderately famous picturesque couple ready and waiting for them to slip into. Since then, their existence had continued at an equally frantic clip, but on a fairly even keel, until the past few months when they'd settled down at Chez Mouche to oversee the final details of Bonsai.

Here in La-La Land, along with the first scrap of leisure time she'd had in ages, had come many unwelcome realizations. But while Cherry Rose was grappling with how to stop her entire life from figuratively slipping away, Miko's life, quite literally, did.

TWENTY-NINE

FRANK CAME IN, toweling his hair. "Hey, where were you, Ava?" The girls were upset mommy wasn't there to see them go through their paces."

I jumped up from the table. "Oh, no! I forgot all about it. I'll come out right now."

"Too late," Frank said. "I've already hosed them down and they're stretched out on the chaises to dry. Baaad mommy."

"Well, Mommy had an unexpected visitor as you can see. But how did they do?"

"I am pleased to announce that Miss Dimples Bernstein and Miss Dumpling Bernstein passed their exams with flying colors and are now certifiably pool-perfect!" Frank declared, and I joined him in applause for their remarkable achievement, which was no small feat.

Frank grinned at Cherry Rose, who was looking blank. "Don't mind us, C.R. We tend to be pretty certifiable ourselves when it comes to those dogs." Tucking the towel into a sarong around his waist, he poured the last of the coffee for himself, added a shake of cinnamon, then joined us at the table.

"So," he said, eyeing Cherry Rose, "is this where we finally get to hear the explanation of why you and Barry lied to us about Nobuo and Miko's mother?"

Cherry Rose twisted uncomfortably in her chair. "I'm sorry," she muttered. "But don't blame Barry. I lied to him, too." Rubbing her eyes she added, "Shit, I don't know where to start."

"Let's take it from the top," Frank advised, director-like.

Cherry Rose heaved a sigh, then gave Frank a condensed version of where she'd gotten to when he walked in. Frank interrupted once, to ask if the reason she'd started to think the D-word was because of her renewed contact with Woo Kazu, but she vigorously denied it. "You're jumping ahead, Frank. Remember, I laid the big story on you guys before we knew there was even going to be a TV movie, much less that we would wind up working on it with Woo."

Frank just looked at her, and she laughed angrily. "Don't you believe me? Okay, so I'd had lunch a couple times with him. And yeah, he offered me coke and tried to make a pass. But like I've been trying to tell you, those days are long gone, as far as I'm concerned. I'm trying to save my life, not throw it away on some coked-up promiscuous little twerp."

"One more thing, long as we're on the subject of Woo," I began. "Oh, is that the subject?" Cherry Rose snapped. "I thought I was about to make my big confession here."

"And golly, we can't wait," I assured her. "But I just wanted to ask about those designs you allegedly stole from him."

She rolled her eyes, and I could see how bloodshot they were. "For your information, Ava, when Woo Kazu and I parted company nearly ten years ago, I left everything—including most of my clothes and all my sketches—behind. And it wasn't just noble sacrifice on my part, let me hasten to add. I'd been living there as well as working there, and he kept track of every line I drew. Whether via nostril or pencil."

She swirled cold dregs of coffee around in the bottom of her cup. "There is absolutely no truth to that rumor he's been trying to spread, and he knows it. Woo's just jealous because of what he thinks I've got, little does he know."

"Okay, C.R.," Frank said, after a long silence. "Please go on."

Although Cherry Rose was sure she'd reached the end of her rope with Barry, she also knew it would be totally suicidal to rock the Bonsai boat at that point. It was then she'd gotten the idea to propagandize Barry with a story which was based partly on truth: that Nobuo had been married to Toshiko but left her behind with their infant while he moved out to California, became rich and famous, and was estranged from his family for many years.

What Cherry Rose neglected to tell Barry was the entire truth.

Roy and Nobuo Huwei were the youngest sons of a influential and very strict New York Japanese family. When their parents died within a very short time of each other, Roy went nuts with his first taste of freedom, which culminated in eloping with an Italian girl, thereby reneging on his long-arranged marriage to a Japanese bride.

Thoroughly outraged, the remaining Huweis all but disowned Roy. Then, in order to retain at least some degree of family honor—not to mention appeasing the wrath of the bride's family—Nobuo's older relatives insisted that he step into the breach created by Roy.

"Uncle Nobuo was so devastated by Daddy's desertion, he didn't know what to do," Cherry Rose said. "This all happened on his sixteenth birthday. He was just a little kid! I guess he thought about that poor, abandoned bride and felt like they were birds of a feather," she conjectured. "At any rate, he agreed to go ahead and marry Toshiko, not that he really had a choice."

Apparently Toshiko had no choice in the matter, either. Nor had anyone guessed what rejection and resentment festered beneath that beautiful face.

"Mama said that nobody ever once saw her without full-on traditional makeup," Cherry Rose recalled. "I remember her only as the most fabulous creature I'd ever laid eyes on, and wondered why my own mommy didn't look like that!"

Roy's wife Francesca gave birth to Cherry Rose about a year before Miko was born to Nobuo and Toshiko. But Miko's birth had triggered a reaction in Toshiko which climaxed a year later with her attempt to poison Nobuo. "Fortunately, he noticed a strange taste in his tea," Cherry Rose commented dryly. "There was a terrible scene, where Toshiko became hysterical and totally unable to explain why she'd done it, begging forgiveness."

Nobuo had forgiven. Then within three months, Toshiko tried again. Twice. And once more, for the sake of family honor—both his and Toshiko's—Nobuo Huwei had departed for California, allowing himself to be branded as a wife and child deserter. "It was the most face-saving thing he could do," explained Cherry Rose. "Far better to be perceived as a heartless bastard than to bear the shame of being known as a man whose wife attempted to kill him three times.

"Of course, Daddy promised Uncle Nobuo to look out for Toshiko and Miko, but it was hard—he had a wife and baby of his own to worry about.

"So you see, there really was an estrangement, but it was mainly because my dad felt so guilty for what happened to Uncle Nobuo—which he was—that he was too embarrassed to get close to him again, even though Uncle Nobuo kept trying. It was only a couple of years ago, after Toshiko died in the fire, that Daddy was able to really forgive himself, and Uncle Nobuo was waiting with open arms."

Frank addressed Cherry Rose in a hard, sarcastic voice I'd never heard him use before. "Hey, it's been mesmerizing and all that, C.R. Obviously the guy hadn't suffered enough for forty years, so now I understand why you found it necessary to bash him in order to make sure we'd do your dirty work."

Cherry Rose's lips trembled and tears filled her eyes. "I know I deserved that," she admitted, "but you see, Barry would've gotten suspicious if I'd suddenly gone to visit my wicked uncle who deserted his wife and little baby girl." Her tone mimicked the one in which she'd told this lie with such apparent sincerity.

Frank was growing angry. "What the hell difference would it make?" he demanded, banging his fist on the table.

She flinched, but held her ground. "Because, Frank. I not only want a divorce, I want out of Bonsai. I don't have a nickel to my name that isn't tied up in our business." Her voice softened. "I still care about Barry, and I didn't want to create a big stink and ruin Bonsai for him. My plan was to present him with a fait accompli."

"Which was?" Frank prompted.

Cherry Rose smiled wanly. "I knew if you gave my message to Uncle Nobuo he'd instantly know there was something behind it—a code, sort of—and call me."

"Providing you with the perfect excuse to have a private meeting with him which Barry would've been only too glad to skip since he thought the story was true?" Frank guessed.

She nodded. "At which time I would grovel with apologies for slandering him, explain my reason, then offer him a chance to buy me out of Bonsai."

"What made you think he'd be interested?" I asked curiously.

"Oh, under the circumstances I was positive he'd be very interested," Cherry Rose replied, meaning Rikka and Guido.

"You guys came into it because Sonia said Henny told her you'd done some kind of work for him."

Frank looked at me and shook his head helplessly.

"So, where are we here?" I inquired. "Something tells me Barry doesn't know he's about to lose his wife, but gain a new partner."

Cherry Rose shrugged. "That's because so far, he's not. Uncle Nobuo listened very attentively to my tale of woe, then told me to cool off and give it some time. If I still felt the same way, he's consider my offer. Talk about deflating!

"Then, when Lil got in a bind over Tex Wing, Uncle Nobuo insisted on bringing us both in on the job. He told me maybe we just needed a different environment." She laughed. "Can you believe it? Nobuo Wei, the Relationship King! As if he's not caught like a fly in Rikka Tring's silken web."

"How did Rikka get into the picture anyway?" I wanted to know.

"Simple," said Cherry Rose. "Not only was she a popular runway model around the New York fashion scene, she also worked part time in a very expensive Park Avenue boutique. Then she moved out here to do that soap role, but a bunch of new writers came in and killed off her character. Miko and Rikka used to hang out a lot in New York, so when Bonsai finally went through and we needed somebody experienced to help us put things together in a hurry, Rikka was naturally the first person Miko thought of.

"And, of course, I had complete faith in Miko's business judgment, even though we weren't very close personally." Cherry Rose stood and began to pace the kitchen. "In fact, I wouldn't have trusted anybody else to manage Bonsai. At least at its delicate embryonic stage."

All I could say to that was "Oh, really?" while privately thinking I wouldn't have trusted Miko Hayashi with anything or anyone, under any circumstances.

Cherry Rose glanced swiftly from Frank to me and chuckled. "Oh, she made a pass at Frank, did she? Don't take it personally,

Ava. Miko was on automatic pilot where men were concerned, especially Caucasian men. I guess Ashkenatz counted as Caucasian with her because she even came on to Barry, if you can believe that!"

"Taking Freudian revenge on Uncle Vitello, no doubt," I retorted nastily. "Any old roundeyes is the same in the dark."

"Ava!" Frank exclaimed, surprised at hearing me talk that way.

Cherry Rose gazed at the floor a moment then replied, "I can't blame you for getting upset, Ava, and I'm not about to lapse into SallyOprahJennyRickiMontel speak, or anything. But what I am saying is, you don't have to approve of someone's actions to care about them. I understand—understood—Miko's behavior because I knew where it came from. I saw the abuse she went through."

After Toshiko and Nobuo split, Cherry Rose told us, Toshiko began to reject Miko. Then, when Guido was born, Toshiko contracted puerperal fever and nearly died, triggering the complete breakdown to follow. The first sign she was about to really crack occurred when she shut herself and the children away in her apartment, refusing to see anyone for over a month.

Finally, after many attempts, Cherry Rose's mother Francesca persuaded Toshiko to let her come inside. What she saw shocked her so badly, she immediately snatched up Miko and rushed her away. "Guido was a fat, pampered little prince while Miko was skin and bones, tottering around in a filthy diaper with bruises all over her body," Cherry Rose said, in a voice choked with ugly memories.

We listened numbly as she recounted how Miko came to live with them for a while, then was circulated among Toshiko's proud, insulated Japanese relatives. "They were too high-and-mighty to do anything in the beginning"—she curled her lip—"because it would make everybody 'lose face' to admit there was a problem at all. Anyway, since it was my Italian mother who exposed the situation, that made it okay for them to step in and take over."

It was soon after Miko had been removed from her mother's custody that Toshiko made the violent attack on Octavia, in her madness convinced that Vitello truly loved her and their son, and was committed to an expensive nursing home in Connecticut.

As Miko grew older, though still a child herself, she insisted upon taking care of Guido, which was fine with the rest of the family as the boy presented a serious embarrassment to them. Gradually, Miko became as fiercely possessive of Guido as Toshiko had ever been, carefully recording his every birthday, his every outing on film, sending prints to her mother in the vain hope of gaining some sign of approval. Though no response was forthcoming, Miko seemed to sense a silent demand from Toshiko for even more pictures of Guido, and strove to fulfill it.

"I think Miko told me she'd probably mailed Toshiko prints of more than three hundred pictures of Guido over the years before the place burned down," Cherry Rose recalled.

In effect, Miko became a surrogate mother to Guido, who, at nearly forty had remained unmarried and firmly under her thumb. Until eight months before, when they arrived in Los Angeles. Obviously, he could not stay at Nobuo's home with his sister, so she had rented him an apartment in Brentwood Village. But Miko was far too busy to keep her usual eagle eye on him, so he had happily run amok in the streets of Beverly Hills and across the campus of UCLA.

Unsurprisingly, he succumbed to the wiles of Rikka Tring and war broke out—Rikka on one side, Miko on the other, while Guido vacillated in the middle and Cherry Rose and Barry frantically attempted to umpire while enmeshed in the legalities and technicalities of opening Bonsai.

Finally, a furious Miko gave Rikka an ultimatum: Stop sleeping with Guido, or get out of Bonsai.

Rikka did stop sleeping with Miko's brother. Then she started sleeping with Miko's father.

THIRTY

NO, IT WASN'T A DREAM. I really was stretched out buck naked on a table, while a hefty Korean woman named Mrs. Tho, garbed only in black bra and fuchsia lace panties, vigorously scrubbed me from stem to stern with what felt like steel wool. She was chattering in her native tongue to three other women, identically clad and similarly engaged. Periodically, they'd break into giggles, no doubt critiquing and comparing the physical attributes—or lack thereof—of their respective clients.

When Mrs. Tho began sloshing me with buckets of water, deliciously warm and fragrant, I assumed she was done with the front, but instead she started all over at the toes and worked her way up again. Then she flipped me over like an egg and repeated the entire double performance on my back.

Next I was coated with a mixture of honey, crushed almonds, and milk, which was then kneaded into my skin by a deep-tissue massage. After that, Mrs. Tho packed my face in fresh cucumber pulp, which she'd personally mashed just moments before with mortar and pestle, and left me to marinate while she took a well-deserved break. At some point during these proceedings, I went into an alpha state and didn't come to until she had nearly finished washing my hair.

A few more sloshings of water and it was all over. Reluctantly, I dismounted the table to make way for the next lucky gal and staggered over to where Cherry Rose was sitting up to her chin in a steaming pool of inky black water. A sign on the wall announced it was filled with skin-beautifying dunghi herbs, which sounded terrible but smelled divine, rather like ginseng tea with honey. When I climbed in, whatever it contained fizzed like Perrier bubbles over my freshly scrubbed epidermis, making it tingle.

Cherry Rose acknowledged my arrival by fluttering one eye halfway open. "So how do you like it so far?" she asked drowsily, and seemed to comprehend the ecstatic little moans and groans which were all I was capable of uttering just then.

When Cherry Rose had invited me to come along as her guest to a Koreatown bath house called Seoul and Body, I had been a little leery. "Ava, it's not an oriental massage parlor," she'd laughed, correctly divining my hesitation. "Rather, it is, but not a naughty one. Trust me, you'll love it."

Naturally, I was squeamish and self-conscious about being the only bare-assed white girl in a sea of Asians, and realized I was getting a taste of what it was like to look different from everyone else around you.

"Don't feel bad, Ava," Cherry Rose comforted me as we passed a pair of identical Korean twins with identically perfect bodies, their jet-black bikini lines waxed into identical two-inch-wide racing stripes. "There are only two other Japanese women here besides me."

Startled, I demanded to know how she could possibly tell and she went into a whole rigmarole about nose-bridges and eyelid folds which I didn't even begin to grasp.

We were scheduled to get "the works," which included unlimited use of the sauna, steam, and waterfall rooms, then the hour-long body scrub and massage, but other ladies, who were apparently regulars, elected to scour themselves and assisted each other at the communal trough. There was a touching scene of a grandmother, mother, and daughter tenderly scrubbing down the ancient great-grandmother as if she was their most prized possession. Contrasting this respectful ritual to the harsh, utilitarian bathing procedures practiced at certain American homes for the elderly I'd had the great misfortune to visit, I shuddered.

The tingling black water was causing me to snap out of the trancelike state induced by Mrs. Tho. "What's in here, anyway?" I asked Cherry Rose, who responded by groping along the bottom of the pool with one foot, then lifting her right leg to display an enormous cheesecloth bag dangling from her toes. It was stuffed with sinister-looking vegetation, the vaunted dunghi herbs in action.

Cherry Rose let the bag plop back into the water, then we did a few minutes in the sauna followed by an ice plunge, a blast of steam, then a pummeling from the natural mineral springs thundering down through ceiling pipes in the waterfall room. Afterward, we collapsed onto a couple of plastic chairs lined up in a row against one wall.

"Well, what's next?" I asked my hostess.

"Your choice of shiatsu or accupressure massage, plus a facial," she said. "But first, we eat."

We slid into our Seoul and Body robes, and left the wet room, passing into a lounge area with a raised platform where several women were dozing on bamboo mats. The sleeping platform was flanked on either side by a giant TV. On one screen there flickered what appeared to be a Korean soap opera, while the other broadcast international stock market news.

Several sofas and chairs were arranged around the foot of the platform, where a few women in robes were eating and talking. We found empty chairs and were immediately served plates of melon and a pot of tea by a round little woman in a pink smock who seemed to materialize from nowhere.

"Mmm! Cherry Rose, this is the best treat I've ever had," I told her. "Thank you so much, kid."

She shook her head. "Ava, it's the least I could do, especially after what I put you through with Uncle Nobuo."

I gnawed a cantaloupe rind thoughtfully. "Speaking of Nobuo. He said Miko acted very happy at his house for several months, and that they were really enjoying each other's company. Then she suddenly shut down on him and moved out. Do you have any idea why?"

Cherry Rose frowned. "No, I don't. Miko wouldn't discuss the subject at all except to say she needed a more intense Japanese experience than she could get living with her father, who was so Americanized and Hollywoody. But the tone she started using when referring to him was completely different than it had been. It was almost like she'd come to hate him."

Pouring herself a cup of tea she added, "That's when Miko went on this 'I am so totally Japanese' kick, something she'd always rebelled against because her mother's people who'd raised her had been oppressively traditional. Would you believe, she even insisted she and I speak only in Japanese, but I told her that was ridiculous, and I was frankly fed up with all these groups wanting to separate themselves into little clumps against each other."

"Do you think she got angry at Nobuo because he had something going with Rikka? Could that have been the reason she moved out?" I asked.

"Well, she certainly wasn't happy about their affair, but that couldn't have been what triggered her move because those two didn't get together until after Miko bought that place in Little Tokyo," Cherry Rose said. "In fact, Nobuo was still trying to convince Miko to move back to Wei-Side when he met Rikka. He came over to Bonsai one day while Miko and I were having a meeting with Rikka to plan the fashion show, and *kaboom*. Ironic, huh? As you can imagine, there was no more talk of coming home to daddy after that!"

For the past few minutes, I'd become aware that an Asian woman—one of the two Cherry Rose had earlier pointed out as Japanese—seated on the sofa nearest to us, had grown increasingly interested in our conversation. When she realized I'd noticed, she blushed.

"Please excuse me," she said hesitantly to Cherry Rose. "I didn't mean to eavesdrop. But I heard you mention Mr. Nobuo Wei."

Cherry Rose was amused. "That's right. Would you like me to get you an autograph?"

The woman seemed taken aback. "I'm afraid you don't understand. My mother was his cook for many years, but—"

"Aha!" I exclaimed. "The one who just suddenly walked out on him without a word of explanation. He was very upset about that. Why did she leave him in the lurch?"

I was astonished when her eyes filled with tears. "Now I understand. He didn't fire her after all!" she sobbed. "I was wrong to be so angry at him."

The other ladies were staring over at us now. Cherry Rose and I managed to get the woman calm enough to tell her story.

Her name was Pat Tata, from Seattle. She and her mother, Kim Beraku, only spoke long-distance one or twice a month because Pat's job with an import company required extensive foreign travel. However, Pat's last trip had lasted much longer than usual and she hadn't talked to Kim for eight or nine weeks. Upon her return to

Seattle a few days ago, she'd immediately phoned her mother on her personal line at Nobuo Wei's home, only to have it answered by a complete stranger, a woman who informed Pat curtly in Japanese that Kim had not worked at Wei-Side for two months, then abruptly hung up; Naki exercising her usual charm.

Puzzled and concerned, Pat boarded the next plane to Los Angeles. "Mom always kept the apartment in Little Tokyo she and my dad shared until he died," Pat explained. "But when she started working as a live-in, she had the phone taken out. Said it was a waste of money to pay for it when she was there only a few days each month."

Pat blew her nose. "I figured she'd be at the apartment, but she wasn't. None of her neighbors had seen her for weeks, either. I was worried sick by then, so I went to the police."

And Pat had found her mother. In the morgue. She'd been hit by an express bus in Chinatown, around 4:00 p.m., the rush hour. Pat took a deep breath. "According to the police report, the driver said one second she wasn't there, the next she came dashing off the curb right in front of him. There was nothing he could do.

"And to make it even worse, some bastard stole her handbag when the crowd started gathering, so they had no idea who she was until I showed up."

After Pat made the final arrangements, she decided to visit Seoul and Body in honor of Kim, who had been a weekend regular, though Japanese of her generation rarely crossed Asian racial lines to mix with Koreans.

But, as Pat explained, her mother was a tightfisted lady who also loved her luxuries, and Seoul and Body was cheaper than comparable baths in Little Tokyo.

However, the few Japanese women who patronized the place sought out each other's company. Kim had introduced Pat to a couple of her friends, also employed as domestics. "Mom and I had a tradition of coming here together whenever I was in town," Pat concluded dejectedly. "I was hoping to spot one of her cronies, but I don't recognize anybody today."

"Pat, I'm so sorry about your mother," Cherry Rose said quietly. "Nobuo Wei is my uncle, and I know he'll be distressed to learn what happened to her. He'll also want to know if there's anything he can do for you."

Pat Tata smiled sadly and shook her head. "I've handled everything, thank you. But you might tell him for me I'm just relieved to find out he really is the decent man my mother always said he was."

THIRTY-ONE

THE NEXT DAY WAS Sunday and, somewhat to our surprise, Frank and I found ourselves en route to Wei-Side, where Nobuo had requested our presence as witnesses at the reading of Miko's will. For two people without the remotest hope of profiting from any demises in the Wei family, we were certainly becoming intimately involved with their various last testaments.

The swift location of Ms. Hanae Joon, the lawyer who'd drawn up Miko's will, had posed no difficulty for omniscient little Mr. Masumo.

By now, our car could practically drive itself from Encino to Brentwood. The only thing different about this particular trip was that Dimples and Dumpling had been left behind. After their strenuous expeditions into the heart of Nobuo's estate, one or both dogs always tried to sit on my lap on the way home, and I didn't want to deal with muddy paws on the linen outfit I deemed suitable for this sober occasion—my ancient, irreplaceable Mary Ann Restivo, featuring a jacket covered with leaping blue and gold panthers, paired with a blue basketweave skirt.

When we wheeled into the driveway, Mr. Masumo's Hawaiian

bodyguard/chauffeur was leaning against the black caddy limo reading a magazine, exactly like the first time we'd seen him.

One of the houseboys opened the door, then turned us over to Naki, who beckoned, rather theatrically, for us to follow her. As she led the way, we couldn't help noticing the new bounce in her step, the lively swing of that heavy pigtail, the suggestive little wriggle of hips.

Frank grinned. "Hooray for Hollywood!" he observed, sotto voce. Yes, indeed. For just prior to last week's wrap, Marty and Sam had suddenly discovered Naki, pronounced her and her pigtail picturesque in a *Good Earth* kind of way, and given her a tiny, nonspeaking role as Major Leland Temple's maid. So far, she'd voiced no complaints about being typecast.

Once again, our little parade halted at the library. Naki, who really was making the most of her big break, flung the doors apart in a dramatic gesture, motioned us to enter, then made a show of sliding them together behind us.

Inside the library, Cherry Rose and Barry were sitting on a sofa next to Manfred Walter, while like a moth, Mr. Masumo had once again been drawn into the clutches of that devouring chair. A stout, youngish Asian woman with stringy hair, slightly buckteeth, and horn-rimmed glasses hovered protectively over a somewhat battered leather satchel and a long, blue-backed document. Evidently the lawyer Joon.

Nobuo strode forward to greet us. "Frank, Ava! Thank you for coming on such short notice." He indicated the bar. "Will you join us in a Bloody Mary?"

Frank accepted the offer, muttering something about "hair of the dog," and rolling an accusing, red-rimmed eye at me. Cheongsam, Bonsai style, and sake had left their marks on him.

"Good morning, good morning!" Manfred Walter, tan, dapper and very pleased with himself on general principles, stood as we approached. "Ah, the director! And his lovely bride!" he boomed jovially, pumping Frank's hand, then holding mine far too long. Manfred fancied himself quite the ladykiller.

He blotted his perfect white mustache, then smoothed it sensuously with a forefinger. "I believe I hear my cue to take a little stroll in the rose garden," he announced. "Ta-ta for now, all!"

When he had gone, I took his vacated spot on the sofa by Cherry Rose, and Frank perched on the sensible straight chair which Mr. Masumo should've selected.

Plainly, Barry wanted to demand what we were doing there, but he just mumbled a greeting and returned to chewing his thumbnail. Cherry Rose raised her eyebrows inquisitively, and I shrugged a reply.

As far as I knew, witnesses were not required at will readings, so the only reason I could suggest for our presence was Nobuo's love of staging scenes, and scenes required an audience to watch them.

Hanae Joon rubbed her pudgy hands together and picked up the blue-bound document, but scowled at the slight negative movement of Mr. Masumo's head, which was as if a leaf had barely stirred in the faintest breath of air.

The room was unnaturally quiet. I caught the curve of amusement on Nobuo's lips, and wondered what we were waiting for.

Voices in the passageway heralded a new arrival, then Guido loomed into the library, escorted by a radiant Naki. Dear, oh dear. The girl had it bad.

"Ah, come in, Mr. Hayashi," Nobuo Wei invited. When Naki showed no signs of leaving, he added curtly, without looking at her, "That will be all, Naki."

She inclined her glossy dark head in a submissive gesture, treated Guido to another smouldering look, then melted silently from the room, pulling the doors to with a *snick*.

A little self-consciously, Guido swaggered to take the chair Nobuo indicated, keeping a wary eye on his rival. One swift glance around the gathering revealed the object of his lust was not among us, and he relaxed slightly. Where was the Tring, anyway? Morning sickness, perhaps?

Once again, the crumpled leaf stirred, and Ms. Joon went into action. First, she made a big deal of polishing her glasses, then cleared her throat nosily. Finally, after as much rattling of papers as possible, she began to read Miko's will in an unexpectedly pleasant voice.

After all, there were no astounding revelations. Miko, as predicted, left virtually everything to Guido, including the percentage of profits from Hayashi Tea Importers she'd inherited upon her mother's death. Which probably explained why Toshiko had naturally turned to tea as her weapon of choice in those attempts to murder Nobuo.

Now, thanks to Miko, Guido was not only completely free of restraint for the first time in his life, but rich enough to travel in the fast lanes of L.A. for a while. I watched that self-absorbed blob of testosterone in designer clothing sit there without displaying the slightest sign of grief or gratitude, and felt a sudden flare of anger.

But then, I glimpsed a strange expression lurking behind Guido's frozen features. Of course I couldn't be certain, but it looked like fear to me.

THIRTY-TWO

FRANK AND I CHOSE the restaurant this time. Helene's was a small, French Provincial cafe—mittel-European style—on the fringes of Beverly Hills. Or, as the ads in the *Los Angeles Times* real estate section prefers, Beverly Hills, adj.

At Helene's, the rolls were hot and crusty and the vin rouge maison smooth as silk on the way down, but dry enough to make your teeth grow fur.

Frank and I waited in the car until Barry and Cherry Rose pulled their Range Rover into the curb behind us on the secret little side street off Olympic where we always parked. Outside, dark clouds were gathering and it seemed likely we were about to get one of our rare thunderstorms.

The four of us walked wordlessly up the short block to Olympic, where Helene's was wedged unobtrusively between a Chinese laundry and Sylvia's Shmatas. As we entered, Cherry Rose's delighted squeal broke the unnatural silence.

"Oh, you guys! How terrific!" she exclaimed, waving an arm around the dining room, which was just kitschy enough to be authentic. The black-and-white mosaic tiles, only slightly chipped, were the 1920s original flooring, surviving from its first incarnation as a speakeasy, as did the mahogany bar, paneled walls, and ornate fireplace.

The gigantic cuckoo clock ticking above the mantel, plus mounted shofars and pen-and-ink drawings of the Holy Land dotting the walls were more recent additions to the decor—say mid-1950s.

Since it was too late for lunch and too early for dinner, we were the only customers in the place and had our choice of any of the small round tables.

When we were seated at the only one by a tiny, none-too-clean window (which Barry sardonically dubbed the power table) Frank ordered a basket of hot bread, bowls of onion soup, and a carafe of vin rouge from the French waiter, who'd been studying an English grammar book behind the bar when we walked in.

Upon tasting their soup, the Lehrs awarded high praise to the simple fare, but soon the heavy silence that had been hovering since we'd left Wei-Side enshrouded us again.

Cherry Rose crumbled a piece of bread abstractedly. Her troubled eyes kept straying to the worn briefcase resting at her feet. She'd been aghast when Ms. Joon had read the short passage, "I bequeath the photograph albums to my cousin, Cherry Rose Lehr, who will know best how to use them." Curious phraseology, I'd thought at the time.

So Miko had kept a complete set of those prints of Guido's life in pictures she'd sent to Toshiko. Knowing what I did now, I sensed how Cherry Rose dreaded going through those albums.

That was why, as we were all milling awkwardly around Nobuo's library afterward, I'd impulsively asked the Lehrs to join us for a drink and a bite somewhere. Frank had given me a look of surprise, but gamely backed up the invitation.

Now, under the influence of hot bread and butter, at least Barry was beginning to relax. Frank ordered another basket declaring, "Never underestimate the power of good bread on a Jewish boy!"

Cherry Rose remained quiet as she spooned steadily away at the onion soup, which revived her somewhat because near the bottom of the bowl, she slowed down and spoke. "Ava, before you and Frank came in, I told Uncle Nobuo about meeting Pat Tata at the spa yesterday. He was absolutely horrified to hear what happened to Kim Beraku."

She scraped the last shreds of onion from the sides of her bowl, then repeated, "Absolutely horrified. I think he feels he should've known, should've been able to do something to prevent it."

Barry grunted cynically. "A little late to start playing the great caretaker, isn't it? I mean, after what he did to his own family, how come he's suddenly so concerned about somebody else's mother?" Barry sloshed the last of the wine into his glass and waved the empty carafe at the waiter. Of course. He wasn't paying.

"And his cook, yet! Am I the only one who's noticed how he talks to the cook he's got now? I bet he wouldn't even recognize her if he ran into her on the street in real clothes instead of those black pyjamas. And now we're supposed to believe old Nobuo's broken up about some expendable domestic? I don't think so."

Barry paused until the waiter resumed his post after pouring wine for all of us. "If he really cared that much about this Kim person, seems like he would've tried to find out what happened to her weeks ago. Not to mention getting in touch with the daughter. You ask me, I think he was just trying to look good in front of that actor friend of his."

Cherry Rose traded glances with Frank and me, knowing she couldn't put off Barry's revised family history lesson much longer.

With a sigh, she reminded her husband that Nobuo had indeed FedEx'd a letter to Kim Beraku's apartment, which was still waiting beneath the doormat where it'd been left when Miko went to check personally. Rather than just leave it sitting here, Miko had brought it back with her to Nobuo's.

Naturally, he had met Kim's daughter, but couldn't recall her married name, if he'd ever known it. Nor did the cook's employment forms show any other point of contact, except the Little Tokyo address.

And though one might have expected to discover an address book or other important information in Kim's room, a thorough search conducted by Miko and Naki, who'd already been installed as a temporary measure, failed to unearth anything. Whatever there had been, Kim must've had it in her purse, which was stolen while she lay dying on the street.

In fact, none of Kim's personal belongings were to be found and since some of her clothes were also missing, Miko's conclusion that the heretofore reliable woman had perhaps received an emergency call from her daughter and left an explanatory note which somehow got lost or misplaced, made the most sense. Until now, that is.

At any rate, Cherry Rose had put Nobuo in direct touch with Pat Tata. Hopefully, between the two of them, they'd be able to fit enough pieces together to make sense out of what happened to Kim.

A sudden peal of thunder made us all jump. By golly, it looked like rain after all! And, wouldn't you know, the night before we shot. But then, as Frank reminded us, we were doing mostly interiors tomorrow, anyway. Specifically, Major Leland Temple's houseguests arriving.

"Actually, I almost hope it does rain," Frank said. "It could be nice and moody."

As if in reply, a bolt of lightning cracked the patch of purple sky we could see through the grimy window, followed by a gigantic boom.

"Moody? Ha!" Barry Lehr had managed to slip beyond relaxation into uninhibitedness without us noticing. "You've been so focused on the fiction, Frank old pally, you never even noticed the stranger truth going on, right under your nose!"

Frank shrugged. "Oh. If you mean the Rikka and Nobuo and Guido thing—"

"Hell, no!" Barry interrupted, laughing. "That's old news. Anyway, that's only a trois of it, so to speak. There's Naki, who's suddenly blossomed into this red-hot mama-san, only we can't decide if it's for Nobuo or Guido.

"Then, Rikka hates Ava's good buddy Davida, because she's obviously weak for Nobuo. And of course, Naki can't stand either one of those women!"

Barry chuckled, generously splashing more wine into our glasses. "Now we have C.R.'s ex-beloved, Woo Kazu, who, when he's not hitting on my wife or fag-hagging around with Rikka, has started mooning over that big Brazilian guy."

His goofiness was contagious, and before long we were all in hysterics, coming up with the most outrageous scenarios we could think of, including Manfred Walter backing Naki into the pantry to play a little sahib-and-the-native-maid.

Meanwhile, what afternoon light there was had vanished completely behind the heavy black clouds, and sporadic grumbles of thunder began to erupt.

Behind the bar, our waiter put away his English book and crossed the dining area to the large fireplace, glancing at our table as he passed to make sure we were well supplied. Almost as soon as he got a fire blazing, the rain started to fall, and several people scurried inside. Somebody punched a Piaf tune on the jukebox, and the place took on a party mood.

We were wrapped in a sort of suspension in time and space with the rain outside, a roaring fire inside, and constantly in the background, Edith Piaf singing songs of love and death. One of them was, to the best I could decipher in my rusty French, about a hotel bellhop who had a hopeless passion for the beautiful woman who wore expensive jewels and lived in the penthouse suite with her poodle.

Barry continued to wax entertaining, this time with a long, involved account about some adolescent misdemeanor of Frank's. I saw that Cherry Rose was listening to him ramble with a gentle smile on her lips. Could it possibly be that Barry was starting to look pretty good to her again, after all? Talk about happy endings.

The sudden clamor of the cuckoo clock alerted us to the time, seven-thirty, which we couldn't believe. Certainly Mr. Cuckoo had been dutifully announcing the quarter-hours ever since we'd walked in, but after his first few appearances, we'd tuned him out.

Helene's was packed by now, and after Frank had paid the bill, a pushy group at the bar, who'd been covetously eyeing our table surged forward, ready to take possession. In the ensuing scramble, I hit my ankle on Cherry Rose's inherited briefcase. She'd almost walked off without it.

Deliberately? Is that why she hadn't just left it in the car?

Snatching it up from the floor, I was startled by the case's unexpected weight. Miko must've photographed Guido's ever waking moment.

I hurried after the others, calling, "Hey, Cherry Rose! You forgot something!"

"Oh. Thanks, Ava," she replied unenthusiastically.

Outside, we huddled together under the striped awning, debating whether to make a dash for our cars, or wait a few minutes to see if the rain let up.

Cherry Rose started complaining about how heavy the briefcase was, but didn't want to put it down on the wet sidewalk.

Barry flexed his wiry biceps. "I'll take it, C.R.," he offered, reaching for the bag. "After all, what's a husband for? Beast of burden, source of pl—"

Wham! Something banged into me, and Barry and I went crashing to the sidewalk in a heap.

If I'd thought anything at all about the running footsteps I'd heard approaching, it was that someone was understandably in a hurry to get out of the downpour. And since it was raining heavily and quite dark, except for a dim bulb in the carriage-type fixture outside Helene's door, none of us saw the attacker.

And then Frank was helping me up and I was hoping my cherished outfit wasn't ruined, at the same time trying not to laugh at Barry's embarrassed protests as Cherry Rose helped him up.

And then we realized that the briefcase was gone.

THIRTY-THREE

FRANK GOT HIS WISH. The rain, which had continued off and on through the night, was now floating down in a soft drizzle, creating an eerie, Hitchcockian ambiance as various cars and limos rolled wetly around the circular driveway.

The idea was to deposit Major Temple's houseguests at the ornately carved entrance door where Naki waited, then do reverse shots over her shoulder, which would serve as closeups for the main guest stars as they arrived, upon which opening credits would be superimposed.

I happened to be standing to one side as the vignette of the entrance of Dr. Upharsin and Lotus was being filmed, and witnessed a choice moment of unfeigned animosity between Naki and Rikka. I made a note to watch for that in the dailies, because it would introduce a mysterious nuance to the story right off the bat.

As the morning wore on, I could see Frank was really cooking; rarely did any one scene require more than three takes. Naturally, Marty and Sam were ecstatic since by the time the crew was breaking down that setup, we were already ahead of schedule.

While they were preparing for the next scene, which was in the living room where Major Temple would be receiving his guests at a cocktail party, Woo Kazu and the Lehrs fussed around with the costumes, ordering an attractive assistant hither and yon with a steamer.

Presley Shores's expression, as he observed the young lady zap wrinkles and creases, was besotted, and the girl was clearly aware of it.

Woo Kazu adjusted the Armani lapels of Jose the hunka-hunka burning Brazilian appearing as Fero, the Baron's assistant, and pouted prettily up at the big man. I hoped we didn't have another Tex Wing situation brewing.

Meanwhile, Barry had discovered one of the silver tassels on the Cloak of Death was loose, but Axel Muntz, who was playing the Baron, had already grown quite attached to the garment and was loath to surrender it for the necessary repairs.

Axel, an actor friend of Nobuo's from their mutual WWII movie days, was really something else. The German came equipped with a bald bullet-head and (so it was rumored) real dueling scar, which, added to the monocle worn by the Baron would've tempted a lesser actor to throw away the role as a caricature. Not this guy, though. He was dead serious. And the way he swirled that cloak around his burly body gave me cold chills.

Davida, who'd lately shown signs of emerging from her protective shell, had been doing the usual paparazzi's dash, duck, and shoot maneuvers, but now I became aware of a prolonged series of camera-type explosions, one right on the heels of another, coming from the same direction. Intrigued, I tracked the sound to the small coatroom off the entrance.

It was empty except for Nobuo and Davida; dark except for the strobing of her camera. He stood spreadeagled, back against the wall, immobile, unblinking, while she flashed shot after shot, right in his face, sobbing hoarsely. It was the most strangely erotic, heartbreaking sight I'd ever seen, and I had no right to be there.

Fortunately, Davida and Nobuo were so intent on each other they never noticed me. As I skulked off, I thought they probably wouldn't have noticed an earthquake.

THIRTY-FOUR

THE CREW FINISHED setting up for the Major's cocktail reception scene just in time to break for lunch. Ordinarily, these things drag out so long, it didn't seem possible we'd gotten this much accomplished already.

While almost everyone stampeded out to the covered patio where Challah Dolly had laid out the food, certain others were intent on satisfying different appetites.

Guido Hayashi, for instance, who was not on call today because his scenes were to be shot at the end of the week, turned up for what appeared to be the express purpose of groveling at Rikka Tring's feet.

And why had she finally allowed him to corner her after all this time? Because she wanted him to, that's why. Rikka was watching Guido with the anticipation of a cat about to lap up a bowl of cream. It reminded me of one of Henny's old sayings: "He chased her until she caught him."

"Hey, Ava." It was Presley Shores, who wanted my opinion on an idea he had for his self-appointed project, *The Making of Dr. Upharsin,* which was to be a spoof on those behind-the-scenes documentaries. At some point during our brief discussion, Guido and Rikka vanished.

Naki stalked by, obviously looking for Guido, or possibly Nobuo, but she was out of luck on both counts; Davida and the man playing Dr. Upharsin were also among the missing. However, Naki had her own admirer, Manfred Walter, no less, hot on her little slippered heels. It looked like Barry's makee-outee scenario hadn't been so far offbase after all.

As to the Lehrs, I suspected a little second honeymoon in the works from the way they'd been going around hand-in-hand today. We might as well have been shooting a soap opera.

So what was I doing, just standing here like a lox while Wei-

Side was throbbing with nooner madness? I started out the door to look for Frank, and collided with Lieutenant Bernard Weinberg.

"Oh! Sorry, Ava," he apologized perfunctorily, but his real attention was focused on a point over my shoulder. I turned to see Barry and Cherry Rose walking toward the back of the house. Holding hands again.

"Mr. and Mrs. Lehr!" Weinberg called out, and they wheeled in surprise. "I need to talk to you, please."

The couple approached apprehensively. "What is it now, Lieutenant?" Barry sounded impatient.

Weinberg studied them for a moment before answering. "I thought you might be interested to know how your cousin died, Mrs. Lehr," he said finally.

Cherry Rose put her hand to her throat. "You mean, you know whether it was the knife wounds or...or the broken..."

"...neck," Weinberg finished for her. "Or last, but not least, the congestive heart failure due to the cocaine she ingested. You forgot to mention that."

Barry made a strangled noise and Cherry Rose's almond eyes widened. "Coke?" she shrilled. "I never heard about any coke. Miko swore she wouldn't do drugs until the show was over!"

"Calm down, Mrs. Lehr," the lieutenant advised. "It's more than likely she kept that promise until right before she died. We've known about this for a couple of weeks, now," he added, not mentioning he'd already informed Nobuo.

Nor did I mention that Rikka had also known because she'd eavesdropped when he'd told Nobuo, or that I knew because I'd eavesdropped on Rikka and Woo.

But why was he telling Cherry Rose all this now? Surely the real reason he was here was because of last night's mugging. Frank and I had felt duty-bound to persuade them to report the incident, on the off-chance it could be connected to Miko's murder in some way.

Also, after much discussion, Frank decided we should privately inform Weinberg of Cherry Rose's convoluted plan to divorce Barry. Because, he argued, Cherry Rose, by her own admission, was too strapped for cash to cut loose from her husband. However farfetched it might seem as a motive, she could've killed Miko to try to get control of Guido and that lovely Hayashi tea money. Although it was hardly likely she'd go to all that trouble only to scrap the whole project in favor of patching up her marriage.

Now Weinberg mused, "I wonder how your hit-and-run bandit felt when he discovered he'd gotten nothing but a bagful of old photographs for his trouble. That is all that was in the briefcase?"

Cherry Rose shrugged listlessly. "I guess. Actually I hadn't even gotten around to opening it yet."

"Ever do any coke, Mrs. Lehr?" Weinberg asked suddenly. His voice was deceptively soft, inviting confidences.

Barry exploded. "You sonofabitch! First you accuse my wife of murder! Now you're saying she did it for a bagful of cocaine disguised as old family albums!"

The policeman frowned. "That's odd. I don't recall saying any such thing."

"Huh!" Barry snarled. "Very funny."

"Barry, stop it." Cherry Rose laid a slim hand on her husband's arm. "You have to admit, there must've been something else in that bag we didn't know about. And somebody wanted whatever it was badly enough to take such a big risk."

She was right. It had to have been a calculated risk, not some random, impromptu snatch as I'd been unrealistically trying to convince myself. And who would chance a thing like that unless they knew for a fact there was a valuable commodity inside the bag?

Cherry Rose continued. "And to answer your question, Lieutenant Weinberg. Yes, I used to do quite a bit of cocaine. In fact, I was pretty much your basic addict. But that was a long time ago. I haven't touched the stuff for ten years."

"Anyway," Barry said angrily, "what's all this got to do with how Miko died? I thought that's what you came to tell us."

"I'm sorry if I gave you that impression, Mr. Lehr," Weinberg replied stonily. "Perhaps I was hoping maybe you could tell me."

"What the hell do you mean?" Barry demanded. "That maybe

we could tell you because one or both of us did it? Is that what you meant?"

Weinberg raised a hand for silence. Surprisingly, Barry shut up. "Let me put it his way, Mr. Lehr," he said. "It is the coroner's opinion that the double knife wounds, left unattended, would've definitely been fatal. The right kidney was punctured, you know.

"The tricky thing about lumbar stabbings is that victims have been known to walk around feeling fine for up to half an hour after sustaining the injury, without realizing anything is wrong. Until they're actually dying, of course. But by then, it's too late.

"On the other hand, the cocaine-induced heart attack was sufficiently massive to kill her. And the broken neck speaks for itself."

"So how did she die?" Cherry Rose's voice was a raspy whisper.

Weinberg shook his head. "In the coroner's own words, 'You pays your money and you takes your choice.'"

THIRTY-FIVE

MAJOR LELAND TEMPLE'S welcome cocktail party was going splendidly against background glissandos of Vivaldi, the clink of ice on crystal, the splash of expensive liquor, and the satisfied hum of chatter among his guests as they mingled around the marble fireplace where pine logs crackled cheerily, signaling a successful gathering.

The calm before the storm, of course. Gradually, each character would come to realize the unexpected presence of that sworn enemy, faithless lover, suspected murderer, or long-lost relative was no coincidence, but a complex equation calculated by Major Temple. And they were going to have to do the math.

Resplendent in a navy cashmere blazer and silk ascot, gesturing lavishly with a big cigar, Manfred Walter looked every inch the Major. And Frank's merciless direction exposed Temple's lecherous bonhomie toward his more toothsome female guests as being shot through with the fearful whiff of incipient impotence, for which he compensated by achieving penetration into the woman's psyche, simulating copulation with swift, brilliantly cruel thrusts of innuendo.

And Russ was right there with Frank, beaming the camera like a searchlight into the Major's heart. Was it Manfred's own, as well? He was almost too believable as his character.

Manfred knew exactly what was going on, and didn't like it much. But he was torn between an actor's need for honesty, and a human's need for subterfuge. Two or three times shooting came to a halt so a makeup person could powder away the perspiration beading his brow.

However, our Freddy, as he'd instructed us to call him, was a real trooper, ultimately surrendering himself completely to Leland Temple, resulting in some very ripe stuff.

I was sitting on the front steps, waiting while they shifted position to shoot the first encounter between Dr. Upharsin and the Baron, when Bernard Weinberg returned.

Earlier, a call on his cell phone had interrupted him in the middle of giving Barry and Cherry Rose a hard time. It seemed the Beverly Hills police station was having the unprecedented experience of being picketed by the Asian League, who didn't feel enough effort was going into the search for Yamiko Hayashi's killer.

Since Weinberg was officer in charge of the case, his superiors had ordered him to the location to field accusations of discrimination.

His arrival back on the set coincided with Davida Yedvab's. Trying not to be obvious, I searched my friend's face for some clue as to whether that wild camera foreplay in the coatroom had led to a more hands-on encounter with Nobuo, but her expression betrayed nothing beyond irritation when she caught sight of Weinberg.

"Hey! You never gave me back that film I shot at Bonsai like you promised," she reminded him in a belligerent tone.

Evidently, Weinberg's encounter with the Asian League had taxed his patience to the limit because he snapped, "I'm beginning to understand DeNiro's point about paparazzi." As an exit line, that one was pretty much untoppable. Recognizing this, Weinberg did the sensible thing and exited.

Davida shrugged and plotzed down next to me, not seeming too disturbed about the fate of her film. Maybe things had taken a turn for the better with Nobuo, at that. If so, I wanted to hear all about it.

"Davida, I looked everywhere for you at lunch. I was hoping we could eat together and catch up on stuff."

Davida conveniently started to fumble through her camera bag. "Oh, I was just in a sushi mood today. There's a great little place in Brentwood Village."

I shuddered. I had ventured into a sushi bar only once, and was traumatized by the sight of desperately wriggling fish being eviscerated in full view of their prospective diners.

The friends I'd gone with tried to explain that this method of preparation is culturally significant because it guarantees the freshness and integrity of what actually ends up on one's plate.

In response to that line of reasoning, I say, gimme anonymity over integrity and cultural significance, every time. If I'm going to eat something, I don't want to have previously made eye contact with it. I am emotionally incapable of boiling a lobster, and I can't eat a fish that doesn't arrive at the table incognito.

I suddenly remembered Cherry Rose had grown up working in her dad's Sushi Shogun restaurants. I don't care what anybody says about fish not having the same capacity to experience physical pain as humans. How do they know? And even if it's true, I still think it requires a certain amount of nervelessness to commit sushi. Could Cherry Rose have taken that same approach to killing Miko?

Davida's voice recalled me from these unwelcome thoughts. "...know I haven't been much of a bud lately, Ava," she was saying. "I've been going through a whole lot of shit, but I can't get into it right now..."

I couldn't keep up this farce. "Davida, I know about you and Nobuo," I said flatly.

That upset her. "How could you? I never said a word. Did you see us out together, or something?" Her thick brows met suspiciously. "Is that why you got me on this job? Playing Cupid?"

"Don't get your kishkas in an uproar, Davida," I told her. "First of all, no, I swear I didn't know a thing about you two until after you got here."

"So how did you figure it out? God, don't tell me I was that obvious!" she wailed.

I toe-danced around that dangerous topic, not about to admit I'd been an unwilling spy on her confrontation with Rikka in the maze.

"Oh...there were signs a friend would notice," I said vaguely. "And you did mention you'd been considering marrying an Asian guy."

Davida's scowl faded. "Yeah. I sure can pick 'em, can't I?" she asked rhetorically. "One dies on me, the other dumps me. No matter what, I wind up with a heart like a flat tire."

I turned to look at her and all at once, the situation struck me as funny. There sat Davida Jochabed Yedvab, sabra, born in Jerusalem yet, who'd ended up in Hollywood as a glitzoid photo hound, madly in love with a Japanese man old enough to be her poppie, and moaning about her flat tire heart like a bad country song.

It was the first good laugh I'd had since Miko's murder, and I didn't attempt to suppress it.

At first Davida looked puzzled, then angry, but when I managed to gasp out what had set me off, an unwilling chuckle escaped her. Next thing, we were both making up the grossest metaphorical country lyrics we could think of to go with "heart like a flat tire." It wasn't too hard. Before long, we were howling our oderous ode for some of the crew.

Well, just look at me now / big as a cow
Because you went and broke your vow.
Every double-chocolate malt / was all your fault
Not to mention the extra added salt.
You left me with a heart like a flat tire / refrigerator thighs
A great big jelly-belly full of your lies
Uh-huh, a heart like a flat tire
The spare's around my waist
Two buns the size of real estate

Making silly curtsies to our audience, which was equally generous with applause and jeers, Davida looked like a much happier camper.

And speaking of camp. Out of the corner of my eye, I spotted Woo Kazu and Rikka Tring, snickering as they slipped off toward the maze for an afternoon nose job.

Davida had seen them, too.

"Can you believe she's still doing cocaine?" I marveled. "Doesn't she even care about hurting the baby?"

Davida whipped her head around at me so fast her long, springy curls struck like a cat-'o-nine-tails across my face. "What baby?" she asked.

I was surprised. This set was such a hotbed of gossip, I'd just assumed everybody knew Rikka was pregnant. "Rikka's baby. And Nobuo's, or so she claims, and he's admitted it. Obviously though, he's to have no say about whether or not it's going to be a baby addict. Her body, her choice."

Davida stared at me, her face the color of ashes. "She can't be pregnant."

"Well, I agree she sure doesn't look it, but—"

"You don't get it Ava," Davida growled, gripping my wrist with her steely warrior's fingers, black eyes burning into mine. "She can't be!"

THIRTY-SIX

DAVIDA'S SHOCK AT discovering another woman's pregnancy by a lover she had been reunited with less than three hours, was certainly understandable. That secretive glow hinting perhaps sushi wasn't the only thing served raw during their lunch hour was replaced by a dulling look of despair.

She was on the verge of saying more when Presley buzzed up in his golf cart, the cute little wardrobe assistant by his side.

"Hey, ladies, I caught your act on tape! Now, lemme get some shots of y'all talkin' to Tia, here. Go on, honey," he urged the girl. "Just stand there with Ava and Davie and act natural."

Davida, who'd probably never been called Davie in her life, gazed blankly at the sweet young thing alighting gracefully from the cart, then turned on her heel and stalked into the house.

Which, of course, meant I had to stay behind and make excuses for her rudeness. All I could come up with on such short notice was something she'd had for lunch disagreed with her. The literal truth, if nothing else.

"Well, hell! Whaddya expect with that sushi stuff?" Presley exclaimed, busily videotaping Tia and me to insert somewhere into *The Making of Dr. U.* "Down home, ain't but two things we do with raw fish. Fry it, or use it for bait!"

By the time I finally escaped his clutches (not until I'd heard all about his mama's incredible black pepper and cornmeal batter for deep-fried mullet filets), Davida was nowhere inside. But when I looked out the window facing Snapdragon's parking lot, I saw her car was still there.

So she'd taken off somewhere on foot, and though I felt compelled to go after her, I was in no mood to wander aimlessly over Wei-Side today. Then I remembered the staircase landing was surrounded by glass.

Having gained that vantage point, however, I was so distracted by the glorious views coming at me from all directions, I almost failed to notice Davida, creeping stealthily into the maze, a camera slung around her neck, fitted with a large protuberance even I recognized as a zoom lens.

The logical conclusion was that she intended to keep a safe distance while snapping candid closeups of Rikka and Woo playing snowman, but then what? Use the photos to blackmail Rikka into leaving Nobuo alone? Or show them to Nobuo like some vindictive little tattletale?

The Davida I'd known would never have done either of those things. The obvious response to that being, she was no longer the Davida I'd known.

But could the Nobuo I was getting to know very well indeed have trysted with Davida, whom he'd often proposed to, while he was still shacked up with a woman he'd impregnated and made a major heiress? Apparently so.

I decided I'd already butted in to such an extent, I might as well keep au courant, so moments later, I was outside and heading into the maze after Davida.

It seemed reasonable to suppose that Woo would be serving coke to Rikka on that same convenient rock, only I couldn't remember how far along the trail it lay. Consequently, I was so focused on being ready to duck out of sight each time I rounded a corner, the sudden yank on my T-shirt from behind caught me completely off-guard.

With thudding heart, I turned to face my captor. It was Davida, who'd reached out from her hiding place behind the bamboo to snatch me as I went by. Ignoring my indignant gasp, she whispered, "Hurry. They're getting ready to leave."

Unceremoniously, she hustled me back in the direction I'd come until we reached the spot where several false trails fanned out invitingly. Quickly, she pulled me beneath a bower of climbing roses that arched over the one parallel to the true path, and none too soon. Just as we'd concealed ourselves, Rikka floated past, trailed by a glowering Woo, moodily kicking at the soggy bamboo leaves before him.

We waited in silence until they were safely out of earshot, then Davida spoke abruptly. "Don't say it, Ava," she warned. "Just don't."

"No problem," I assured her. "At this point, words fail me."

She scowled. "All right, I'll say it for you. What was I thinking, sneaking around like some cheap keyhole peeper? Since we both know the shameful answer to that one, let's just skip it, okay?"

"The what is easy," I replied. "The why isn't."

"Well, I'm not sure I know why, myself," Davida hedged, avoiding my eyes. Then she looked directly at me. "But there is another what, Ava. I heard Rikka tell Woo that, after this movie aired, his line was going to be hot, hot, hot again. And then she not only demanded he launch a heavy print campaign using herself as the exclusive image for WooWoo Wear, but that he give her a big piece of the company, too!"

I had to acknowledge that Rikka's single-mindedness was impressive. Evidently, this chick would stop at nothing to feather her nest, which seemed to be expanding by the moment.

"And what was Woo's response to her propositions?" I asked.

Davida gave a real laugh. "Ava, I've heard some rancid language in my day, but nothing like the verbal bomb of Japanese, Chinese, and English he exploded at Rikka! And you know something? It just rolled right off her like she was Teflon."

Her brow creased. "What I don't get is why she thinks she can just order Woo to hand over all this control to her."

Of course, Davida hadn't been present at my own eavesdropping session, which made it clear Rikka had every reason to think she could tell Woo to do whatever she wanted.

Because she knew he was responsible for Miko's death.

THIRTY-SEVEN

OUR SECOND DAY of shooting dawned miserably, and went rapidly downhill from there.

All the progress we'd made the previous day was gobbled up by hours of extensive downtime as we waited for the weather to break.

The problem was, we had to shoot two rather complex outdoor scenes today. Had to. One was an elaborate tea party on the high terrace with the deep fishpond; the other below on the lawn next to a tall grove of oleanders.

There was no possible way to adapt them for indoors, and no margin of time to allow any alterations.

About the only ones not pacing restlessly up and down the terrace steps and back and forth across the damp green grass to raid Challah Dolly's buffet was a little knot of dress extras, who were to be dispersed at tables between those of the featured players. Inured to the interminable waiting of this strange avocation, they plied their individual pastimes of needlepoint, crosswords, reading and, in one case, tapping away on a laptop computer. A screenplay, no doubt. A year from now we'd all be working for him.

The other three people not moving around were Mr. Masumo and Bobo, his Hawaiian chauffeur, and Hanae Joon, sitting quietly at a table just out of camera range. Nobuo had invited his attorney to meet the Japanese actor, Vic Tahara, who would be featured in the second scene, should we ever get the first one done. Masumo's party could be in for a lengthy vigil.

Finally, a frustrated Russ, who'd been dickering with arcs, keys, spots, and reflective panels for hours, trying to transform the gray gloom of morning into perfect sunny afternoon tea party brightness, to no avail, called an emergency prayer session with Lil. And, lo and behold, as the saying goes, this produced what they called a divine inspiration. Which, at that point, no one was inclined to dispute.

Russ had remembered a seventies film of Nobuo's—Ninja Marines—where a handpicked team of jarheads endures what amounts to a martial arts bootcamp in preparation for their encounter with a deadly Asian drug gang running opium into Chinatown. The only thing I recalled about the movie was its promo line: "The Marines are looking for a few good Ninjas."

In any event, Ninja Marines had been shot at Wei-Side, and the Marines had lived in tents on the grounds. Sure enough, those tents were still available, piled up in one of Snapdragon's outbuildings. Soon, Russ, Lil, and team had canopied the entire terrace in khaki canvas, which enabled them to reset the lights in an entirely controlled environment.

Apparently, it is far simpler to create bright sunlight against a totally dark backdrop, than when entirely surrounded by leaden natural light, which Russ eventually realized had been sucking up every last amp he'd been able to crank out of his considerable equipment, like a giant sponge.

I felt relieved that problem was being solved, but beyond technicalities, there was something unusually oppressive about the color of the day, which made me acutely conscious of the weight of Miko's unsolved murder, and all the powerful emotions—suppressed and otherwise—infusing this production.

What the hell was wrong with everybody, anyway?

I wandered down the stone steps and squished across the spongy turf, looking for Frank, glad I'd worn my bright green molded plastic gardening clogs, which had never done a lick of gardening and probably never would.

On our second trip to France, when we'd been shooting some exterior footage to weave through our fashion designer's new runway presentation, it had rained incessantly. One of the PA's had shown up wearing a pair of these plastic clogs—neon red ones— and I was an instant convert. In wet weather, they were far better than sneakers, providing higher elevation and superior traction. Plus, they came in as many colors as a fistful of lollipops, and looked very hot.

Frank was not among the feeders at the catering table, so I trooped on toward the row of inevitable Winnebagos.

While bit players and extras had to make do with changing in the wardrobe workshop—which meant a trek back and forth to the set—Nobuo, Rikka, and, as Nobuo's guest, Freddy Walter, were able to use their own suites in the house as dressing rooms. But the remaining featured actors had to be accommodated in trailers, just like on any other movie set.

The door of the second-from-last Winnebago stood ajar, and I spotted Frank, together with Marty and Sam, deep in conference with Vic Tahara, none of whom noticed me.

Sighing, I turned and started to walk back, feeling bored, lonely, and oddly apprehensive despite the activity swirling around me, all maladies peculiarly common to writers on sets. I concentrated on the relatively cheery flashes of my shiny green shoes, not really paying much attention to where I was going, until I bumped into the wide form of Hanae Joon.

She had no right to be in this area. It was posted Restricted because our insurance did not cover civilian injuries due to close encounters with the generator truck or dozens of other, equally unpleasant, scenarios.

All the while I was tactfully apprising Joon of what, as an attorney, she certainly must have known, her tadpole eyes were darting around those fishbowl lenses, not seeming to find what they sought. I could tell she hadn't paid the slightest attention to a word I said. Though Joon didn't strike me as the obsessed female fan type, I could think of only one reason why she was here. Anyway, who knew but what behind that unprepossessing facade, she might be seething with unspeakable passions.

"If you're looking for Vic Tahara," I said gently, "he's in conference right now. But Mr. Wei's already arranged a special introduction for you guys, remember? In fact, I think he's even planning to get our photographer to take some pictures of you with Vic."

The eyes swam to a halt and gazed at me. "Oh, really? That's great!" Joon exclaimed enthusiastically. "I'm sorry," she added, baring unlovely teeth in the semblance of a smile. "I guess I just got a little overeager. All this waiting, and everything."

I shrugged. "Yeah, well. That's showbiz."

The door to the trailer we were standing next to banged open abruptly, and Woo Kazu stuck his head out. His long black hair hung loose around his face. "Tia!" he shrieked. "Tia!"

"I just saw her getting a bagel, Woo," one of the makeup people volunteered in passing.

Woo twisted his hair into his trademark topknot, skewered it with a pair of rhinestone chopsticks, and screamed, "Tia!"

This effort succeeded in producing the girl, who came panting up to the wardrobe trailer, clutching a half-eaten blueberry bagel. "What is it being, Mr. Kazu?" she inquired breathlessly.

"It is being," Woo mimicked her rather charming accent, "that I want you to take these things up to Rikka at the house." He thrust a zippered garment bag at her. "And also, this is for that pompous windbag." He draped a heavy-looking retro maroon silk tie, patterned with white chess pieces, over Tia's arm.

Tia looked worried. "Please, what is pom-poos windbug? I am speaking very good English, but this I never hear."

In response, Woo smoothed an imaginary mustache, then guffawed loudly.

Tia's face cleared. "Oh, of course!" she said wisely. "You are meaning Mr. Freddy." And with that, hurried toward the house.

"These damn foreigners!" Woo clucked, shaking his head. "Oh! Sorry, Ava. Didn't see you two ladies there," he added mischievously, watching Joon's offended back as she stalked away. "Liar," I contradicted. "And how are you, Woo?"

He struck a pose. "Absolutely fabulous, as always."

I lowered my voice. "Listen, Woo. What you do on your own time is up to you, but while you're on this set, I'd take it as a personal favor if you'd lay off the recreational substances. Haven't you noticed? We receive regular visits from a police detective."

Woo's face seemed to shrivel. "I have nothing to hide," he whined.

"Another lie," I said. "But the main thing that concerns me right now is that you do nothing to screw this picture up. You keep on like you've been, and you could just ruin things for the rest of us. Plus, people might start mentioning you in the same breath as Tex Wing."

"Tex Wing!" Woo exclaimed, horrified. "That disgusting little pussy!"

I smiled. "I rest my case."

Woo started to say something else, but I wasn't listening. I'd glanced over at the house and spotted Hanae Joon slipping furtively through one of the side doors.

Belatedly, I acknowledged I hadn't really believed her thin tale of wanting to see Vic Tahara so badly she'd entered a restricted area. In fact, I'd been the one to hand it to her on a silver platter.

I took off after Joon, but even in my trusty clogs, haste caused me to skid in a patch of mud. I went flying into the arms of Axel Muntz, who was just about to enter his trailer.

Large and sinister in the Baron's Cloak of Death, not even the melting look in his icy blue eyes when he realized it was me could completely dispel the menacing aura he'd conjured up around himself.

"Ava, mein schatze!" Axel cried merrily. He grasped my arm to steady me, managing to sneak in a tingling caress along the sensitive underside with his thumb. Those blue eyes twinkled knowingly down into mine.

Axel Muntz, who looked much younger than his actual years, was an aryanized version of Nobuo Wei, still enormously vital and, I had to admit, exceedingly attractive in a rather alarming manner. Again, I thanked God for my husband, and felt a genuine wave of compassion for unattached women in this often lonely business. With irresistible forces like Axel and Nobuo around, no wonder so many of them embarked upon such destructive relationships.

"May I get you some coffee, mein schatze?" Axel offered, thumb still stroking.

"Ah, no thank you, Axel. I was just—" I looked over at the house, but Joon was already inside. Oh, well. There were plenty of people around to stop her from, what? Stealing something she'd seen on her first visit? I began to wonder why I'd been alarmed in the first place.

"On second thought, I will take coffee, thank you, Axel." At

least he'd have to let go of my arm, which was threatening to develop some undeniably delicious goose bumps.

Axel returned with my coffee, then confidently embarked upon
one of those peculiarly Teutonic flirtations which, quite honestly,
I encouraged, and thoroughly enjoyed. Between Axel's blandish-
ments and Challah Dolly's house-blend dark roast, my spirits were
beginning to rise.

Suddenly, the loudspeaker crackled and Presley Shores's voice
echoed grittily across the area. "Okay, listen up, y'all! Russ Meyers and his gang decided if God said let here be light, there's
gonna be light, so guess what? Now we got light! Amen, believe
it, brethern and sistern! Everybody in the tea party scene, you got
five minutes to hustle those butts to the terrace and look like the
onliest thing on y'alls itty-bitty minds is whether you gonna drink
Darjeeling or Lapsang Souchong!"

Axel, who'd instantly morphed back into the Baron, abandoned
me and made for the terrace, leaving me to trail behind. After all,
this was one of his juiciest bits.

The gist was, at some point during the tea, the Baron manages
to corner Lotus and begins to put the moves on her. For which, as
I had good reason to know, he'd be all warmed up. A ten-minute
delay occurred while we awaited Rikka Tring's appearance.
"Trouble with the costume," she explained, slightly breathless. But
I thought she must've been getting stoked from her own heat
source because from the moment Frank called, "Action!" she and
Axel blasted off like twin rockets. When I saw Guido lurking
around on the fringe of the crew, I was sure of it.

The Baron's motive in trying to seduce Lotus, of course, is not
merely to score sexually over his powerful rival, but also an attempt
to persuade her to part with secret information about one of Dr.
Upharsin's most impressive illusions. Then, Lotus turns the tables
on the Baron, and before he realizes it, he is almost ready to tell
her his own secrets—anything to get her into his bed.

Flash cuts of the Major watching knowingly, Upharsin watching the Major watching them.

But Lotus, suddenly afraid she's overplayed her hand, is trying to find a way to gracefully get herself off the Baron's hook while keeping him dangling on hers.

Just when it looks like they've reached the point of no return, Fero slouches sulkily into the party, spots his boss with Lotus, and jealously breaks up the tête-á-tête. Fero is so self-centered, he thinks Lotus is after his job.

"Cut! Print!" Frank shouted exultantly.

The burst of applause was so spontaneous, unanimous, and heartfelt, it brought tears of pride for Frank to my eyes. Marty and Sam, predictably, were screaming, "Stars! Stars!"

Later, I was so glad Frank had been able to savor his moment in Russ's makeshift sun, because that's as good as it was going to get for a long time.

THIRTY-EIGHT

EVEN THOUGH THAT SCENE with the Baron and Lotus had galloped home like a thoroughbred, there remained several vignettes of featured actors seated at various tables, plus the spectacular illusion involving the terrace's deep fishpond where Dr. Upharsin and Lotus, accompanied by Combat Studs, were to perform for the assembled guests. And they all had to be shot on this set.

If we could've just kept going without having to break it down, we might have been able to make up some time.

This, however, was impossible, because Vic Tahara's scenes had to be arranged to accommodate his performances in a new production of *Miss Saigon,* which was opening at the Pantages tomorrow. Therefore, we had to shoot his critical encounter with Nobuo today, and just hope we could beat the schedule somewhere else along the way.

While Russ and his lighting gang were trying to work the same miracle they'd done on the terrace out by the thick oleanders where Vic's scene was to take place, Nobuo, as promised, brought the actor to visit with Mr. Masumo and Bobo. That unmatched pair seemed equally enchanted at the opportunity to meet Vic, whose presence drew a cluster of fans. Though not very well known in his native Los Angeles, he was quite a star in the international film community.

Among Vic's admirers, about the only Asians not hanging around to meet and greet him were Joon, who'd feigned such wild enthusiasm; Rikka, who'd gone up to change; and Naki. Even Woo Kazu hovered ingratiatingly with the others as Vic generously signed autographs and posed for pictures, which Davida snapped with all the animation of a rag doll, deliberately moving away from Nobuo every time he approached.

This couple seemed determined to hit every last pothole on that bumpy road to love.

Frank and I had arranged to rendezvous at the buffet, so I made my way down the steps along with the extras, who were through for the day. They were the only ones delighted at this unscheduled serialization of the scene, because it meant at least one more day of work for them.

Crossing the lawn toward the "trailer park," as I thought of it, I marveled, not for the first time, at the sea of humanity necessary to mount a production. I didn't recognize half the people scurrying to fulfill their mysterious appointed tasks, from the Go-Go Gofer bike messenger who'd just narrowly missed swerving into me, to the guy spearing trash into a fluorescent orange plastic bag.

I did, however, spot one familiar face in the mirror of an outdoor makeup table. Naki, in preparation for the less than twenty-second shot she was about to do with Nobuo, was beginning to rebraid her pigtail. A group of hair and makeup folks had gathered to witness this event, mesmerized by the thick, black tresses that, unleashed, hung nearly to the ground.

Naki's reflection betrayed as little emotion as ever, but the way she slowly, sensuously, handled the sections of her hair was almost a form of strip tease. She was reveling in all the attention, and who could blame her?

I found Frank filling his plate with pasta salad, looking preoccupied. As he ate, I gave him kisses between mouthfuls and told him how wonderful he was, but I could feel him tensing up by the moment.

In this entire film, the imminent scene with Vic was probably the most taxing upon his technical skills as a director.

Nor were his apprehensions misplaced. Less than an hour later, after getting Naki's and Nobuo's quickie in the can, I was watching helplessly as he struggled against the twin forces of nature and Japanese phonetics for what seemed like forever.

Though the television viewing audience was to be enlightened by my deathless subtitles, it was difficult for Frank to feel secure about directing Vic's speech inflexion, which took its toll on his ability to extract the essential emotion. Nobuo was helping, but it was uphill all the way.

I noticed Rikka on the sidelines observing the struggle with a superior little smile on her lovely face that made me want to slap it. But even in the midst of my irritation at her attitude, I had to admit, that woman looked good in anything. I certainly could never get away with a snaggly old white terry robe held together around the waist with what looked like a purple necktie.

And though Russ had again tented the area and lit accordingly, it wasn't working as well, simply because the scene had to be framed with the top of the oleander bushes, about three feet above the actors' heads, against the sky. There was just no way to achieve the same control as he'd had on the terrace.

Added to this, a watery sun now kept trying to break through, which resulted in erratic shadows, requiring Russ to call numerous halts.

Then, on the tenth take, everything seemed to come together all at once, and we held our collective breath—to no avail, as it turned out. An esoteric fritz with the sound equipment just before Vic's final speech ruined the whole shot. However, I could tell Frank had at last gotten a grip on something solid, which boded well for the next pass.

He called a break while Andy, the sound man, ran a check on his delicate instruments to see what the problem was.

Meanwhile Naki, having stumbled onto a crowd pleaser and clearly determined to milk it for all it was worth, was yet again rebraiding her pigtail. I thought a repeat performance so soon would dim its mystique, but I was definitely in the minority. This show was being videotaped before an even larger audience than she'd drawn for the first by Presley, maximizing downtime to acquire more footage for his spoofamentary.

As usual these days, he had Tia riding shotgun in the golf cart, but for once she didn't look at all happy to be sitting there by her man. Her piquant little face was scrunched in a worried expression, and I hoped Presley hadn't tried something we might all regret.

Eventually Andy, who couldn't find anything wrong with his equipment, announced he was ready to go again. But when Frank called, "Action," he got far more of it than he wanted.

Suddenly there erupted a hideous racket, like an alarm bell and police siren simultaneously blaring at maximum decibels—Nobuo's elaborate security system, which was straight out of James Bond.

When triggered, all doors and windows were automatically sealed, effectively detaining the culprit and proceeding to shatter his eardrums. Not only could no one get out, but not even Nobuo could get in to silence that demonic wail until the security force that serviced the system arrived.

Presley surmised it had been inadvertently activated by somebody in the crew moving cables around. This was confirmed when the offender appeared in an upstairs window, conducting a sheepish pantomime.

More startled faces—Naki, Rikka, and Cherry Rose among them—peered from other windows, clueless as to what was happening.

Nobuo remarked calmly, "Well, this will give me a chance to see how rapidly these people respond to an alarm."

It took them under ten minutes, which sounds pretty fast unless you happened to be there.

Finally, on Take Twelve, everything came together again.

Thanks to Nobuo, Frank had grasped the nuances to emphasize as he directed from the phonetically transcribed speeches of the script.

Thanks to God, the lighting was holding consistently enough to satisfy even Russ.

"Quiet, y'all!" hollered Presley.

"We're rolling," Russ announced.

"Speed," said Andy.

"And...action!" Frank called tensely.

Dr. Upharsin began his dialogue with Vic as the hostile gardener, who was engaged in pruning the oleanders.

Dr. Upharsin brings Vic to the point of imparting information, only to have him nimbly sidestep to call attention to various things he'd accomplished in the garden, all spoken with enigmatic significance. One of his greatest achievements, he says, in a nonsequitur to a question from Dr. U, is how he has managed to protect his rare and delicate varieties of lilies, screening them from the sun's harsh rays by planting them behind the oleanders.

"Those leaves," he observes dreamily, "can cause death to a man, as you know, Doctor. And yet, those same leaves can filter in just enough light to give life to a flower."

"Ah, but their beauty remains unseen," Dr. Upharsin points out.

The gardener agrees that is so, but only while they are growing. When they have bloomed, then they will be cut and placed in the house for all to see.

"But in fact, they are already dead by then, though they may not yet appear so!" protests Dr. Upharsin. "Are you, then, the only one who has the privilege of seeing them alive?"

Vic turns to face him. "To share such a privilege, one must be a special friend." Beat. "Or a special enemy." A pause. Then, "You are not a friend..."

I gnawed my lip. This was the first time we'd gotten through that part.

Upharsin merely waits in silence. Suddenly, the gardener smiles, bends down the oleander branches, and beckons Dr. Upharsin to look. But even then he reserves for himself the first glance, as if to demonstrate his possessiveness of the flowers.

Though I knew this script sideways, I was seeing it truly come alive for the first time. The words were hammering like heartbeats in my head.

Oh, no. Something was wrong. Vic wasn't supposed to do a doubletake and grow rigid.

Or turn around and let the branches fly up, narrowly missing Nubuo's startled face.

Or turn nearly white and yell, "Oh, my God!" Then start throwing up.

"Cut! Cut!" Frank cried frantically, and dispatched a gofer to the trailer park where our bored nurse was most likely playing her umpteenth game of gin rummy with a prop man.

Russ, Frank, and I scrambled over to the retching Vic Tahara. "What's wrong, Vic?" Russ put a large calming hand on the other man's shuddering back.

"It wasn't something you ate? God, I hope not!" That was Marty, visions of mass food poisoning and lawsuits rising up to haunt him. A pasty-faced Sam dithered in his partner's wake.

Vic shook his head and gestured toward the bushes. "In...there!" he gasped.

"A snake!" squealed one of the PA's hysterically, and a murmur swept through the onlookers as they watched in horrified anticipation for Vic to drop dead of snakebite.

Nobuo, who'd been staring at Vic in perplexity, turned and cautiously pulled the branches aside, peering behind them. His head jerked back in astonishment.

"Don't let the snakes get us!" the PA shrieked, and somebody sensibly slapped her face.

The nurse arrived and began tending to Vic. Russ, Frank, and I edged warily toward where Nobuo stood, the branches still frozen in his hand. Marty crept behind us, puffing in panic down my neck.

All too quickly, we were able to understand why Vic had collapsed.

Lying on the ground, squat legs splayed obscenely, fists

clenched uselessly, tadpole eyes frozen sightlessly, lay the strangled body of Hanae Joon.

THIRTY-NINE

THE QUESTION WAS, into whose jurisdiction did Hanae Joon's
homicide fall?

Logistically, it belonged to the West Los Angeles Division,
having been committed upon Brentwood soil.

Technically, there could be no doubt this murder was somehow
linked to Miko's death in Beverly Hills.

Weinberg, ignorant of the most recent corpse, had returned
from his latest encounter with the Asian League to find a new investigation already in progress, the oleander grove being cordoned
off under the direction of West L.A.'s Lieutenant Harvey Prescott.

After discussing the matter themselves, followed by consulta-
tions with their respective superiors, it was agreed that this case
would be shared between both departments.

That settled, Weinberg and Prescott withdrew to bring each
other up to speed. Their captive audience had observed the cop
scene with professional appreciation. After the snake rumor proved
to be a false alarm, the presence of a dead body in the bushes was
accepted with stoic resignation. After all, Joon was unknown to
almost everyone in the cast and crew. Or was she?

The discussion between Weinberg and Prescott concluded with
an exchange of brotherly backslaps. Then, Prescott resumed his over-
sight of the forensics activities, and Weinberg dispatched Meacham
and Forrester, who'd just arrived, to begin interrogating the witnesses.

Meacham, already puffing on a pipe and looking his deceptively benevolent self, headed for the fringes of cast and crew, while Forrester took Andy, Shelly (the screaming PA), Angela, the script supervisor (who'd developed an irritating habit of squeezing unnecessarily close to Frank during the monitor playbacks), and Presley. All of them had been right up front when the body was discovered. So had Tia, but at some point during the uproar, she'd taken the opportunity to detach herself from Presley. What had our pet Swamp Thing done to upset her so?

Accepting Nobuo's offer of the library as headquarters, Weinberg led Frank and me, Russ, Nobuo himself, and a shaky Vic Tahara toward the house, along with Marty and Sam, who'd fastened themselves like burrs.

Once inside, I went first, relating my earlier encounter with Joon in the restricted area. Weinberg seemed skeptical. "If you were so suspicious of Ms. Joon, why didn't you follow through on your decision to keep an eye on her?"

"Um, well, I did try," I said defensively. "But I was in such a hurry that I slipped in some mud, and..." I felt my face grow warm.

Marty came to my rescue. "...and," he finished for me, "she slid right into the clutches of Baron von Luzt, Lieutenant! I saw it all!" Marty and Sam had christened Axel "von Luzt" for obvious reasons.

"Der Graf put der grip on Ava's lovely arm, and I'll bet he invited her to 'Come lie mit me in die edelweiss, mein schatze!' "

I was embarrassed at his accuracy, but Frank winked at me and looked complacent. Yet another confirmation he'd married the most desirable woman in the world, bless his heart.

"That's basically what happened, Lieutenant," I confessed to Weinberg's interrogatory brows. "By then, Ms. Joon was already inside, and I figured there were enough other people around to keep her from stealing the silver, or whatever."

Weinberg's expression conveyed that as Pam North, I was a washout.

Frank acknowledged having first met Joon, as I had, at the reading of Miko's will, but said he hadn't seen her at all today.

Vic Tahara flatly denied any acquaintance whatever with her.

So did Russ, though he did remark he might've vaguely noticed her on the terrace while futzing around with the lights.

Nobuo told Weinberg that since Joon was sitting with Mr. Masumo and Bobo, who were there at his express invitation to meet Vic Tahara, he'd naturally assumed Masumo had generously thought to bring the woman along with him.

However, a phone call to Mr. Masumo refuted this. While the elderly attorney had accepted her presence, he'd not been responsible for it.

Which meant Hanae Joon came to Wei-Side today for her own private reasons, whatever they had been.

Weinberg turned to Vic again. "Mr. Tahara, you were in position by the oleanders for some time, were you not?"

"I'll say," Vic agreed, with a wry glance at Frank.

"And you didn't hear or see anything suspicious during that period?"

Vic shook his head. "No. I was totally concentrated on staying in Japanese mode, because I was going to be speaking Japanese, which I don't use that much. Plus, the speeches are all very old style—poetic and obscure—because that's how the character is. Which made it doubly demanding."

With the ghost of a smile he added, "Aside from Pat Morita, your average modern Japanese doesn't usually go around chanting haiku riddles."

Weinberg deflected Vic's feeble stab at humor with a stony look, then addressed me. "You said your encounter with Ms. Joon in the restricted area occurred at approximately twelve-thirty?"

I hesitated. "Well, give or take a few minutes on either side."

"And Frank," he continued, "you, your crew and the principals remained in the same general area from shortly after 3:00 p.m. until when the body was discovered at around 5:00 p.m.?"

"Correct," Frank responded, accompanied by a short amen chorus from Russ, Vic, Marty, and Sam.

"That's sure as hell quite a gap. Where was she all that time? And not one of you noticed a damn thing!" Weinberg glared at us impartially.

Frank was starting to boil. "Hey, what our company is doing may be only a movie to you, Lieutenant. Nevertheless, there's a lot of real live asses on the line here, including my own, and I'm afraid I didn't come to work at 5:00 a.m. on what has turned out to be the mother of all bitches of a day, expecting to have to stay alert for murder evidence. People usually don't."

"Don't they? I wouldn't know anything about that!" Weinberg snapped bitterly, then fell into a brooding silence nobody felt inclined to break.

Finally, he stood and began to pace the room. "Since we won't know the crucial time period until we hear from the CI, let's just work with what we have from the moment Ava saw Ms. Joon until when Mr. Tahara discovered the body."

When Vic shuddered at the flashback those words conjured up, my mind began to stray into a warped groove. Was Vic perhaps protesting too much his ignorance of Hanae Joon's existence? With her gone, there was only his word for it now. After all, she had been wandering in the direction of his trailer, definitely looking for someone—a someone who proceeded to demonstrate, in no uncertain terms, just how much they did not want her to find them.

Granted, it would give any actor quite a shock to discover a dead body in the middle of his big scene. But mightn't Vic's subsequent hurling performance have been just some smoke and mirrors, to coin a metaphor?

Weinberg's voice recalled me from my morbid speculations. "All right," he announced, "here's what's about to happen, folks. You're gonna make me a time line, from twelve-thirty to five, which includes everything you can remember that's relevant about everything that happened up until you found the body.

"Then, I'll give copies of it to the investigators who can use it as a guide to question other witnesses."

Marty and Sam looked impressed at Weinberg's approach.

Russ suggested, "In order to maximize this particular session, Lieutenant Weinberg, you'd better include our AD, Presley Shores, and Angela Slater, the script supervisor. They would've been keeping separate logs on the continuity."

While Presely and Angela were being summoned, an uncharacteristically subdued Nobuo volunteered to feed our findings into his computer.

Presley entered warily, looking concerned, but Angela strutted in with a self-important smirk, then made a beeline for the sofa where she squeezed cozily between Frank and Russ.

What follows is the initial basic timeline our collective memory produced for Weinberg. The only deletions I've made are some of Angela's specific comments for every scrubbed take. For example, Take 8 NG—Director Error.

12:30	Ava sees Joon in restricted area, has conversation.
12:35	Woo Kazu interrupts Ava and Joon from wardrobe trailer, yells for Tia to deliver Rikka's costume and Manfred's tie to house. Joan leaves.
12:40-12:45	Ava has conversation with Woo Kazu; notices Joon entering house. Begins to follow. (This is the last known time Joon is seen alive.)
12:45-12:55	Ava slips in mud, caught by Axel Muntz. Notes Joon has disappeared into house. Coffee and discussion with Muntz.
1:00	Presley Shores announces five-minute call for extras and principals to report to terrace for tea party scene.
1:20	Shooting begins. (Delay of five to seven minutes because of Rikka's costume trouble.)
2:00-2:45	Tea party set broken down, oleander scene set up; Frank and others take lunch break; Ava almost hit by bike messenger; Naki puts on hair show.
3:00-3:15	Shooting begins. Oleander Scene (Part I—Nobuo & Naki) in can.
3:20-4:02	Shooting resumes. Oleander Scene (Part II—Nobuo & Vic), 9 NG takes due to lighting problems and Director Error.
4:03	Take #10 NG due to sound glitch.

4:05-4:20	Break for Andy to test equipment; Presley shoots outtakes; Naki gives another hair show.
4:22	Shooting resumes. Take #11 NG due to security system malfunction.
4:24-4:34	Break for security company to arrive and service alarm.
4:45	Shooting resumes.
4:50-5:00	Take #12 cut due to discovery of Joon's body.

Nobuo printed out the timeline, then Xeroxed it. Each of us received a copy, and I think we were all unpleasantly surprised to see how lame it looked on paper.

Of course, there were many moments from many people as yet unaccounted for, but Meacham, Forrester, Prescott and other investigators would soon fill in those gaps.

Certainly none of us suspected that unimpressive larva of a list we'd labored so hard to produce was even then trying to tell us something.

FORTY

"LIEUTENANT WEINBERG, does this situation mean we're going to have to...shut down?"

Everybody connected with *Dr. Upharsin* went into instant panic. Sam had just uttered the two ugliest four-letter words in show business.

But Weinberg acted as if the thought hadn't even crossed his mind. "I don't see any reason for that," he responded, in a tone of mild surprise.

Lieutenant Harvey Prescott, who'd entered the room as Weinberg was speaking, concurred. "Hell, no! You boys and girls keep right on making your picture. It's not every case we know exactly where to find everybody!"

Then he frowned. "Except for one of the wardrobe girls, who seems to have suddenly gone missing." He glanced down at the piece of paper he was holding: "Name of Tia Borko."

All eyes turned to Presley, who looked like somebody had punched him in the stomach, but he merely said he couldn't recall seeing her after the break when the security people came to shut off the alarm. "Young lady was right interested in learning all about AD work," Presley elaborated. "So I was kind of letting her help me get outtakes for this little behind-the-scenes thing."

West L.A. and Beverly Hills gazed steadily at Northwest Florida until he squirmed. "Okay. Truth is, Tia and me been sorta dating for a while. Only, today she got real upset about something and ended up bugging out," muttered Presley, red-faced.

"Now, don't you worry, Mr. Shores," Prescott said comfortingly. "We'll find her." Then he turned to Weinberg. "Couple of things, Bernie. Doc Sedler says time of death is iffy since the ground was still fairly damp and the sun in and out all day. Pending the autopsy, he's saying no earlier than two o'clock, but no later than four and don't hold him to any of that."

"Tell him thanks for narrowing things down for us," Weinberg growled sarcastically.

Prescott shrugged. "Also, there's signs of a struggle for sure, but only one set of footprints in the muddy flowerbed. Joon's. Looks like whoever it was made sure to keep a solid position on that border of iceplant, which is as good as standing on foam rubber for all the prints you can get. Only one or two depressions, but my guess is they won't tell us a damn thing."

He went on to explain the geography of the murder site in relation to the house and set where we'd been shooting. At the rear of the house, the kitchen, dining room, and a small lounge sometimes used for breakfast all had doors that opened onto a flagstone terrace, which narrowed into a walkway that wound through several small gardens. These were bordered on each side of the walkway by dense iceplant of the Red Apple variety, screened to the north by Italian cypress and to the south by those fatal oleanders.

As Prescott spoke, I began to visualize that area. There was a point, he said, where, unless somebody had just happened to glance from one of two upper windows at exactly the precise second, a person could move along that flagstone path as if wearing an invisible cloak.

Which meant a person would've had to have known about that peculiar blind spot. Which meant the killer had designated the rendezvous location for just that reason. Which meant total premeditation.

Hanae Joon must've been lulled into a false sense of security by the close proximity of so many people, never recognizing how truly isolated the murderer had rendered her. She couldn't have been up to any good, keeping such an assignation. It hadn't done her any good either, poor thing.

Although Weinberg had made his opinion of my detecting abilities perfectly clear, I couldn't resist speculating as to what Joon had been up to. The only thing that would seem to require such secrecy was blackmail. Which, from what I'd observed, certainly seemed to be Rikka Tring's favorite outdoor sport, next to snorting cocaine. Might it not have been Hanae Joon's as well?

If so, then she had come to Wei-Side today because her damaging information was about someone who was either on the grounds because of the filming, or was simply here because they lived here. Or both.

Of the cast and crew, Vic Tahara, Guido, plus assorted Combat Studs and technicians were Asian. So were Nobuo and Rikka, the primary residents of Wei-Side. Of the six service people, Naki lived on the main premises, two of the houseboys occupied small cottages behind the mansion, and three commuted from their own homes to their jobs at Wei-Side on various days of the week. Again, all were Asian.

True, race was not necessarily a prerequisite to blackmail by another Asian, but Nobuo had specifically told me about Miko's mysterious extreme cultural kick shortly before her death. Since it was during that period she'd engaged Joon as her attorney, it stood to reason most of Joon's life and associations would have revolved around the Asian community.

Then I remembered, Manfred Walter was staying at Wei-Side as Nobuo's guest for the duration of the shoot. It was entirely possible—nay, probable—Freddy baby had a past strewn with incidents he wouldn't want revealed, and the enterprising Joon had unearthed a particularly rancid one.

Prescott's gravelly voice continued his narrative. "All we know so far about the murder weapon is that it's something at least two inches wide and was pulled so tight it totally crushed her windpipe. Couldn't have taken more than thirty seconds, especially if she got caught by surprise. Which seems pretty likely, as there's no sign she brought along any means of defense. Of course, she might have done and the killer could've removed it from the scene."

Prescott heaved a dreary sigh. "A lot of force went into the strangling, but if the attack was a surprise it wouldn't necessarily have taken a great deal of strength. So this murder could've been committed by a man or a woman. Probably righthanded, as there seems to have been more pressure exerted on the left side of the victim's neck."

He went on to say that Joon's briefcase, resting behind the front seat of her unlocked Toyota Land Cruiser, seemed undisturbed. Prescott appeared to have finished, and Weinberg, who'd been jotting notes as the other officer spoke, rose in preparation to presenting him with our skeleton timeline.

"Oh, just one more thing, Bernie." Prescott forestalled him, sliding a small plastic bag from his breast pocket. He tossed it over to Weinberg, then leaned back against the bar and smiled, rubbing his shadowy chin.

Weinberg picked up the bag and held it to the lamp, affording most of us a clear view of the contents: a narrow yellowish scrap or fragment of something. It was maybe one or two inches long, and looked to be torn on one edge, but uniformly jagged on the other.

"This was gripped in her right fist," Prescott said, referring to the unidentified article.

Such an insignificant piece of paper or plastic, or whatever, might mean nothing at all. On the other hand, it could mean everything.

I knew I'd seen something like it before, but where?

For no apparent reason, a sudden image of Henny and me materialized. We were seated at the chrome-legged dinette by the kitchen window, late-afternoon Amsterdam Avenue traffic fighting its noisy battle toward 87th as Henny pointed at something.

"This was Frank's mother, Baila, may she rest in peace. She had the most gorgeous, natural copper-red hair I ever saw in my life, Ava. Beauticians used to stop her in the streets of Antwerp and offer to style it for free if she'd let them take pictures to put in their windows."

In my mind's eye, I followed Henny's bony, nicotine-stained fingertip to the photograph of a plumpish, smiling woman, anchored to the back page of a scrapbook by corner mounts. The once-glossy deckled borders of Baila's picture had tarnished to the slick, unhealthy yellow of age.

The fragment Joon clutched in her death had been torn from an old photograph.

FORTY-ONE

THE FOLLOWING DAY brought revelations of a link between the victim Joon and several of our players, which supported William Goldman's contention there are only X number of people in the world and half of them know each other, or something like that.

Since Prescott seemed to have no problem with Weinberg's unorthodox investigative technique of disclosing acquired data to all and sundry, suspect or not, everybody soon learned that Hanae Joon had been a spinster, age thirty-two, with no known male companion; the sole owner of a luxurious condominium just north of Wilshire on Kenmore; no known living relatives, pets, or close friends. Colleagues at her law firm described her as tough, tenacious, rather crude and pretty much a loner. Her late-model Land Cruiser had been paid for in cash a year ago, and there were no outstanding debts or liens on her property.

The surprise was that Joon had been one of the attorneys handling a class-action against the soap opera, *City Love,* on behalf of those Asians who were fired when new writers took over.

City Love was the sudser Rikka had acted in, playing Betty Pom, scheming mantrap daughter of Papa Pom, gangster owner of a popular Thai restaurant called Family Thais.

One white media critic, finding the traditional field of political correctness overcrowded, began steadily sniping away at the show for portraying Asians as wicked and manipulative. Meanwhile, white actors and actresses on the exact same show bemoaned, to any entertainment reporter who would listen, how they were routinely denied sufficient opportunities to flex in those juicy, wicked manipulative bitch and bad-boy roles they so craved.

But when there was a shakeup on the existing staff and a fresh team of writers and producers voted to send off the show's entire Asian population with a bang—a good, old-fashioned restaurant massacre occurring on the premises of Family Thais, including Betty (Rikka) and everyone unfortunate enough to have had an urge for mee krob that night—the very critic who'd strenuously denounced offensive Asian stereotypes such as restaurant owners and vicious mobsters did a complete about-face.

Now his theme became that whites felt threatened by an Asian such as Papa Pom, who was smart and canny enough to operate a legitimate business—like a successful, gourmet Thai restaurant—while maintaining his position as a kingpin in the highly competitive Asian underworld. The headline for this column was a masterpiece: "Thai, Die!"

At that point, Joon's law firm had jumped on the bandwagon by persuading the unemployed Asian actors in question to endorse a class-action suit, anticipating the network would cough up millions of dollars to avoid a court case.

They were wrong. The complaint was reviewed in a closed courtroom by a judge.

The network's lawyers quickly deflated charges of discrimination by putting the two new head writers on the stand, a husband/wife team named Bill and Miranda Wong.

All this happened two years ago and had been water under the bridge. Until now.

Because not only was Rikka a former cast member of *City Love* and among those named in the class-action suit Joon worked on, so were two of our Combat Studs—Ronald "Mister" Moto and Bob Yee.

It didn't end there. Woo Kazu's *City Love* credit was wardrobe consultant exclusively for the Asian cast, and Davida had been on staff at the network's PR firm, suppressing fallout during the litigation.

But perhaps the most startling news of all to me, since I am not a watcher of soaps, was that on *City Love,* Vic Tahara once played a cop from Papa Pom's 'hood whose yen for daughter Betty warred with his earnest desire to bust her daddy.

So Vic had already known Rikka, Mister Moto, Bob Yee, and Woo Kazu before he ever signed on for *Dr. Upharsin.*

"So what?" Vic demanded angrily when confronted. "Most Asians in this business know each other because we're bound to work together sooner or later. What's that got to do with anything?

When Prescott pointed out Vic's name was listed in the class-action suit Joon had worked on, he'd gone ballistic, claiming to have asked for his role to be written out before the new writers ever came on board *City Love* because it was going nowhere and he had a shot at a very good part in an upcoming Van Damme film, which he'd gotten.

The only reason Vic allowed his name to be included was because he'd spoken to some female attorney on the phone (for all he knew, it could've been Joon) who convinced him that:

a) He had a legitimate claim because eliminating the Asian storyline meant his own established Asian character would also be Precluded from Returning to *City Love*. (Preclusion from Returning is a very serious matter, since Returning on soaps occurs as frequently as Replacement—which is when the actor/actress portraying a certain character one day is Replaced literally overnight.)

b) His moral obligation was to support his fellow Asians.

Vic remained adamant this was the entire extent of his involvement in the suit, and that he had never, to the best of his knowledge, ever laid eyes on Hanae Joon at any time prior to finding her body.

Rikka acknowledged she first met Joon when she'd given her deposition at the law firm filing the suit. During the course of litigation, there had been several other occasions for contact with Joon, who, among others, assisted Rikka in preparing her testimony.

"But I hadn't seen her since, until she turned up here at the house with Miko's will."

Marty, who was present at the time, told me later that Rikka, having realized Weinberg was a lost cause, had then tried out her babydoll games on Harvey Prescott, who, as the latest gossip had it, seemed to be heavily smitten with Shelly, the screaming PA.

Foiled again, Rikka huffily denied speaking to, or even seeing, Joon at any time yesterday, the day of her murder.

Woo Kazu was defensive about his involvement in the *City Love* contretemps, but readily admitted that's how he'd met Joon. "My dear, what a ripe candidate for a makeover!" Woo exclaimed. "If ever there was a female more appearance challenged than our Hanae, I have yet to encounter it!" But Joon had rejected his good intentions, Woo said sorrowfully. Yes, he had seen her briefly yesterday, several hours before she was killed.

"Having an argument of some kind with Ava Bernstein, as a matter of fact."

Mister Moto and Bob Yee both said though they'd been introduced to Joon when "all that legal stuff was going down," their main contact at the law firm was the male attorney who'd taken their depositions.

Yes, they'd noticed Joon sitting on the terrace with an old man and some big guy that looked like a bouncer, but hadn't spoken to her. That was the only time either actor had seen her because both left Wei-Side for the day when interminable delays mandated breaking down the terrace set. Which, of course, meant their scene with Lotus and Dr. Upharsin couldn't be shot until it was rebuilt.

When Weinberg questioned Davida about her employment by the PR firm for *City Love's* network, she'd laughed in his face and reminded him that she was a photographer, and the network had paid big bucks to stop pictures of anyone connected with *City Love* from appearing in the papers.

Davida denied having any previous acquaintance with Joon or anyone else currently working on *Dr. Upharsin* who'd been involved in the *City Love* situation.

Yes, she thought she'd noticed Joon on the terrace earlier the day of the murder. And no, she was positive Joon had not been present on the terrace when she was taking photos of Vic Tahara with his fans. Would Weinberg care to see those pictures? And incidentally, where the hell was her film from the fashion show, anyway?

The reason I knew all this was because Weinberg, in keeping with his screwy Freedom of Information policy, offered the statements for my reading pleasure. Maybe he was hoping I would spot something that didn't jibe with what I knew to be true, but he was destined for disappointment.

I handed the papers back with nothing more than a tiny, niggling feeling of having been surprised by a certain phrase. Not necessarily because it was untrue, just unexpected. But since the momentary impression had evaporated immediately upon exposure to my consciousness, I couldn't remember what few words triggered it in the first place.

Obviously, I wasn't about to mention a fuzzy-wuzzy semi-thought like that to Weinberg.

FORTY-TWO

"WOULD YOU BELIEVE this is the very room where they screened the dailies of *Enemy Lover?*

Marty—or maybe Sam—uttered those words with reverential awe from the darkness.

Enemy Lover (1954) had been Nobuo Wei's first big picture. Playing a Japanese spy masquerading as a wealthy Chinese businessman from Hong Kong, he wines, dines, and attempts to seduce a gorgeous Chinese-American girl who is secretary to some bigshot in American Intelligence. No dummy she, the Chinese chick strings him along, then turns him in.

That film also marked the debut of many such vehicles Nobuo and Axel would go on to work in together.

And now, forty-something years later, at not quite 7:00 a.m., a small group of people were gathered in the screening room of that same studio lot on a seedy Hollywood side street where *Enemy Lover* first flickered, watching the same two actors appear in disjointed reels of film. Looking for a real murderer. Because late last night, Lieutenant Bernard Weinberg had gotten this crazy idea about viewing the dailies.

Two rows ahead, the outline of his broad shoulders visibly slumped with disappointment and sheer fatigue from scanning endless feet of film MOS—without sound—that so far, had failed to reveal the face of a killer.

From our perspective, however, the screening was a smash. Marty and Sam were exchanging happy whispers, while to my left, I sensed Russ expand in gratification as the pictures glowed like jewels in their settings.

A disembodied voice spoke from the control booth. "One more, Frank. Want me to rack it up?"

The house lights (original deco wall sconces which tempted me to bring a screwdriver next time) flared on and the rest of our little audience—Angela, Shelly, and Andy—jerked guiltily awake.

Frank leaned forward and asked Weinberg, "Ready, Lieutenant?"

Weinberg half-turned, massaging his forehead. "Fine, fine," he mumbled wearily. Poor guy, but had he really expected the culprit all neatly wrapped up in film?

Soon, new pictures washed across the screen, and I felt Frank wince. These were the twelve takes of the oleander scene between Nobuo and Vic which had ended with the discovery of Joon's body.

As each new slate displayed a higher number, the tension in the room grew more palpable.

Take 10 was the one where Frank had finally gotten a handle on Vic's performance, and it showed. The intense complexities of his character—talented Japanese gardener of the new century with a prewar mentality, bound by the painful awareness that his low caste makes his lust for the highborn Lotus doubly futile, visibly struggling against the temptation to plunge his pruning knife into Dr. Upharsin—all these colors spread over Vic's face like oil paints applied by a master.

Clearly, as Vic had stated, he was totally intent on being this particular Japanese; he wouldn't have, couldn't have, noticed anything else. Particularly if he'd already killed Joon and had been playing the entire scene with the object of discovering her body.

"Stop the film!" Weinberg shouted suddenly. "Now, back it up to—there—and run it again," he commanded.

The footage in question was a luscious semi-closeup of Nobuo and Vic in three-quarter profile, oleanders directly behind them. You could literally feel the emotion pouring from Vic while Dr. Upharsin kept his cool. And then came that heartbreaking cut. The two actors had abruptly turned in confusion toward the camera.

"That was the sound equipment glitch, Lieutenant," Andy informed Weinberg.

"Again," Weinberg ordered, ignoring him.

This happened four times before we finally comprehended what Weinberg, who had a whole different perspective on viewing dailies, had reacted to immediately.

A big oleander branch behind and between the two men had swayed heavily, causing its shadow to dip across Vic's face. Not even Russ, to whom any unplotted shadow was an evil force to be banished by correct lighting, had realized its significance. None of us had.

Until now. Because the only movement was in that single branch. The others remained completely motionless, so there was no wind. And neither Vic's nor Nobuo's hands were touching it.

A word from Weinberg brought the lights up, and we sat in stunned silence, not wanting to believe what that shadow meant. Finally, Russ spoke. "I saw it happen. But the performances were so good, I didn't want to stop Frank for something so relatively minor."

Weinberg twisted around in his seat. "Tell me again why the hell this damn film doesn't have sound on it?" he demanded.

Andy stirred. "It does, Lieutenant. But you said you were mainly interested in the picture, so we didn't synch it up yet."

The voice from the projectionist's booth drifted out. "Want me to do an interlock, Frank? It'll take only about five minutes."

While the phantom synched up sound to picture, Weinberg asked Andy, "Why did you say you killed that take?"

"At first I thought it was a big chunk of zoo doo-doo."

Weinberg's blank stare at Andy's automatic response provided our only comic relief.

"It's a nicer way of saying animal noise shit," Andy explained, slightly red of face. "Happens all the time when you shoot around lots of trees. Birds and squirrels and horses and cows have ruined some real magic moments.

"But when it didn't happen again, I had to run an equipment check just to make sure we weren't about to have a major breakdown."

With that, Andy retreated into self-conscious silence. After all, he was a listener by profession, not a talker. It wasn't often he was called on to be so verbal.

Weinberg shook his head. "Zoo doo-doo. Now I've heard everything," he murmured.

When the interlock had been set up to synchronize the sound with Take 10, we all heard it the first time. After five repetitions, the sound echoed endlessly in my ears and probably would for as long as I lived.

The only way to describe the noise that followed the dip of the branch is somewhere between a gargle and a croak, which could've been anything from a crow's throaty gargle of victory as he swallowed a yummy mockingbird egg, to the panicky chipmunk chatter made by hideously expensive magnetic tape being shredded alive by a machine.

It was now horribly clear that the shadow and the sound meant Hanae Joon had grabbed at the other side of that huge oleander just before she'd been strangled to death while at least thirty-five people agonized over a TV movie without the slightest idea murder was happening in the real world about twenty yards away.

I huddled close to Frank and let the tears come. I felt miserable. Of course, everyone else did too, since they'd all been right there and noticed nothing.

But I was the one who'd spotted her where she shouldn't have been and suspected she was up to mischief. If only I'd stayed on her trail and hadn't let myself get sucked into that self-pitying, nobody-loves-a-writer-on-the-set syndrome. Then my ego wouldn't have required me to dilly-dally with Axel.

It wouldn't have mattered if Joon realized I was following her. It might've even caused her to cancel that fatal rendezvous and she'd still be alive.

Andy was moved to speech again. "When the equipment checked out okay, I thought it'd been a hawk or something after all, and what a pain because we'd have to do a loop session if that turned out to be the best take."

We endured several more replays of the scene before Weinberg was finally satisfied and allowed the projectionist to move on.

Despite the macabre circumstances, our professional instincts took over as we watched the two remaining takes. By some miracle, there was going to be enough coverage within the existing twelve that would cut together beautifully into an entire scene. The only thing we didn't have were the flowers Vic had been about to reveal to Nobuo when Joon's body was discovered, and that could be easily solved with a quick pickup shot.

I studied Vic's face very carefully as he pulled back those oleander branches for the last time, and if his violent reaction to the sight of Hanae Joon's corpse was a performance, then every Oscar-winning actor should just fork their statues over to him right now, because they couldn't have possibly been as good as he was in Take 12 of *Dr. Upharsin.*

Shelly whimpered and didn't uncover her eyes until it was over and Presley's Second Unit shots, which the lab had tagged onto the end of the big reel, appeared onscreen.

After the usual mishmash of exteriors, interiors, plus principals and extras eating, drinking, and talking, came the fun footage he'd done for *The Making of Dr. Upharsin.* Most of the latter had been taken over several days from the golf cart, tracking and veering through the cast and crew, catching some offguard while others were alert and eager to hog the lens.

What looked like a glossy black sheet that briefly filled the entire screen was puzzling until the pullback revealed it to be an extreme closeup of Naki's hair, as she sat rebraiding it at the outdoor makeup table. The process was fascinating, and plainly demanded infinite patience and stamina to accomplish such a feat every day of one's life. I didn't even want to think about the amount of labor required for a simple shampoo.

At this point, Weinberg requested a copy of Take 10 and ex-

cused himself, clearly feeling there was nothing further to be
learned by sitting through silly stuff like braiding, Axel swirling
his cape, Nobuo looking stereotypically inscrutable, or Rikka
Tring slinking in her ratty bathrobe held together with what I now
recognized as the maroon chess piece necktie Woo had selected
for Manfred Walter.

He was wrong.

FORTY-THREE

FRANK AND RUSS DROPPED me off at the house to pick up our car,
then proceeded to Wei-Side.

It was good to be home, even for a few minutes, and I experienced pangs of guilt familiar to every dog owner at the joyous reception that greeted my unexpected arrival. We hadn't been
spending much time with Dimples and Dumpling lately, since
Frank had temporarily barred them from the set so he could totally concentrate on work without distraction.

But now that his most difficult ordeal—the oleander scene—
was over and the worst possible thing had already happened—in
the form of Joon's murder, I figured a couple of springers for
comic relief might be just what the doctor ordered.

I informed the girls they could accompany me when I drove out
to Wei-Side. They thanked me with toothy grins and went off to plan
their itinerary while I changed into a pair of Bonsai's brand-new
Streamline sweats, courtesy of Cherry Rose. These were steel gray
and severely tailored, creating the effect of a sexy prison uniform.

A half hour later, the three of us were identifying ourselves to one of Prescott's men in a uniform not nearly so stylish as mine.

Dimples and Dumpling, in no mood to dally once they'd caught Wei-Side's wondrous scent, expedited matters by curling their lips and snarling at the cop when he leaned too far into my window to suit them.

About midway up the long drive, their delirious shrieks of anticipation were posing a threat to my hearing, not to mention what their scrabbling paws were doing to the tinted glass, so I pulled over. I'd no sooner gotten the door open than they streaked past me and bounded into the woods like kangaroos.

I parked and started up a flight of stone steps which led behind the house where they were shooting today. This particular scene, featuring Dr. Upharsin and Lotus performing one of their most famous illusions, was tricky—in every sense of the word—but at least promised to be lots of fun for a change, thank God.

At the top of the steps, I encountered Woo Kazu. "Ava, darling! You're just in time!" he greeted me, with an unaccustomed cordiality which probably owed much to whatever left that tiny white fleck clinging to his upper lip.

Woo was swathed—there's no other word for it—in a garment of his own design that seemed to be a hybrid of sari and monk's habit, and his topknot was skewered with two slender, jeweled daggers which could've served as Liberace's letter openers in a previous life.

"Your husband's a genius, Ava, simply a genius!" Woo gushed, clomping alongside me perched on tall, elaborately carved tatamis. "He's going to do an Altman kind of thing in this scene."

Oh, dear. That could be...okay, or very, very bad. "Meaning?" I asked apprehensively.

"Meaning"—Woo twirled a slender hand—"Frank wants to get these almost subliminal peeps of me as Lotus's costume designer, fussing around with her draperies and acting campy, just before she goes into her thing with Dr. Upharsin."

"In other words, just being your own sinful self," I said, relieved.

Woo emitted a pleased screech, and slapped playfully at my arm. "You meanie!" He giggled, then went into a spate of wickedly funny gossip, ending with "And somebody ought to tell that Zionist paparazzi pal of yours to lay off the free bagels. She's starting to pork up. Definitely unkosher, darling!"

When we reached the flagstone terrace curving around the back of the house with its wonderful view of the Santa Monica mountains, Woo abandoned me for the only makeup table with a vacant mirror. It remained vacant, I thought bitchily, as his face appeared in the glass.

I turned my attention to the location, which was far more worth looking at than Woo's decadent reflection. Masses of bougainvillea climbed from below, and spilled magenta profusion over the waist-level iron railing.

Off to one side, a thicket of giant birds-of-paradise had drawn two iridescent hummingbirds to sip, while to the other side, I could see an edge of the oleander grove where Hanae Joon had met her fate.

Today's scene was to be shot around the ornamental pool sunk six feet deep into the terrace. Its current tenants, a family of rare *kohaku* koi, had been evicted for the occasion, and were temporarily boarding with their downscale, so to speak, *sanke* relatives in the maze's crescent pond.

Dr. Upharsin's famous illusion was geared to whet the taste buds of the most jaded of audiences, what with its dark, erotic symbolism of relentlessly pursuing a beautiful woman, then imprisoning her in a golden cage from which there was no escape, thanks to an unnecessarily large, jewel-encrusted padlock.

The illusion's true brilliance, however, lay in its impossible simplicity, which rendered it simply impossible.

After a sexy skirmish, Dr. Upharsin corners Lotus, locks her in the golden cage, then lowers it into the pool. A minute later, the cage is hauled from the pool—empty, and with that phallic lock still intact!

Suddenly, Lotus reappears, bone dry, with every hair in place.

Now, an eerie mist—dry ice—hovered upon the water's surface, creating a deliciously menacing ambiance. Above it, the glittering cage hung suspended from a winch, swaying slightly in the breeze, as if awaiting some large, exotic bird.

And here she came. Lotus, wearing a deep gold shatung robe trimmed with gilded ostrich feathers.

Presley Shores clapped his hands. "Okay, places y'all. And settle down!"

I watched as he efficiently whipped the set into shape. Presley suddenly seemed to be in pretty high spirits for someone whose girlfriend had gone mysteriously missing. So far, there had been no sign of Tia Borko. I studied his attractive, good ol' boy face more closely. Could he have some hidden motive for killing Joon, and Tia had found out? I recalled how upset she'd been the last time I'd seen her. Maybe Presley knew exactly where Tia was.

Nonsense! I shook those creepy thoughts out of my head as the actors and extras quickly found their marks, and Dr. Upharsin took his place near the cage.

"We're gonna run through this once," Presley informed them, "or maybe even twice. And y'all better act like them cameras are actually recording your every thought for Judgment Day!"

Nobuo seemed to expand in height and breadth, visibly transforming into Dr. Upharsin as he moved toward Lotus. He was wearing a luxurious brocaded black silk kimono which made him look quite extraordinarily sexy in an untouchably ceremonial way. Most intriguing.

As they began to perform their carefully choreographed, erotic chase, I ran down the shot list in my mind:

CU Major Leland Temple, stroking his moustache with a trembling hand, barely containing his sensuous excitement.
CU The Gardener, gazing at his golden goddess reverently from the shadows.
CU The Baron, hood of the Cloak pulled over his head, cobalt eyes watchful, determined to miss nothing.
CU Fero, glaring jealously from Lotus to the Baron.
CU Naki, observing with enigmatic animosity.

All these closeups and others, plus every move, had been skillfully, intricately, plotted by Frank and Russ so that the spring of suspense would continue to wind ever tighter.

Even in rehearsal, I could already feel the powerful effect the sequence was going to induce and became so absorbed that when somebody touched my arm, it literally gave me a jolt. But it was only Lil, who wanted to share the experience of watching our men at work.

On the second run-through, I glanced over at Davida, cameras hanging across her chest like a shield, observing Nobuo and Rikka with grudging admiration for their undeniable chemistry, yet by her expression, not about to concede defeat. Woo was right, though. Her normally lean trunk seemed to have been stuffed with difficulty into those expensive black jeans. If she wasn't careful, she was going to personify the lyrics of "Heart Like a Flat Tire." Guido, who was featured in the next scene, slouched like a brooding Samson against the wall, loving and hating his beautiful, evil Delilah.

"Perfect!" Frank called after the first actual take. "Let's do it again."

Though this "perfection" happened several times, four to be exact, the repetition of Dr. Upharsin capturing Lotus and carrying her struggling in his arms toward the cage, served only to heighten the energy.

Next they did the B-part of the shot, where Upharsin thrusts Lotus into the cage and snaps that enormous jeweled padlock shut. Frank wrapped it up in three takes.

Then came the inevitable anticlimax, when everything had to be shifted for that highly dramatic shot of Lotus being lowered down into the pool.

While the crew was scurrying around to set up and Presley rearranged the actors and extras, Frank and the technical advisor on the illusion, a trendy magician named Benn Kwik, wrangled about how to proceed.

The TA was shrilly maintaining it was vital, absolutely vital, that the camera show Lotus actually descending under the water to maximize authenticity, while Frank patiently maintained that we were still playing catchup on the schedule, and fortunately this was one long, drawn-out shot we could eliminate.

His alternative plan was to track along with the cage contain-

ing Lotus to the instant its bottom touched the pool, then reverse
to show the top of the contraption sinking below the surface. Frank
pointed out this technique would be just as effective, especially
since the opacity of the dry ice mist provided practical as well as
dramatic value. This was evidently purist Benn's first movie job,
and he yanked at his curly blond hair in high artistic funk, to
everyone's sincere enjoyment.

While all this was going on, Lil had joined Russ at the far end
of the terrace, where they were having a serious word with Rikka
Tring, who evidently didn't want to hear it. She cut them off with
a mocking little laugh, then turned her back.

Lil called, "Rikka!", and just for a moment, Rikka seemed to
hesitate. But instead of responding, she continued to move away.
Russ and Lil exchanged very grave looks.

What on earth was that about?

I didn't have time to ask because just then, Presley bellowed
for everyone to take their places.

Lotus, exotic in golden silk, now hung suspended in the golden
cage, looking down at her captor, Dr. Upharsin, knowing it was
really she who had the power.

Suddenly, out of nowhere, two flying bundles, one liver and
white, one black and white, came charging hellbent for the pool.
Oh, no! Dimples and Dumpling, unable to resist temptation. Frank
would never forgive me if they caused a delay, since time was so
precious. But Frank, after one startled glance as they went galloping by, shouted, "Dimples! Dumpling! No!" Amazingly, they
skidded to an obedient halt.

Frank jerked his head at me. "Call them, honey." Well, at least
I was still "honey," probably because he was so proud his intensive training had paid off for all to see.

The girls, ears dragging sheepishly, came to sit with me, followed by a ripple of amusement.

Finally, we were ready to go again.

A bare-torsoed Guido, whose chest hairs glistened as if sprayed
with oil, turned the winch to lower Lotus into the foggy pool. He
was to lock its handle the instant the cage touched the water.

Russ, perched on the crane, was getting great shots, tracking up, down, and around for closeups of Lotus's impassive face between the gilded bars.

Woo hovered, clearly hankering for more camera time than his Altman-type cameo had afforded him.

Davida was busily orbiting the pool, clicking away. Once she nearly missed her footing.

Benn, whose lower lip jutted petulantly, was observing with interest despite himself, as Guido cranked and Lotus serenely descended. "Okay, cut!" Frank called finally, and Guido dutifully reversed the handle to lock it into place. Except that it wouldn't lock.

Instead, all traction seemed to disappear completely, and the crank came off in Guido's hand. He stood staring at it foolishly, as the cage plummeted ungracefully into the water.

So much for saving time by eliminating the need to dry Rikka out!

There was a moment of shocked silence, followed by a gust of nervous laughter, but I knew Rikka would be humiliated and couldn't help feeling sorry for her.

A grinning Davida, who clearly did not share my sympathy, stood poised and ready to shoot the instant our reluctant Venus was hauled from the sea.

Nobuo had turned his back to conceal any amusement he might be feeling, but Woo chortled delightedly.

Naki, without the slightest change of expression, nevertheless managed to convey her day had just been made.

Guido was the first to recover. "For God's sake, somebody!" he shouted desperately. "Help me haul the cage up. She can't get out—it's locked!"

Contrite, Frank, Russ, and Presley all sprang forward, found handholds on the flaccid chain, and began to tug. Then, more people rushed to assist.

Dimples and Dumpling, sensing the sudden urgency, pitched in by dashing around and barking excitedly.

Given their extremely physical and emotional natures, I was

very impressed at how instantly they'd responded to Frank's command not to go into the pool, as yet unaware that his obedience training had literally saved their precious little lives.

The dry ice haze had taken on a sickly brown tinge, and the water foamed unpleasantly until finally, after the longest ninety seconds in the history of time, the golden cage with its jeweled padlock emerged from the water.

The wardrobe assistants rushed forward with towels, then, as one, fell back with terrified shrieks, sounding the first notes of the horror chorus we all became when we saw what they'd seen.

Where Rikka's vertical eyes had been, gaped empty sockets.

Her nose, the left side of her face, and her entire throat were missing.

"Piranhas!" Shelly's scream rose above all the rest. Then she fainted dead away.

FORTY-FOUR

THE POLICE DIDN'T ALLOW any of the cast and crew, other than those who actually lived there, back on the grounds of Wei-Side for two days.

When the ban was lifted, Frank and I returned to discover security had been tightened during our enforced hiatus. The police guard on duty, who knew us by sight, nevertheless demanded to see picture identification.

This irritated Frank, who, like everyone else involved with the movie, was terribly concerned with what would happen now. He was poised to launch into a diatribe about horses and barn doors when Harvey Prescott pulled up behind us.

That once genial detective honked impatiently, and motioned for the guard to admit us. But after we drove through the gates, he cut around our car, aiming a grim, unfriendly glance as he sped past.

Well, he certainly had his reasons. Not only had Beverly Hills and West L.A.'s cooperative efforts failed to solve the two previous homicides, but a third had taken place practically under their noses.

If there is such an oxymoron as a "normal murder," I guess those of Miko Hayashi and Hanae Joon would fall under that heading.

But the diabolical creativity employed in Rikka's cruel and unusual death was something else again. It argued a consuming hatred, and desire to inflict intense suffering upon its victim.

I had not yet succeeded in erasing the horror movie that kept rewinding and replaying itself on my internal video monitor.

Guido, raging like a wounded bull while the production nurse worked to revive Shelly...Woo Kazu, who seemed to have instantly withered from his very roots...Davida, controlled by sheer instinct, automatically snapping a picture of the pulpy mess in the cage, her own expression obscured by the camera...Nobuo, standing as if turned to stone, an implacable ancient pagan deity in his billowing ceremonial robes...Naki, her crackling black gaze shifting speculatively between Guido and Nobuo...all the other familiar faces which had suddenly taken on the sinister, secretive distortion of characters in a Fellini film.

Prescott and Weinberg arrived on the scene within seconds of each other, and one of them ordered the pool to be drained immediately.

And there, writhing on the bottom were the murder weapons—later identified as twenty-five razor-toothed, rare black Amazon piranhas. So rare, in fact, that even the marine biologist consulted had never seen any in the flesh and rushed over to take these into protective custody.

The one and only light moment came when the biologist quite seriously informed Prescott she would hold the fish in a tank at her Santa Monica aquarium for as long as necessary and he'd quipped, "You mean a holding tank?"

Since then, however, Prescott had completely lost his sense of humor while Weinberg, over the stretch of three consecutive murders, looked like he'd lost nearly twenty pounds.

Granted, Brentwood has unfortunately become notorious as the scene of dramatic death, but for a beautiful woman to be eaten alive by carnivorous fish in an ornamental pool while shooting a movie was really pushing it.

Like many other exotic and dangerous creatures, black Amazon piranhas are illegal for private ownership. But as everyone knows, there is always somebody eager to cater to appetites for the exotic, dangerous, and illegal.

To date, however, all known traffickers in contraband species who'd been rounded up had emphatically denied access to these particular piranhas. Indeed, several went so far as to brazenly request the police inform them when they discovered the source.

The Brazilian actor who played Fero spent some uncomfortable moments until his passport proved he hadn't left America for nearly three months. Moreover, he'd been raised in a Sao Paolo ghetto and never once in his thirty-two years had so much as set foot in the Amazon jungle—not even when Sting was there promoting rain forest preservation.

Now, as Frank and I trailed along in Prescott's dust, we reflected on the irony that if we had written a thriller script based on these real-life murders exactly as they'd occurred, it would've undoubtedly been rejected by every studio for contrived plotting, unrealistic dialogue, sloppy evidence gathering, and politically incorrect racial stereotyping.

Or, as Frank pointed out, the same exact reaction, prior to June 1994, accorded to any original screenplay with a storyline of a famous black football pro on trial for slashing his beautiful, blonde, white ex-wife to death.

The terrible truth about real murder is that it's neither well written nor politically correct; the evidence is often far more confusing than enlightening—even sometimes unrecognizable as such and overlooked altogether—and there's no such thing as cutting scenes for length.

Since Rikka's murder, our leaner, meaner Weinberg had not been so forthcoming with the facts as before, so we had only a rough idea as to the current status of the investigation.

Of course, the first thing he'd done was insist on viewing the dailies again, but this time, there was no miraculous revelation.

Guido, who'd been operating the winch, was temporarily held as a material witness. Apparently he'd used the opportunity to throw suspicion onto Nobuo, claiming the older man was insanely jealous because he'd discovered Rikka was planning to return to Guido, her former lover.

Benn Kwik came in for his own share of grief because of his vehement argument with Frank about Rikka actually entering the water, and thus could've had a motive for tampering with the winch, if not of placing lethal creatures in the pool.

But both Guido and Benn were let off the hook on that score by the forensic team's discovery of a progressive structural defect in the winch's reverse mechanism, something called "interior rust," leaving the equipment rental company shuddering at the prospect of a wrongful death lawsuit.

The only thing perfectly clear at this point was that Frank's decision to cut the scene where the caged Rikka is actually lowered all the way down into the water, had been taken at virtually the last minute. That meant whoever put those piranhas into the pool fully expected Rikka to be submerged for the predetermined thirty seconds and thus would have no reason to sabotage the winch. Consequently, the murderer wouldn't even have had to be on the set, so even Vic Tahara, reportedly packing them in at *Miss Saigon*, was technically back in the running.

But if the killer had been present, I could just imagine his or her frustration upon discovering the critical scene was cut and it seemed they'd set that fiendish trap in vain.

Until a simple mechanical failure had delivered Rikka directly into the jaws of death.

The unpleasant truth about Rikka's murder was that motives and suspects sprang to mind far more readily than with either Miko or Joon.

Jealousy, for instance, could have driven Davida—or even the unlikely Naki—to eliminate such a powerful rival for Nobuo's affections.

I'll never forget that terrible look on Davida's face when she'd learned Rikka was to bear Nobuo's child. Among her eclectic circle of acquaintances and connections, there undoubtedly lurked a character who knew exactly where to procure those piranhas.

Meanwhile, the Asian markets where Naki shopped for groceries most of us have never heard of, might also have access to more bizarre gourmet items, like a certain type of fresh Amazon fish.

There were two other faces of jealousy, both of them masculine.

Guido may have had nothing to do with debilitating the winch, but what if he'd decided Rikka's pregnancy by Nobuo was the last, intolerable straw and debilitated the *wench?*

And while the ways and means might appear a bit Machiavelian for someone like Guido, Frank reminded me he'd turned out to be a better actor than anyone had suspected and therefore should not be written off just yet.

Then there was Nobuo himself, to whom paradoxes, parables, and riddles were second nature, a man who'd dramatized his last will on videotape and designed an intricate maze to be planted on his property. He'd never remarried since his own murderous wife had gone up in smoke. Could he have taken belated revenge on her by disposing of Rikka so spectacularly?

Recalling the various occasions I'd noticed him observing her with such irony, it was clear he'd seen his mistress for the manipulative bitch she was. Such a diabolical booby trap as piranhas in a pool would appeal to his flair for the devious and obscure, a device worthy of his best martial arts film ever, *Monkey See.*

But was Nobuo Hayashi actually capable of inflicting the same punishment on his own unborn child?

Fear could've motivated Woo Kazu to strike back at Rikka. She'd been blackmailing him—I knew this for an absolute fact—and, according to Davida, her demands had increased to gargantuan proportions. But what hold did she really have over that strange little guy? Surely not just the certainty he'd seen Miko dead in the sedan chair and never admitted it to the police?

Could it be Rikka had possessed solid evidence that neither Davida nor I had heard about in our respective eavesdropping sessions, that Woo was actually Miko's killer?

At any rate, whatever it was made Rikka confident enough to issue Woo an ultimatum that he cut her in as equal partner and exclusive model for his new fashion line.

Something like arranging for Rikka to be eaten alive underwater while wearing one of his own creations would definitely appeal to Woo's decadent sense of humor, a fitting end for his beautiful nemesis.

"And last, but not least," Frank concluded, as he stopped the car in front of the house, "there's the money thing again. And we both know what that means, don't we?"

I nodded silently as I hauled out my briefcase and a new box of Balance Bars, which I'd almost entirely subsisted on lately.

What it meant was that the cops would be taking another very hard look at Barry and Cherry Rose. Which, to our way of thinking, was ludicrous. If these people were really trying so hard to get away with multiple murder, they'd hardly have committed another one which shined the spotlight directly upon themselves.

They might just as well have announced it in the trades.

The fact remained, however, that Rikka's death was two more down—if you counted the unborn baby which I definitely did—and none to go.

Because now, as far as we knew, there was nobody left standing in Cherry Rose's way to inherit the lion's share of Nobuo's fortune.

Except of course, Nobuo himself.

FORTY-FIVE

FEAR, MINGLED WITH ANXIETY, hung like smog over Wei-Side.

Piranhas no longer posed a threat, but now the sharks were starting to circle. Network sharks, bred for the sole purpose of scenting productions leaking money, then moving in for a swift kill.

Though the entire cast and crew were present on location, no work could begin until after our imminent shark encounter. Never, if they pulled the plug on us.

People stood around in restive, murmuring clumps, or perched uneasily in pigeonlike flocks along the wide steps leading up to the front door.

Frank and I crossed the driveway and approached the house, acknowledged by muted greetings and few hopeful thumbs-up. They knew their director would do his best.

My heart was hammering as we made our way to the library where the critical decision was to be taken. I glanced up at Frank's handsome profile and felt the sting of tears when I saw the expression of resignation. This might very well be his last chance. You simply never know how things will play out in Hollywoodland.

For example, one director who, due to circumstances completely beyond his control, is linked with a project during which a couple of murders occur could easily find himself blacklisted; another may demand unnecessary and perilous helicopter shots (overriding the aerial cameraman's strenuous objections), resulting in several tragic deaths, yet somehow manage to be exonerated by those who have the power to decide such things—while continuing to shoot a picture every year.

Of course, since somebody must be blamed for the loss of life, most likely it would be the aerial cameraman who ended up on the blacklist.

Because everybody had pitched in and worked such long, hard

hours, *Dr. Upharsin and the Flying Cloak of Death* was able to recoup all that lost time—until the two-day shutdown for Rikka's murder investigation.

Unlike Joon, Rikka was personally known—at least by sight—to everyone involved in the production, which pretty much eliminated any chance of an outside perpetrator. Consequently, the cops had taken an entirely different attitude toward both murders, ordering shooting suspended while they combed the house and grounds for evidence in Rikka's death, and relaunched the search for Joon's murder weapon as well. Though I personally didn't see how they could possibly tell if a specific scarf or rope or cord was responsible.

The library was nearly full when Frank and I entered. We joined Marty, Sam, Nobuo, Russ, and various union representatives to face four network "jaws" salivating over a bundle of spreadsheets with the anticipation of hungry diners choosing from a hearty menu.

Weinberg and Prescott leaned against the far wall. Both their faces were set in identical, blank-but-watchful cop expressions, betraying no clue as to whether they would recommend we be allowed to continue to shoot, or not.

I'm going to skip over the details of that meeting, which lasted three hours and was even more excruciatingly painful, unfair, and humiliating than any of us could've imagined. Suffice it to say that, because we had at least managed to break even thus far, and because law enforcement weighed in on our side, we won a very grudging okay to begin the last ten days of shooting.

However, even one more off day meant we were down the tubes.

Only Russ seemed unsurprised at the decision. "Lil and I got the Beth Messiah Jeshua Prayer Chain on the case," he informed us, after Frank announced the go to a cheering crew. Beth Messiach Jeshua is the messianic congregation they attend, where Russ often fills in as cantor.

And so, we embarked on an even more backbreaking schedule than ever. Early calls were pushed forward to 4:30 a.m., and the union reps grew increasingly blinder and deafer.

Marty and Sam ceased their cries of "Superstar!" and "Spin-off!" They were suddenly older and wiser, and had developed cheekbones, as well as impressive backbones.

Nobuo approached his scenes from an ethereal, otherworldly corner of his soul, which was great for the texture of Dr. Upharsin, but rendered the man we had come to respect—even love—unattainable. He would give a stunning performance, then drift off to his quarters without a word to anyone, staying there incommunicado until he was needed again. On one of these occasions, I saw Axel gazing after his old friend, a suspicious gleam of moisture in those cold blue eyes.

But on the fifth day, two incidents occurred that yanked Nobuo back into the real world.

The first happened right after he finished a brief, pungent scene with Manfred's Major Temple. As had become his habit, Nobuo was heading silently off the set when Davida fainted.

One minute she was fine. The next, boom. She was down.

Before anyone else could react, Nobuo had scooped Davida up in his arms and was carrying her toward the house, curtly rebuffing the nurse, who had certainly seen more action than she cared to on this picture.

Business as usual was resumed, but curiosity gnawed at me until I had to satisfy it. Nobody noticed when I slipped away from the set. Once inside, I moved stealthily from one room to another, but the house seemed deserted.

Then, I began to hear noises. Retching, gagging, miserable noises. My God! What was going on?

Cautiously, I peered around an arched opening into the hallway that led to the powder room. The door stood ajar to reveal Davida, crouched over the toilet, vomiting her guts out while Nobuo knelt beside her, stroking the springy black curls.

In a choked voice he said, "Oh, my darling! Why didn't you tell me?"

I withdrew, knowing this was one time when to listen would be an inexcusable, unforgivable, violation. Anyway, I'd heard enough to answer all my questions about Davida. All but one.

What an idiot I was not to have realized she was pregnant by

Nobuo! Hadn't her shocked reaction after I mentioned Rikka's pregnancy (Pregnancies by Nobuo, Inc.) practically screamed out her secret?

But could Davida have done something so insanely terrible as to destroy her rival and her (their) lover's unborn child?

The second event came later that same afternoon. Cherry Rose wanted to get my opinion on a costume for Major Temple's aging movie star houseguest.

Manfred Walter had courteously allowed the actress to use his room for the final fitting, so Cherry Rose and I cut through the kitchen, intending to take the back stairs.

There, we discovered Pat Tata sobbing wildly at the long pine table, while Nobuo calmly poured her a cup of tea. Cherry Rose and I exchanged guilty looks. Pat Tata! We'd forgotten all about her and her poor mother, Kim Beraku.

Nobuo glanced up as we came in. "We have just received some most distressing news," he said gravely.

Pat Tata regarded us through swollen eyes. "After you put me in touch with Mr. Wei," she droned in a ragged voice, "he hired some private investigators to look into my mother's death."

She was interrupted by Naki's entrance into the kitchen through its connecting door to the garage. Naki was carrying a couple of plastic grocery bags from Vincente Foods and was not at all pleased to discover her territory occupied.

Plunking the bags onto the counter, she scowled at the disproportionate litter inevitably generated by the production of a simple cup of tea, and made shooing motions with her hands. "Out!" she ordered, in one of the few words of English I'd ever heard her speak.

Nobuo lifted his brows in haughty astonishment, then addressed a curt remark to her in Japanese, no doubt something to the effect that if anybody leaves this kitchen it's going to be you.

Naki responded with sullen submission, black eyes darting irritably at Cherry Rose and me, then widening a fraction as she noticed Pat Tata hunched down in her seat at the end of the table. Apparently Naki, unaware of the presence of a stranger, acted so high-handed only because she thought it was just us. Without further ado, she scuttled from the room.

Pat gazed at the swinging door through which Naki had made her abrupt exit with some perplexity, then attempted to take a sip of tea. But her hand was shaking too badly and the cup clattered as she replaced it in its saucer before continuing.

"Mr. Wei also had an independent forensic pathologist perform a second autopsy on my mother."

What it boiled down to was that Nobuo's pathologist had discovered horizontal bruises behind Kim's knees, which indicated she had been struck—or kicked—from the rear. Which meant Nobuo's former housekeeper hadn't simply fallen in front of a bus. She'd had her legs knocked out from under her.

Kim Beraku had been murdered!

FORTY-SIX

THERE OCCURS A CERTAIN moment during any production, large or small, when it ceases to be a mere workplace, and becomes a parallel universe where you actually live, breathe, eat, and sleep. It's a self-contained world populated with fictitious characters brought to life by master craftsmen, and it is dangerously easy to begin relating to people based on the characters they portray, or the technical functions they perform.

On the set of *Dr. Upharsin,* this dreamscape aspect was even more convoluted than most, due to the now four murders that swirled around our little world. Four deaths that were appallingly bizarre, yet we were strangely lacking in the violent impact we should have felt.

While we certainly didn't have the luxury to observe even one day of mourning—much less sit shiva for four people—our corporate lack of emotional reaction to these tragedies was very disturbing. Not that it would have helped if everybody suddenly started shrieking with horror.

I wanted to believe it was just me, that I had done my usual turtle thing and withdrawn to avoid feeling or confronting unpleasantness, but was forced to abandon that theory when Russ and Lil confessed they were experiencing the same sensation.

"There's something very wrong here," Russ observed in a troubled voice after we broke for dinner the seventh night. Then, catching Frank's sardonic eye, added, "I mean, beyond the actual murders. There's a specific root this is all coming from that we can't see in the natural realm."

Lil slipped her little arm around his solid waist. "But, the good news is, there is a God in heaven who reveals secrets, so it behooves us to get busy and get some revelation happening around here!"

Apparently, the Meyers planned to use their dinner break for just that purpose, and set off to meet three "prayer warriors" from Beth Messiach Jeshua at their rabbi's home in nearby Bel Air.

Meanwhile, it was difficult to determine how the earthly powers, represented by Weinberg and Prescott, were responding to the evidence of Kim Beraku's murder, which Nobuo had turned over to them that afternoon.

While neither man was foolish enough to dismiss Kim's death as unrelated to the other three, it had transpired in southeast Los Angeles, where the case had been officially closed. Now, they had to decide whether to pass on Nobuo's information to that overworked division, where it might—or might not—be welcomed, much less acted upon.

Or whether to just keep it to themselves for a while.

Thankfully, police protocol wasn't my job, but I would soon have to begin earning my onscreen credit of supervising producer, a conveniently ambiguous title which can mean just about anything. In this case, it meant that I would be the one sitting up until

all hours with the film editor, putting together a rough cut and ordering a justified script. Which is a script revised to conform precisely to the resulting picture.

Because we were so under the gun, Frank wanted to make sure
I went into the edit bay as current as possible, so I got a turkey
sandwich and spent my own dinner hour plowing through reams
of script changes with Angela.

Russ and Lil returned from their prayer meeting—or whatever—with a News Bulletin from Beyond, and just in time to grab
the last congealed chicken quesadillas.

"Two people saw the same exact vision," Lil reported, between
bites. "You tell them, Russ."

Her husband chewed thoughtfully and extracted a shred of
jalapeno from his beard before replying. "Well, the first object
looked like a small globe, rotating in darkness. Only, not of the
whole earth. Reva's impression was that it represented a certain
sphere, or kingdom."

"A certain sphere..." I felt a strange chill. Just a few hours ago,
I'd been thinking how this film had become a world unto itself.

"And then," Lil intervened, "there appeared in the distance
something shaped like an anvil. It began to slowly orbit this sphere,
coming closer and moving faster each time around."

As if on cue, Russ took up the tale. "What happened next is really weird," he cautioned us, wiping his greasy hands on approximately a yard of paper towels. "As the anvil-shaped thing rotated
closer and closer, it began to strike against the sphere. This happened five times, you guys!"

Frank and I looked at each other. The object had struck five
times. But there had been only (only?) four murders. So far.

Russ nodded at our expressions. "Exactly," he said, his brow
furrowed in concern. "But this last part gets really strange. Because
both Reva and Ben saw that the object was covered in such thick
green velvet, they couldn't make out its true shape. That's why,
whenever it struck the globe thing and wreaked havoc, the globe
not only couldn't feel how badly it was injured, but—"

"But it never even knew what hit it!" Lil finished excitedly.

Then the rabbi had brought an interpretation of the vision,

which though I'm definitely no expert on such matters, rang absolutely true to me.

He said that the anvil appearing from darkness represented a heart—weighted down with hatred that had remained hidden in the past—that had now been sent forth as an instrument of destruction, but in disguise so no one recognized it for what it was.

The velvetlike cushion that concealed its true shape, also served as an anesthetic to prevent the kingdom from feeling how deeply it was injured.

The green color indicated it was driven by the forces of jealousy and greed for money.

Frank cleared his throat. "Um, was there anything else?" he inquired, making an unsuccessful attempt to inject his usual dose of cynicism.

"Well, yeah," Russ admitted reluctantly. "There kind of was."

"So?" Frank demanded.

Lil sighed. "The fifth time, this object crashed into the sphere or kingdom and—exploded."

We didn't wrap until nearly midnight, so by the time Frank and I got home, walked the dogs, had a brandy, and collapsed into bed, we might just as well have stayed at Wei-Side.

I fell into a light doze, only to find Wacko, Yakko, and Dot Warner dropping green anvils and giggling, "Hello, nurse!" while Nobuo's beautiful estate exploded into flames.

Indeed, these were perilous days we lived in. It was entirely possible that a terrorist, bent on exacting revenge on Nobuo Wei for some past offense, was hidden in plain sight among us, concealing murderous plans to blow everybody to kingdom come behind a deceitful smile.

Such a plot would require extensive technical expertise, and Wei-Side was crawling with people who had it.

My dreams segued fitfully from one nightmarish scenario into another.

Andy, the sound man, a neo-Nazi in league with Presley Shores...Russ's substitute gaffer, who actually was a Vietnam vet, reaching critical Asian mass on this picture and suddenly snapping...the Asians themselves, engaged in some esoteric turf war to control Nobuo's property and fortune. Cherry Rose at her drawing board, designing some evil in green velvet...Barry, the engineer, putting it together ...

Then, from a distance, I heard soothing words I'd forgotten in all the confusions—what Russ had told us was Rabbi Ben's understanding of the vision:

> When the root of hatred is exposed
> that has destroyed so much it will
> in turn be destroyed by that upon
> which it fed and healing will flow.

I had no idea what it meant, but after that, I slept like a baby.

FORTY-SEVEN

THE EIGHTH DAY is very significant in Judaism, particularly to male infants.

Dr. Upharsin, though by no means Jewish, was nevertheless subjected to a form of bris, as every remaining nonessential page was mercilessly cut from the shooting script.

Frank had moiled the thing until it was as slick and kosher as a dairy restaurant, then made some final notes for me to reference when I started the rough cut tomorrow morning.

If all went as scheduled today, there would be only two more scenes left to shoot tomorrow, which meant we'd be able to wrap one entire day ahead of our allotted time!

Overnight, my husband had been transformed from workmanlike plowhorse into sleek racing stallion, about to gallop round the bend into the home stretch. His new excitement filtered into the ranks, and the set buzzed with fresh energy.

But every moment, that green anvil was whirling closer.

Its final orbit began at lunch. Frank and I were on the verge of plunging happily into a succulent b'stella of shredded chicken and pistachios, unmoved by Stu, the makeup man's severe admonition that it was a total miscombination of foods and therefore an enemy of the colon.

"This," Frank retorted, dissecting a flaky segment of filo to release heavenly, nutmeg-scented steam, "from a man whose idea of gourmet paradise is a Fatburger washed down with Fat Weasel."

Stu's pudgy face took on a sanctimonious expression. "I've changed," he declared. "I've been reading The Zone."

Which left him wide open to the barrage of good-natured ridicule that followed.

Suddenly, Lil was speaking urgently in my ear. "Ava, come with me," she ordered, under cover of the Stu-baiting. "Now!"

"Oh, Lil," I protested. "Can't it wait? I'm starving and this b'stella is fabulous."

But she'd already pulled me out of my chair. "I'll bake one just for you," Lil promised. "Only, come on!"

She dragged me inside, then looked around cautiously. "Have you seen Weinberg or Prescott anywhere?" she muttered.

"Not since early this morning," I told her. "They probably went off to drink their lunch and who could blame them?"

Lil breathed a sigh of relief. "Good! Although—we're going to be needing them pretty quickly, and we're going to need them on our side."

"What are you being so cryptic about?" I complained, as she herded me upstairs.

"Don't worry, you'll see," she replied.

We reached the spectacular glass-enclosed landing, but turned left instead of right. I had never realized the far wall curved around to form a hidden corridor.

The tile floor was laid in a stunning trompe d'oeil design of an oriental runner, and the marble walls were pale gray and blue-veined. An ornately carved rosewood door was set on either side of the hallway. Evidently, the master—and mistress—suites.

Lil knocked on the right-hand door. When it was unlocked from the inside, I was amazed to see Presley Shores's slightly jug-eared face peer out.

"Y'all hurry up and get on in here," he commanded, hustling us across the threshold.

I knew immediately whose room this had been.

The dry, spicy tang of cedar, sandalwood, and heliotrope that greeted us was visually echoed by a color scheme carried out in shantung, cashmere, and suede—the perfect setting for a deadly, exotic orchid like Rikka Tring.

A tortoiseshell and bamboo table stood next to a chaise lounge covered in iridescent silk the shade of burnt sugar, which faced long French windows overlooking the swimming pool.

The same brulee silk covered a tufted and fringed ottoman in front of the ochre marble fireplace. Upon this ottoman sat Tia Borko, missing wardrobe assistant, crying her eyes out. Cherry Rose Lehr sat beside her, holding a box of Kleenex within Tia's easy reach.

I whirled to face Presley. "You've been hiding her!" I accused.

"Well, didn't you just win the french-fried toenail!" he blustered defensively.

"Presley Shores, I'm in no condition to tolerate your juvenile panhandle palaver," I warned. "Not only did you lie to the police, you let them go ahead and waste valuable man-hours looking for Tia when you knew where she was all the time!"

Tia's wails grew louder and she groped for more tissues in the box Cherry Rose held. Presley flushed and started to say something but Lil intervened.

"Maybe we'd better hear Tia's story as quickly as possible, then we can decide what to do," she suggested reasonably.

I felt scratchy at the quandary Presley had put us in. "Well, okay," I said crossly, watching as Tia dropped another tissue onto the damp, crumpled mound growing at her feet. Finally, she blew her nose and peered anxiously up at me.

Cherry Rose spoke for the first time since my arrival. "Ava, she says she's got important information but she was afraid to tell the police because she's an illegal alien!"

As this, Tia started in panic, as if expecting to see INS men materialize out of the woodwork, but Presley hastened to assure her.

"Now I keep telling you, don't worry your pretty little head 'bout getting deported, Tia honey. There's a real special way to take care of that."

Female to the core, Tia flashed him an understanding sweep of thick black eyelashes that left the poor boy looking for somewhere to sit down.

Lil glanced at her watch. "Out with it, Tia!" she ordered crisply.

Tia sniffed and pouted a little longer, before she finally got down to business.

Oh, Presley! What was your sweet, biscuit-baking mama back in Panama City going to make of this one?

"Rikka Tring asked for me to personally help with dressing because I have delicate touch with Lotus costumes," Tia began, in a husky alto entirely out of proportion to her size.

She was an olive-skinned, delicately built woman in her early thirties, with curly black hair, sloe eyes, and a wide, plum-colored mouth. Another exotic hybrid. Her appeal was not subtle, but it had the great advantage of being undeniable.

"I am at top of stairs bringing costumes from Mr. Woo Kazu for Rikka and tie for Mr. Freddy when I see fat woman coming down from third floor."

Fat woman? "You mean, Hanae Joon, the woman that was killed?" I asked.

Tia nodded. "She begin to follow me. I tell her to leave, but she wouldn't. She ask if this is Rikka Tring's room. I say yes, get out. But she just sit down and say, 'Make me, little girl!' "

Tia was beginning to relax and enjoy her narrative now. After all, four people were hanging on her every word.

"So, I am trying to ignore her and do ironing. Finally, Rikka Tring come in after she finish scene. She very angry like I knew she would be, and say to fat woman, 'What are you doing here? Get out!'

"Then, they start talking Japanese," she said matter-of-factly.

"Oh." I was deflated. Still, it was better than nothing. And best of all, Weinberg would kiss my dainty feet with humble gratitude.

But Tia hadn't finished. "Of course, since I am speaking such good English, nobody know I'm half Romanian. And half Japanese," she added complacently, catching sight of herself in the mirror and fluffing up her curls.

She dropped this bomb casually as a lace hanky, clearly unaware of its impact upon those in her audience who hadn't heard it before—Cherry Rose, Lil, and I, which rendered us equally incapable of little more than staring first at Tia, then at each other in stunned silence.

This little piece of chiffon had actually been present at one of Joon's final conversations!

Presley drawled coolly, "Yeah. Now ain't that just a great big old kick in the digestive tract?" But his normally merry face was sober with an unspoken plea: *Don't make a big deal...she doesn't understand.*

The rest of us did, though, and I apologized silently to Presley. No wonder he'd hidden her! And how smart to focus on Tia's fear of getting deported, in order to distract her from the real danger of being the killer's next target.

Number five hadn't happened yet.

"It was terrible, the things they say!" Tia shuddered pleasurably, then her face flamed as she stammered out that the women began to argue about their one sexual encounter. This incident had meant nothing at all to Rikka, but everything in the world to Hanae Joon.

From what Tia gathered, Joon not only wanted to rekindle the fire, but demanded a regular cut of the loot Rikka was getting from Nobuo.

Rikka asked what she meant by that and Joon pulled an envelope from her bag, waving it in the air and chanting the Japanese equivalent of "I know a secret!"

"Rikka look at that fat woman real weird and say, 'I believe you do. What's it going to cost me?' Fat woman tell her, 'I'll take the first payment right now.' "

Tia blushed again. "Then, Rikka Tring tell me to get out!" she exclaimed indignantly. "So I did. And when I see that big hairy man she likes in hallway, I tell him he better not go in there."

It was a sordid little tabloid tale, but at least we knew where Hanae Joon had been between the time I'd seen her, and the time she was killed. Tia never saw Joon after that, but she'd seen Rikka on the set, watching Frank struggle with the oleander scene. "And you know what?" Tia had just recalled another grievance. "She even took Mr. Freddy's tie for her bathrobe! It was all wrinkled, but what does she care if Woo Kazu yell at me?"

This, apparently, was the final outrage to a conscientious wardrobe assistant, and Tia was still fuming.

My stomach lurched at the sudden thought that occurred to me. I had noticed Rikka wearing Manfred's tie around her waist, as well! Given the nature of her previous relationship with Joon, she might easily have lured her into that spot with the seductive promise of another quick romantic interlude, then whipped off the tie and it was a done deal.

But if so, who had killed Rikka? Could there be two murderers?

Lil had a question. "Wait a minute, Tia. You said you told the big hairy man Rikka liked not to go into her room. When did you see him?"

Tia extracted more tissues, but now she was trying to remove the sludge left by mascara mixed with tears. "Umm...just when I left, I ran into him. He always coming up to knock on Rikka's door. Sometimes she let him in, sometimes not."

Cherry Rose squeezed her eyes shut. "Oh, Guido!" she murmured sadly, knowing Guido would've gladly wiped out Joon to defend Rikka.

I stood up and Presley asked diffidently, "What're you gonna do, Ava?"

When I replied I was going to scour the grounds for Weinberg and Prescott, Tia wailed, "Oh, Presley! They'll deport me!" and flung herself into his arms.

I clutched a handful of my hair in exasperation. "Okay, here's what we do now. Lil and Cherry Rose, stay here with Tia. And Presley"—I consulted my watch—"lunch is over in five minutes and you are the AD, remember?"

Presley objected. "But now, looky here, Ava. I can't leave—"

I cut him off ruthlessly. "Oh, yes you can, Presley. Tell me. Just how do you explain harboring an illegal alien in possession of vital evidence concerning a murder case?"

Presley blinked. He hadn't exactly considered his own position.

"Look, you clown!" Cherry Rose honked at him. "The best thing you can do for Tia and everybody else is to get downstairs and act like this is all big news to you!"

Reluctantly, Presley acknowledged the wisdom of this. "But sugar, if they try to make you say where you were, it's okay if you tell 'em you were stayin' at my house," he offered nobly.

Tia's lashes swept over him again. "Oh, Presley!" she sighed, causing another holdup in the parade until Lil finally managed to push him out the door.

"Guard the prisoner!" I called ill-advisedly over my shoulder, and heard Cherry Rose soothe, "She didn't mean it that way, Tia."

Lieutenants Bernard Weinberg and Harvey Prescott, reeking of garlic and vino, were just entering the front door when I reached the foyer.

"Ah, another big Italian lunch at Vibratto," I deduced, pinching my nostrils.

"Hell, I can afford it," Weinberg declared, displaying his loose waistband.

"While I just plain don't give a damn!" Prescott, who looked constructed of taut brown leather stretched over a steel frame, seemed more affable than lately.

I observed that medical science has proven garlic is good for the blood, adding casually, "Oh, by the way, I believe you gentlemen were trying to locate a certain little wardrobe lady named Tia Borko?"

Weinberg abandoned his laid-back attitude and glared at me suspiciously.

Savoring the moment, despite the dangerous spark in his eye, I continued. "Well, she's waiting up in Rikka's former room right now, with a key bit of evidence in Joon's murder and scared to death."

I smiled as the two policemen shook loose from their post-pasta stupor, then tried to beat each other upstairs.

FORTY-EIGHT

DON'T BE MISLED by the term "rough cut," into thinking it's just a bunch of film slapped together any old way by some unskilled blue-collar. This vital process actually requires a great deal of finesse and an infinite supply of patience to carve a recognizable shape from the gelatinous mass of disjointed scenes and dialogue that every script—wonderful or not—is inevitably reduced to.

One must be endowed with a sharp ear for garbled dialogue, and an eagle eye trained to spot any discrepancy in visual continuity, combined with a sure instinct about which scrubbed takes to include for pickups of facial expressions, speech inflection, or body language perhaps absent from the good takes. This can really cut down on expensive looping sessions later on.

Admittedly, there are also long stretches of undeniably tedious, repetitive, plodding, sweaty labor. Gil Post, owner of The Post Office editing house where we usually cut, is famous for his saying that "Editors are the blacksmiths of showbiz."

But due to recent events, I was viewing the film-editing process as the perfect metaphor for a murder investigation, demanding the same characteristics of patience, tenacity, and instinct to develop a coherent story on the part of those performing the task.

That these parallel points were bound to converge was something I hadn't considered, sitting in that dark cocoon on the Warner Brothers lot, trying to transform this caterpillar into a butterfly show for the network in less than seventy-two hours.

Was it just a fluke of fate that after such ongoing frustration concurrently endured by the police and the production, both sides should suddenly experience a major surge of forward movement at the same time? As if some cosmic laxative had finally taken effect.

So much had happened since yesterday afternoon, beginning with Weinberg's and Prescott's interrogation of Tia Borko.

Naturally, our cops weren't the least pleased to discover Cherry

Rose Lehr, still a big question mark in their minds, babysitting Tia. But when they jumped to the conclusion Cherry Rose had been responsible for Tia's disappearance, Presley immediately owned up to the deed.

It's debatable whether either detective's heartstrings were plucked by Presley's declaration of love for Tia, or her brave story of having brilliantly solved the difficulty of immigrating from her turbulent Eastern European country by becoming an airline stewardess and simply failing to board the return flight from LAX.

But they were definitely pleased with Tia's critical information regarding Joon's whereabouts shortly before her death. Neither Weinberg nor Prescott attached much importance to Tia having initially encountered Joon descending from the third floor. After all, of the seven small servants' bedrooms once occupied by the staff of the house's original owner, a famous radio star, only Naki's was currently in use.

Obviously, the curious Joon had just been unable to resist the chance to snoop.

They were, however, enormously interested in Tia's account of the unexpected facet in Joon's and Rikka's relationship. Certainly, Joon had something major on Rikka, to get her back into bed.

I decided not to mention my theory to Weinberg that Rikka strangled Joon with Manfred's tie, until I knew for sure whether she could've done it within that very narrow time frame. No point in getting sneered at again.

But, just suppose she had. And just suppose the most outrageous scenario—that Rikka also somehow killed Miko, plus pushed Pat Tata's mother under that Chinatown bus. It still wouldn't tell us who'd murdered Rikka herself.

After the cops were finished with Tia, a motherly looking INS agent escorted her downstairs. The agent firmly restrained Presley from accompanying them to headquarters, advising him the best thing he could do was to get back to work and not worry.

Something in the woman's tone must've reassured Presley, because after they'd driven away in an unmarked government sedan, he'd strolled off toward the set, whistling, "Chapel of Love."

Yesterday's second big event occurred when Weinberg and Prescott filed down the stairs a few minutes after the women left.

Woo Kazu had been waiting for them, ready to make, as he put it, his own "afternoon talk-show confession."

And what a tale he told.

For several years, Woo Kazu and Miko Hayashi had drifted in and out of a relationship based on the fashion scene, casual sex, serious coke, and mutual discontent. When Miko moved to L.A. to help Barry and Cherry Rose set up Bonsai, they'd fallen into the habit of seeing each other regularly.

Despite the fact that Woo had been the one to break up with Cherry Rose, he was resentful of the success she and Barry achieved with Bonsai, and somehow saw himself as the wronged victim.

During one of his and Miko's snort and gripe sessions, they'd hatched a scheme whereby Miko would start feeding him information about Bonsai's design direction, thereby enabling Woo to beat the Lehrs to the runway with his own interpretations, which would make it look like Bonsai was imitating him.

Self-centerd little bitchman that he was, Woo seemed pretty vague about Miko's own motivation to shaft her cousin. The only thing he'd really paid attention to was the abrupt feud that sprang up between Miko and Rikka Tring, after Rikka got her hooks into Guido. Before then, the two women had been buddy-buddy.

It was at that point Woo began to notice a big change in Miko. She suddenly became obsessed with "attaining to her Japanese essence," as she'd phrased it. From bragging about her famous father, she began to denounce him as a white man hiding behind a Japanese mask, and finally moved out of his home.

And yet, when Rikka dumped Guido for Nobuo, Miko seemed angry on her father's behalf. She told Woo she knew both men were being had by tricky Rikka. But when Woo attempted to draw her out on the subject, Miko at first became cryptic—something about looking for a star in the east—then clammed up altogether.

As to the night of Miko's murder.

Yes, he had rendezvoused with her in the sedan chair to do coke, using his secret entrance via that eccentric bathroom setup. Since the fashion show had been endlessly rehearsed, he knew exactly where the contraption would be, and was able to slip in through the curtains without being noticed.

At that, he'd had to wait longer for Miko than expected because of the pictures Davida shot for *Vanity Fair,* and he was getting nervous. By the time Miko finally joined him in the sedan chair, Woo noticed she seemed spacy and short of breath, but assumed she was just eager to do some coke.

But Miko's mood had not improved with her drug intake. She kept muttering things like how she'd shown Rikka who was boss, and that the pseudo-Japanese was about to get the shock of his life.

Then, Miko had wrapped herself around Woo and giggled she was really going to fix Cherry Rose's wagon, and explained how. Until that moment, Woo hadn't been aware Cherry Rose planned to use the sedan chair for her dressing room. With one of those deceptive flashes of cocaine clarity, he realized Miko planned for Cherry Rose to discover them in there together, doing drugs and having sex.

Somewhere in her twisted little mind, she was jealous of her cousin's long-ago relationship with Woo, and was using the opportunity to take revenge.

Angrily, Woo tried to pry Miko off him, but she'd clung like a leech. Then suddenly she started gasping and heaving, and he feared she was having a heart attack. Which indeed she was.

He was just on the verge of calling out for help when he saw his hands were wet with blood. At first, Woo was literally paralyzed with horror, then recovered to the extent of being able to sneak out the way he'd come in, fearing he'd be blamed for her death.

Apparently, Rikka spotted him, and she'd been blackmailing him ever since.

And Woo submitted, because for all he knew, the coke he'd supplied Miko with had caused her to hemorrhage, which made him technically guilty of her death. It wasn't until later he learned that she'd been stabbed, on top of the heart attack.

But Woo insisted he hadn't killed Rikka to prevent her from betraying his presence in the sedan chair with Miko that night. To the contrary, he found he derived a perverse sort of pleasure out of his relationship with Rikka. In her own strange way, she filled the gap created by Miko's death.

At that juncture in Woo's story, I left for my editing session with

Gil, which lasted until around 2:30 a.m., so if anything had happened since, I wasn't yet aware of it.

Frank was snoring away when I'd staggered into bed around three o'clock, and wouldn't have even known I was there if Dimples and Dumpling hadn't formed an impromptu welcoming committee.

At six, we exchanged groggy hellos and kissed good-bye before depositing the dogs with Mike and Molly Kirschner, then going our separate ways.

Now, twelve hours and change later, Gil and I were almost over the hump. He rolled his chair back from the console and declared a break. Unselfconsciously, he reached beneath his Animaniacs T-shirt to scratch a furry belly, causing Dot Warner to look like she was about to jump from the water tower.

"Tell you what, Ava," Gil mused. "Frank's got more talent as a director in his little finger than some bigshots in this town—who shall remain nameless—have got in their entire bodies."

I looked up at the big, shambling man with a gray Ben Franklin fringe around his shiny bald dome. His pale blue eyes behind the huge Milos Forman hornrims, were kind.

"Thanks, Gil," I said affectionately. "That means a lot, coming from you."

"Ah, what the hell!" he snapped. "It's all politics, lousy, frigging politics. These no-talent bums with their twelve-picture deals put all the pressure on us postproduction people to make them look good.

"Which means more and more convoluted technology is necessary to turn their shitty pile of film into something halfway decent." He gestured to the banks of elaborate editing equipment surrounding us. "Do you know when I had this system installed? Last year. Last year! And it's already obsolete, wouldja believe? Do you think John Huston or Billy Wilder or any of the great directors would have needed all this scrap metal? They sure as hell would not!"

It was refreshing to get involved with someone else's problems for a change, and I listened sympathetically while Gil vented his spleen about everything from computer animation to the fact that, as dependent as this Hollywood generation was on esoteric technology, they treated the technical Oscar awards like stepchildren.

We swapped a few dog stories (he's got an outrageous Lhasa Apso named Stella) then got back to work.

In Gil Post talk, the next two hours of film cut easy as a birthday cake.

"All done, Ava!" he announced finally. "Unless you want to stick around while I run the Second Unit stuff for my own enlightenment, not to mention amusement."

"You go ahead," I told him, exchanging my rolling chair for the squashy leather sofa. Propping my feet on the coffee table, I said, "I can see fine from here."

Gil chuckled as he punched some buttons. "You mean you can sleep fine from there."

I halfheartedly denied any intention of napping, but my eyelids drooped as I watched pictures of Wei-Side swim past at every conceivable angle, followed by closeups of oil paintings, statues, rain-drenched trees, glowing fireplaces, and groups of actors and extras eating, drinking, chatting...

"Hey! What's all this nutty stuff?" Gil's voice recalled me to consciousness. Presley's outtakes for *The Making of Dr. Upharsin* were romping across the screen.

I explained Presley's project, and Gil guffawed appreciatively at some of the raunchier vignettes.

All at once, there I was, skidding into Axel. Over his shoulder, the camera had caught Joon entering the house. I tried to feel a sense of poignancy that it was the last picture of her alive, but somehow, I just felt...nothing, as the song goes.

But a minute or two afterward, I snapped to attention because Presley had used all those down periods during that fatal oleander scene with Vic and Nobuo to grab more candid material.

And there stood Rikka in her bathrobe, held together with Manfred's prop tie. I noted the counter—3:57—and felt totally deflated. She couldn't possibly have done it before Presley shot this, because Joon wasn't dead yet. Nor did she have time to sneak all the way around the house, up the path to meet Joon, and kill her by 4:03, which is when the sound glitch told us she was strangled.

Thank goodness I hadn't babbled my bright idea to Weinberg.

I gazed dully at the rest: Naki braiding her hair redux, startled faces appearing in windows—Naki, Rikka, and Woo among them—when the alarm was triggered.

And that was about it, except for a bit of Davida taking a picture of Presley shooting her.

"Now, that's what I call a fine-looking female," Gil observed. "Isn't that the same gal you were hamming it up with on the porch earlier, Ava?"

I yawned. "Uh-huh. And you don't want to know, Gil. Trust me."

He tsk-tsked regretfully. "Complex situation, eh? Too damn bad."

I fished around in my satchel for my makeup bag, and felt the envelope Weinberg had thrust at me before I left Wei-Side yesterday.

"Where's your Israeli pal?" he'd asked, and I said I didn't know, not feeling particularly compelled to reveal the last time I'd seen her she'd been hurling into a commode while Nobuo patted her head.

At long last, Weinberg was returning the pictures she'd taken of the Bonsai fashion show behind the scenes. Having gone to all that trouble, he no longer wanted to be encumbered with them. Solution? Dump them on Ava.

While Gil went off to brew a fresh pot of coffee, I visited the ladies' room to freshen my eyeliner, et cetera. If all had gone as Frank and Russ expected, they'd be wrapping tonight and I was determined to be on hand for the final scene. However, I would need a good dose of caffeine before that long drive to Brentwood.

Gil rejoined me in the edit bay. "Here you go, Ava," he said, handing me a steaming mug emblazoned with Taz, Jake, Molly, Hugh, and Jane. "If you hang on just another few, I'll crank the yardage onto a couple of cassettes for Frank. Wouldn't hurt to give him a jump on the suits, would it?"

Impulsively, I kissed his bristly cheek. "Gil Post, you are the best," I told him tearily.

He grinned and got down to business while I sat back and sipped the scalding coffee. Having nothing else to do, I decided to look at Davida's pictures. As I thumbed through the shots, I marveled again at her ability to capture an elusive, quirky instant of time, and infuse it with professional elegance, which gave her work its unique stamp. Annie Liebowitz, watch your back.

It was a shame these hadn't made the magazine's deadline, particularly the ones of the children. There were Barry and Cherry Rose, looking positively fin de siècle; Guido, Rikka, and Miko restaging their successful cower-and-kick pose; some of the other models, Guido and Rikka in the background; another of Guido...

I thumbed back a few shots and my head began to spin in time to the high-pitched Martian gurgle of the dubbing process.

I thought about something else I'd watched being done twice, then seen again on tape tonight. Suddenly, I knew it explained who murdered Hanae Joon, and how.

Much later, I discovered I'd actually seen even more than I realized at the time.

FORTY-NINE

I WAS SO PREOCCUPIED with what was certainly part—though by no means all—of the truth, that I got stuck in traffic on the 101 before I noticed there was a backup. In the far left lane, no less.

The log jam was moving slower than blood through an artery clogged with cholesterol, and it required all my skill and cunning to keep inching right. Faces in surrounding cars quickly grew all too familiar, but one witty guy provided a light moment when he leaned out his window and called, in a British accent, "Pardon me. Would anyone happen to have some Grey Poupon?"

Finally, I managed to slide over to exit on Sepulveda, and was soon sailing toward Sunset Boulevard. Since I know every bump and curve on Sepulveda Pass, I was able to once again turn my attention to what I'd learned.

Yes, I was pretty sure who killed Joon, and how, but drew a complete blank when it came to why. Nor did I see any connection between Joon's murder and the others—Kim, Miko, and Rikka. But there had to be something—or someone—tying then all together.

With a sudden chill, I recognized what the common denominator was. Who it was, rather. Nobuo Wei himself. Kim had worked for him, Miko was his daughter, Hanae Joon was his daughter's attorney, and Rikka was his mistress.

But—no, something didn't track. There was still a vital factor hovering just beyond my ability to grasp it. That's why I needed to talk to Frank and Russ first, before I so much as uttered a squeak to the cops.

My dashboard clock blinked 10:30 as I turned into Wei-Side's driveway, and the guard on duty waved me through the gate in a manner betraying his boredom.

At first, I was surprised to find so many cars parked in front of the house, until I remembered it was our last night of shooting. Everybody on the crew, the stunt people, the extras, and the featured players—including Vic Tahara—had to be available tonight, just in case. Because there was no such thing as tomorrow.

About the only cars I didn't see were Weinberg's and Prescott's, which both relieved and alarmed me. If I turned out to be right, I'd feel a lot better knowing they were already on the premises.

The front door was propped open, providing a clear view of Marty pacing the foyer, yapping like an ecstatic Chihuahua into his cell phone.

He turned as I came in, making comic faces and pointing at the phone with his free middle digit. "Yes, you heard me exactly right, Larry," he informed the caller. "We're wrapping tonight...yes, I knew how happy you'd be about that...okay, love you, bye-bye."

"You toadying, bean-counting bastard," he added, clicking the phone shut.

I felt breathless. "We really are going to make it, Marty?"

He threw back his head and laughed happily. "Make it? Ava,

thanks to Frank, we're not only going to beat the clock, we're going to beat those network house pussies at their own game!"

Marty grabbed my hand and pulled me along behind him, chattering all the way. "Even if we go into major golden time, we'll still come out a day ahead, and under budget! With two down days and a couple of murders, yet!"

He chortled merrily. "If nothing else, we're going to make the bean counters take a long, hard look when certain other producers start boo-hooing for overages!"

Marty steered me outside through the French doors, toward the maze, where the Baron and Dr. Upharsin were to play their final scene. Originally, it was to have been shot in daylight on the lawn, with Lotus and Fero arrayed in full panoply, ready to second their respective masters.

Somehow, Nobuo had dredged up the creativity to do a powerful rewrite, wherein Lotus dies as a result of the Baron sabotaging her underwater escape, and Dr. Upharsin agrees to a showdown to avenge her death.

When Marty and I arrived at the heart of the maze, he promptly abandoned me for Sam, eager to tell him how he'd reamed Larry.

The set was crowded, seeming to buzz with muted excitement. Best of all, the tantalizing fragrance of success perfumed the air.

Frank spotted me and broke away from his confab with Russ and the gaffer. He hurried over and hugged me so tightly, I could feel his heart thumping against my chest.

"Almost there, baby," he whispered, then was gone before I could say anything.

"Frank!" I called, but he had already been intercepted by Presley Shores and Vic Tahara.

I sighed and sat down in Frank's director's chair, which gave me a great vantage point of all the activity. Barry, Cherry Rose, and Woo were fluttering around Axel Muntz and Nobuo Wei, assisted by...goodness! Was that Tia? Yes, it was!

Every now and then, Presley glanced over his shoulder, as if to reassure himself she was actually there. It appeared that true love would triumph at least once, for a welcome change.

The stars, Axel in full magician's evening dress and Nobuo,

draped in a wide silk shogun robe, looked absolutely out of this world.

The actor who played Fero sat on the ground, a little in front of the featured players and a bare minimum of extras, carefully posed to look like more.

Guido, whom Nobuo had ironically scripted to fill Rikka's position, stood on his mark to one side and glared at his benefactor with implacable hatred.

Watching Guido, I wondered just where he fit into the equation I was trying to complete. Math had never been easy for me.

Lil, wearing her set decorator hat, flitzed around with two assistants, misting the plants with water, plucking off imperfect petals, trimming back a clump of vermilion throwing offensive shadows where Russ did not want shadows.

Gradually, all the different gears in motion began to mesh. Various members of the crew moved toward their respective positions. Shooting was about to begin.

Cherry Rose fussily arranged the drape of her uncle's sleeves, then turned to Axel. She frowned. "Where's the cloak?" she demanded.

Axel frowned back and thundered, "That is vat I vould like to know!"

Cherry Rose Lehr, native New Yorker, was not intimidated. "Get real, Axel!" she rasped. "You've been attached to that thing like a turtle to its shell!"

Woo Kazu giggled shrilly.

Axel's eyes froze to a menacing blue. "The last time I saw it, vun of your people said, in very bad English, to give it to her, it had to be pressed," he replied haughtily.

Cherry Rose did not immediately grasp the implications of Axel's statement. Jerking her head around, she said, "So? Where is it, Tia?"

Tia Borko was mortally offended. "Not me, Mrs. Lehr. I am speaking very good English!"

It was Nobuo who interpreted with grim amusement. "I think, Cherry Rose, he means that he was relieved of his cloak by a woman of Japanese persuasion."

Axel nodded in regal agreement.

Cherry Rose stared blankly. "But—there's no other Japanese woman besides me who'd be handling that cloak!" she protested.

"I bet I know who," Tia piped up, anxious to disassociate herself from people who not only absconded with cloaks but spoke bad English. "That mean old Naki!"

Axel, who had been surveying her with a gourmet's eye, abandoned his autocratic pose. "This little schatze is right," he confirmed, and my stomach knotted.

"I haff not vanted to say anything before," Axel added to Nobuo, "but that servant woman you employ seems very odd to me.

"At first I refused to relinquish the cloak to her, trying to explain how my character attributes much importance to that garment, so that is vy I must keep it vit me at all times.

"Apparently, she did not understand me and actually grabbed it from my hands!" he fumed.

Nobuo seemed bewildered. "When was this?"

Axel plucked a massive gold pocket watch from his vestures and consulted the turnip face. "Three-quarters of an hour ago!" he snapped, with Teutonic precision.

Marty pleaded, "Frank, can't you shoot around that damn cloak?"

Frank shook his head. "Marty, you know it wouldn't track at all. They each have a couple of speeches, shot at three different angles, and then Axel—the Baron, rather—whips off the cloak and whirls it through the air at Dr. Upharsin."

That particular action was accompanied by camera directions that called for the cloak to open up and stretch out like a vampire bat before it reached Dr. Upharsin, a chilling sight indeed.

And complex! Just that one movement had taken an entire day and nearly a whole night on a special-effects stage to get down, further complicated by Barry railing against the FX man who was making so freely with the intricate cloak mechanism he'd devised.

That sequence was carved in stone, and all prior and subsequent footage had to correspond.

Of course, there was the little matter of the cloak-in-the-air business having been shot as traveling across an afternoon sky, but a little color correction covereth a multitude of sins.

While Marty and Sam oy-veyed, Frank and Russ huddled over the shooting script. Finally, Frank looked up and grinned. "All right, you yentas. We just figured out a way to get in the first two speeches, but we'll have to lose that wide three-quarter you both loved. And the two-shot."

At this juncture, both producers were willing to sacrifice any number of hard-won angles.

"But after that," Frank warned, "we've got to have that cape, or it's over, folks."

"Meanwhile, I'm going to find Naki and give her hell!" Cherry Rose announced angrily. "She must've gone crazy, or something!"

"I'll come with you," Woo volunteered, but Barry snarled, "I don't think so, little man. I'll go with my wife."

But when they stopped arguing, Cherry Rose was already out of sight.

Presley clapped his hands and bawled, "Places, everybody. Settle down, now."

In the sudden stillness, a wave of exhaustion rolled over me. Where, oh where, was a cop when you really needed one? And did we really need one? I leaned back in Frank's chair to observe the Armageddon between Dr. Upharsin and the Baron.

It was lulling to listen to the exchange, conducted in High German. Automatically, my mind supplied the subtitles I had wrestled with. "And so, the hour has come, Doktor," announced the Baron, with silky menace. "The planet cannot contain two such as ve."

Dr. Upharsin bowed. "It is not fitting," he replied with deadly courtesy, "for one whose small brain occupies so large a head, to speak of time and space!" I was particularly proud of that one.

I glanced at Davida, who caught my eye and nodded happily. Chalk up another victory for love.

"Cut!" Frank yelled, and moved quickly to watch the monitor playback. I noted with satisfaction that Angela had abandoned her customary pelvic thrust. She was all business, and all lady, these days.

When they ran the playback for the second time, the rest of us—who'd gathered round—applauded. It was a perfect take, no need for a cover shot.

Cherry Rose returned, out of breath and anxious. "I searched all over the house for Naki, but I can't find her anywhere," she re- ported. "I even looked in the workshop. Now, I'm worried. I hope she's okay."

"Oh, dear! Not another body, please!" Woo Kazu exclaimed, and Shelly gasped.

"Shut up, you twat!" Barry growled angrily.

Given the number of fatalities on this production, a wave of concern for Naki swept over the set.

Even the self-absorbed Guido managed to display a little anx- iety. After all, Naki had treated him like a king. No, a god.

The lump in my stomach grew larger and colder. How could I have been so wrong?

Frank rounded up a group consisting of Nobuo, Vic Tahara, Barry, Marty, Sam, and Russ. Davida, Cherry Rose, and I gravi- tated over to join them.

"Look," Frank addressed Marty and Sam. "Unless Russ and I figure out something else—and maybe we will—we've gone as far as we can, for the moment. At any rate, we're still ahead of schedule.

"I suggest some of us form a search party for Naki, without let- ting the others know what's going on. If we can't find her in half an hour, we'll have to call the police."

Everyone agreed it made sense.

"Well, then. I'm coming, too," a new voice said diffidently.

"Sure, Guido," Russ agreed gently.

Frank went off to tell Presley what was going on, intending to leave him in charge of the cast and keep them from wandering away. Just in case our killer was on the loose again.

I felt totally confused and frightened. I wasn't the only one, ei- ther.

When Davida shuddered suddenly, Nobuo reached out and drew her to his side. "I want you to stay here with Presley," he told her, and she nodded.

Cherry Rose clung close to Barry, glancing behind her at the dense bamboo. "All at once, I don't like this place," she said. "The way sound gets distorted is really creepy. On my way back here, I even thought I heard somebody laughing and talking Japanese, and it really spooked me. Then, I remembered you guys were shooting!"

Her nervous laugh evaporated as she realized everyone was staring at her strangely. "What?"

Russ spoke very carefully. "But, Cherry Rose. We weren't shooting in Japanese. We were shooting in German."

FIFTY

NOBUO LEFT DAVIDA and strode rapidly toward Cherry Rose. Taking her by the shoulder he demanded, "What did you hear?"

Blinking up at him, she stammered, "I—I'm not sure, Uncle Nobuo. The voice—I couldn't tell if it was a man or woman—spoke of revenge. Naturally, I thought—the script..."

"You will show me where you heard this voice," Nobuo informed Cherry Rose, then glanced at Frank. "We must find this person immediately. Cherry Rose and I will go together."

Ignoring Barry's protests, he propelled his reluctant niece into the maze.

Davida stirred uneasily. "Ava, do you know what's going on around here?"

My head swam, and I felt on the verge of hysteria. "As William Goldman once said, 'Nobody knows anything.' " My voice seemed to come from somewhere else. Maybe I was developing the ability to ventriloquize? Only I was the dummy.

I had been right all along, but what good was it to be right if you didn't understand how? And I still didn't. What had Russ's rabbi said? Something about a heart heavy with past hatred disguised beyond recognition.

Every act of destruction was a conscious, constant progression toward the ultimate target of its destruction.

From a distance, I noticed Lil talking to Davida. Since they were looking at me with alarm, I thought they must be discussing me. The funny thing was, I couldn't seem to hear them. I found out later I had been on the brink of slipping into mild shock.

Suddenly, Frank was slapping my face lightly and I jolted out of it.

"My God, Ava!" he said shakily.

Then, casting all need to be perfectly right aside, surrounded by Frank, Russ, Davida, Barry, Marty, Sam, and Vic, I told them everything I believed to be true.

"We've got to go in after Nobuo and Cherry Rose. Now!" Russ stated.

Marty and Sam were dispatched to call the cops. Lil offered to stay with Davida, but my sabra warrior was bouncing back. "If you think I'm staying here, you're out of your mind," she snarled, brown eyes flashing like one of her cameras.

So we all went, quietly following the lighted path to the point where it divided and split off into darkness. I fought the panic rising in my throat as a late-night breeze rustled ominously through the bamboo.

"Now, what?" Frank muttered.

Russ held up a large, commanding hand. "Listen."

Gradually, the rise and fall of voices became audible. It's always difficult to pinpoint the origin of sound, let alone in a setup like the maze, but everybody felt it seemed to come from the left.

Sure enough, as we rounded a bend, there were three people standing in a wide clearing. Cherry Rose was off to the side as two big men faced each other. None of them had seen us yet.

The first man spoke in Japanese. It was Guido, who had followed Nobuo and Cherry Rose into the maze without us noticing.

Automatically, Vic Tahara began to translate softly.

"You are a murderer, Nobuo Wei!" Guido accused. "You killed Rikka because you could see she loved me. I am young and you are an old man. She told me how you bought her, how you forced her to submit to you!" Guido's voice grew louder and more confident. "But somehow you found out that she was going to have my baby, so, before she could dishonor you, you killed her!"

Then he shouted furiously, "But that wasn't enough, for you to kill her—you made me kill her!"

Nobuo had been standing like a stone statue, kimonoed arms folded impassively. Now, he shook his head at Guido. "There was no baby, Guido!" Nobuo dropped the bomb softly.

At the center of my whirling thoughts suddenly appeared a clear, solid memory of Nobuo's face as he watched Rikka walk away, after we'd taped that bizarre codicil.

He had known all along!

Guido recoiled under the impact. "You are lying! There was a baby, our baby! She said..." He trailed off in bewilderment.

"Did you two really think I wouldn't make it my business to quietly investigate such a claim?" Nobuo inquired rhetorically. "Mr. Masumo quickly discovered that Rikka had undergone an irreversible sterilization procedure nearly ten years ago. The woman had very good reasons—although she was mistaken—for thinking she could fool me," Nobuo conceded. "Her motive in attempting to do so was obvious."

I could hear Davida's shallow breathing. If Nobuo had already told her this, no wonder she'd looked so happy. It certainly explained a lot.

Nobuo paused, and added thoughtfully, "From her behavior, I was certain she had succeeded in convincing you that you were the father of this nonexistent child. And now, you must ask yourself what she hoped to gain by keeping you on the hook."

Guido, who had been staring at his rival in consternation, began to protest, "But—" and stopped suddenly as a ghostly figure, draped from head to toe in something that shimmered in the moonlight, glided out from the shadows to stand between the two men.

Frank squeezed my left arm in a vise, while Davida clung to my right as if she'd topple over without it. Our vision had adjusted to the surreal glow of moon and stars, punctuated by occasional garden lights, and it was like having front-row seats to some particularly macabre performance.

None of us dared to do more than breathe, except for Vic, who continued with his mesmerized translation.

The figure pulled the gleaming fabric of the missing cloak from its head, and there stood a woman in full Japanese ceremonial hair-dressing and chalk-white makeup.

Cherry Rose and Nobuo Wei cried out as one, "Toshiko!"

The head flung back proudly. "Oh, so now you recognize your wife, do you?" She addressed Nobuo, ignoring Cherry Rose. "I have lived for this moment for many years!"

I suppose the paint on her lips was red, but it looked black in the moonlight as she bared her teeth.

"I set fire to the kitchen because they were going to lock me up again. You see, I had stabbed one of the cooks because he reminded me of you.

"It was so easy for me to escape, and let them believe I died with the others. And of course, all the money you paid in your guilt to my account came in very handy, my generous husband. No one realized how carefully I hoarded it, knowing I would need all I could get to live on while I laid my plans."

Nobuo remained motionless as she continued her tirade.

"So patiently I watched and waited for my opportunity. I, Toshiko, became Naki, a valuable domestic, much in demand by the rich and famous. How glad you were when I was miraculously available to replace your other housekeeper, who left so suddenly."

Nausea swept over me. Naki—Toshiko—had been the one to push poor Kim in front of the bus.

"And all the time, you never knew it was I. How I would laugh at you!" She turned to Guido. "At last came the day when my precious son was returned." Naki put a hand to the speechless Guido's cheek. "And I knew the moment had arrived. I must act swiftly."

She turned her head and the heavily darkened eyes seemed to blaze. "My son was taken from me! First by your abominable family, and then by the worthless daughter which was all you could give me.

"I was originally promised to the oldest son," she added, slanting a brooding glare at Cherry Rose, who quailed.

"I found the misbegotten Yamiko and deceived her into believing I would love her—if she helped me destroy you," Naki revealed. "It was a very good thing when she died. But then there was that mongrel Tring, ready to take over."

Guido, who'd been paralytic, stirred protestingly. Naki didn't notice.

"It was very convenient, though, that dog living with you, my husband. I could keep track of what was going on until my plan was complete." Her voice hardened. "But I waited too long. Because your own worthless daughter was scarcely cold before you gave away her inheritance to your despicable concubine and her unborn bastard." She clenched a fist. "That money is rightfully mine, to go to my son.

"You see, my husband? You never divorced me. And I am still alive!"

She was absolutely correct. If she had been able to eliminate Nobuo without being caught as Naki, she would need only to appear and prove herself to be indisputably Toshiko, his widow, to claim her share of the estate.

And, of course, Nobuo's death had been the ultimate goal, right from the start. As I once pointed out to Nobuo in Cherry Rose's defense, neither she nor anybody else had a money motive for committing the other murders—unless he himself was the ultimate target. Because until he was out of the way, nobody got bupkus.

I remembered his unguarded look when I'd said that. He'd scented the same danger, only he thought it was coming from Rikka Tring. Little did he know the wife he presumed long dead, who'd already tried to kill him three times, was alive and spinning a web of retribution and hatred, right under his own roof. Thanks to Miko, at forty-something, still so hungry for her abusive mother's love, she allowed her mind to be poisoned against the father who'd shown her such kindness.

Since Hanae Joon had handled all the legal paperwork connected with Naki's employment, she naturally knew the "housekeeper's" true identity, having been told that mother and daughter were cooking up a scheme to bilk Nobuo. Once Toshiko was installed in her position as Naki, she began to plot Nobuo's destruction. His actual death was a minor detail; first, she intended to subject him to as much humiliation as possible.

Then, while she played the demure servant girl and pondered just how best to accomplish this, Nobuo moved Rikka Tring into his home.

Of course, Naki knew Rikka was the woman who'd enslaved her precious Guido, so she was glad Nobuo had come between them. As far as she was concerned, Rikka's presence only meant one more person to pick up after.

Naturally, she'd have to exercise more caution in her plot to eliminate Nobuo, but since Rikka had no idea of Naki's true identity, she wouldn't be paying much attention to her, anyway.

That was before Naki discovered Rikka had a plot of her own, and it involved Guido.

Meanwhile, Nobuo had gotten his chance to make a big comeback with *Dr. Upharsin*. When Naki heard the pilot was to be shot at Wei-Side, she decided there was no better weapon to crush Nobuo's pride than to sabotage the project and ruin his last chance to regain stardom before she killed him.

But before she could set things in motion, Nobuo threw a curve by adding Rikka and the phantom baby to his will.

After that, events happened too fast for Toshiko to stick to the original plan, beginning with Marty and Sam giving her a role in the picture! Moreover, Guido had been cast and she wasn't about to mess things up for him.

Also, it would give her a chance to see her son at close range every day. For years, she had been able to follow him only from a distance.

However, it didn't turn out the way she planned, because Guido's main purpose for getting involved with the production was to be near Rikka.

And that's when Toshiko realized Rikka was up to something. She began spying on them.

"I heard that whoring bitch tell my son lies about what was going on between her and my husband behind closed doors, knowing it would make him angry.

"I saw how she was goading him to take action against Nobuo, then tempting and taunting him with promises of how she would reward him.

"My son was too...innocent to see this," Toshiko said tactfully. "Only I could protect him from her snare."

The tension was becoming unbearable. Sweat trickled down my

back and turned to ice water. My arms were numb from being gripped by Frank and Davida.

Once, Barry made a slight forward movement, as if to dash in and snatch Cherry Rose from harm's way, but Russ restrained him, his silent gesture speaking louder than words that Toshiko could well be armed, and who knew how she'd react to any sudden activity.

Nothing interfered with the flow of Toshiko's narrative except Vic's barely audible translation.

Now we were hearing how she'd added Rikka to her hit list. She knew enough about the law to determine Rikka and her unborn child, as Toshiko then believed, would have to die before Rikka managed to dupe Guido into removing Nobuo.

Yet, both women had reckoned without Hanae Joon's agenda.

On the day of her death, Joon showed up at Wei-Side, intent on double-barreled blackmail.

Threatening Rikka to tell Nobuo of their sexual encounter was hardly the type of leverage necessary for Joon to pull in the big bucks. No, that had been in the envelope she'd waved at Rikka while Tia Borko was still in the room, "I know a secret!" she'd teased.

Clearly, Joon had known Rikka couldn't be pregnant because she possessed proof of Rikka's sterilization.

Then, Joon had gone after "Naki."

It was Toshiko who'd stolen the briefcase of photos bequeathed to Cherry Rose by Miko that rainy night. Cherry Rose had assumed they were all duplicates of Guido's life in pictures Miko had compiled for Toshiko, but she was wrong.

There were also snapshots of Cherry Rose's family—including her idiot uncle Vitello, Guido's father and technically responsible for the whole mess—plus some formal studio portraits of Toshiko and Nobuo on their wedding day.

Any of them would have proved who "Naki" really was, but Joon, with diabolical instinct, had retained the one she knew Toshiko couldn't fail to react to: the only existing picture of herself with Guido as a baby.

By then, Hanae Joon had figured out that Toshiko was planning to kill Nobuo. All she wanted for her silence was a cut of Toshiko's eventual inheritance.

Toshiko had listened, pretending to consider the proposition. She'd arranged to meet Joon in the oleander grove to discuss the details, but ordered her to bring the photograph, or there was no deal.

Joon had kept the assignation, fearless because she knew Toshiko was unarmed. Or so she thought. Toshiko had easily caught Joon off-guard and strangled her. With that lethal pigtail. Then, ripped the photo from the dead woman's hand and sauntered coolly to the makeup mirror to rebraid her hair for an unsuspecting, admiring audience.

That hammy encore had always bothered me because it seemed so out of character for the reclusive "Naki." Now I understood it, all too well.

But Toshiko's troubles hadn't ended with Joon's death.

Apparently, Hanae's afternoon pillow talk with Rikka included a revelation of Naki's true identity.

When Joon was found dead, Rikka immediately knew who'd killed her. She'd gone straight to Naki and said, "Look. You did me a big favor by getting rid of Hanae, so I'll do you one. If you pack up and leave this house as soon as the film is over, I'll forget all about it. But if you don't, I'll not only put the cops onto you, I'll tell Nobuo who you are and what you've been planning for him!"

Rikka's snotty attitude had prompted the proud Toshiko to arrange a more gruesome demise for her than originally intended. Therefore, her trip the night before Rikka's pool scene, to a very esoteric, very illegal, very lucrative sushi bar located on a certain yacht anchored in Catalina harbor, had served a dual purpose.

Instead of merely picking up the half-dozen blowfish she'd ordered, whose toxic livers were to be used to poison a special gourmet sushi dish destined for Nobuo's plate, she also acquired a plastic tankful of black piranhas.

None of the other servants paid the slightest attention when she'd transferred a load of fresh fish from the back of her Mitsubishi truck to the huge refrigerator in Nobuo's kitchen; she was in the habit of preparing sushi several times a week for Nobuo and his guests.

Much, much later, she'd stolen outside and tipped the piranhas into the pool.

"It was so important," she concluded with horrible fondness, "To release my precious son from bondage to that evil woman!"

Guido seemed to quiver where he stood.

Toshiko moved suddenly, and the Flying Cloak of Death, slid to the ground. She was dressed in a white satin kimono. "And now, my husband, you will join your miserable ancestors, though in a way more merciful than you deserve!" she cried, raising her right arm toward Nobuo. The waning moon gleamed dully upon the barrel of a small, snubnosed gun.

"I will kill you, and my son and I shall live in peace and happiness on your fortune, at last!"

"Just a minute, you crazy bitch!" brayed a familiar voice.

Davida released my arm and stepped between Toshiko and Nobuo.

Toshiko was furious. "How dare you!" she screamed, in perfect English.

Davida Jochabed Yedvab tossed her mane of curls. "It won't do you a bit of good to shoot Nobuo. Unless you shoot me first," she advised Toshiko pugnaciously. "Because Rikka Tring wasn't pregnant with his child. But I am!"

Davida strolled closer. "The ultrasound showed it's a boy!" she taunted deliberately.

Nobuo, who hadn't moved a muscle as he gathered his concentration and strength to anticipate Toshiko's attack, drew in his breath quickly. He hadn't known!

Toshiko screeched in rage, then aimed the gun point-blank at Davida's bulging stomach.

Suddenly, Guido was spinning toward Toshiko, and his right leg shot out in a patented Combat Stud kick which knocked her arm backward, just as she squeezed the trigger.

There was a flash of flame and a loud explosion, then Toshiko crumpled to the ground. Blood poured from her neck and spread to form a glistening black orchid across the white silk bodice.

As if released from a spell, we all ran forward. Barry grabbed Cherry Rose, and Nobuo silently folded a sobbing Davida against his broad chest.

Only Vic Tahara still seemed unable to move, maybe because he'd been a living transmitter, literally experiencing the emotions of a madwoman as they were relayed in Japanese to his brain, then through his lips into English.

Frank and I collapsed onto a stone bench with our arms around each other, while Russ knelt in prayer beside the body of Toshiko.

Nobuo gazed at Guido over Davida's head. Guido wobbled over to him, and opened his mouth to speak, but no words came out. After a moment, he turned and walked away.

It seemed like we'd been there forever and ever, but incredibly, the entire nightmare scene had been enacted in under twelve minutes, according to the glowing blue dial of Frank's watch.

A sudden crashing and shouting heralded the intrusion of the waking world.

"Frank! Russ!" Marty wailed plaintively. "Where the hell did you guys disappear to?"

Everybody tried to call out directions at once, which, given the acoustics of the maze, only created further confusion.

At last Marty rounded a curve and spotted us. "What's going on?" he demanded breathlessly, hurrying forward. "We finally got hold of Weinberg and Prescott. Would you believe, they were at the Santa Monica Civic Center? At a Hootie and the Blowfish concert yet!"

Marty broke off when at last he saw the small, still figure in white lying on the ground. "Oh," he said, in a tiny little voice.

Cherry Rose picked up the shining cloak from the grass where it had fallen and shook it carefully to get all the interior wires hanging properly. Thrusting it at Marty, she grated, "Here's the damn thing. I'm going to call an ambulance. Come on, Barry."

Russ stood up and told her softly, "I'm afraid there's no rush, Cherry Rose. Let the cops handle it."

Cherry Rose bowed her head, then reached for Barry's hand.

Nobuo took a deep breath. "And now, perhaps if we hurry we can finish this film before the police arrive. That is, if no one objects?"

No one did.

FIFTY-ONE

LOOKING AROUND at the merry throng present at Nobuo Wei's belated wrap party for the entire cast and crew of *Dr. Upharsin and the Flying Cloak of Death,* it was inconceivable that so many terrible things had happened on these very same premises.

There was Presley Shores, beaming fatuously at the new Mrs. Presley Shores, the former Tia Borko...Woo Kazu, with shaven head dressed in simple charcoal silk pants, shirt and jacket, in deep discussion with Vic Tahara and his sinuous, Siamese cat of a wife...Guido Hayashi, not looking as delighted as one would expect, given the three women climbing all over him like ivy on a wall...Harvey Prescott, in a sleek, dark suit which imbued him with a certain sinister charm, hovering attentively around Shelly, the sensitive PA...a thinner Bernard Weinberg, standing alone, nursing his Chivas, brooding over his divorce papers, which had arrived that morning...Axel Muntz and Manfred Walter, flirting ponderously with a couple of those unknown, overblown blonde babes who always somehow turn up at any Hollywood party.

Over by the fireplace, it was fertile acres. Davida Hayashi had blossomed like the desert rose, now well into her sixth month of pregnancy. She was glowing with happiness, and from time to time, I saw her new husband gazing at her with a mixture of adoration and something very close to reverence. As well he might, the woman was a saint.

Barry and Cherry Rose Lehr were sparkling because they'd just discovered their own little identity crisis was on its way to earth. "If it's a girl, we'll name her Emma and call her Emmy," Cherry Rose babbled.

"What if it's a boy?" asked Frank and Barry instantly replied, "Nobuo, what else?"

I laughed. Nobuo Lehr had a nice, ethnic ring to it.

Later on, Nobuo pulled Lil and me aside. "I have drawn up plans to convert the third floor into a photography studio for Davida," he revealed. "Also, Rikka's former room is to become the nursery."

He stopped and shook his head. "Not only to find love, but to become a father again at my age must mean God is giving me a second chance. I can only pray I will do a better job this time."

All three of us got tearful for a moment, then Nobuo cleared his throat. "What I wanted to ask was if both of you would be so kind as to come over tomorrow and go through the rooms of Toshiko and Rikka? You know, pack their things and arrange for some charity to pick up the clothing and furniture?

"I have made sure there are plenty of boxes, newspapers, and tape for everything."

The dark shadow of recent days passed over his virile face. "I want nothing left behind!" he said fiercely.

Davida met Lil and me at the door the following morning, Nobuo at her heels. "Darling! I told you not to upset yourself with this!" he protested worriedly.

His wife snorted. "Do I look upset?" she demanded rhetorically. "Look, if I help it'll just get done that much sooner, honey," she pointed out reasonably.

Nobuo was still dubious, but he capitulated. "Well, okay. If you're really sure."

"What's the Hebrew word for 'pussywhip?'" I wondered aloud.

Davida's rich hee-haw drowned out Lil's giggles. "It's the same in any language!" she retorted saucily.

We turned out Toshiko's room first. Since she'd confessed to her crimes in front of eyewitnesses before she died, the police obviously hadn't felt it necessary to conduct much of a search in here.

At the bottom of a garment bag, we found the briefcase full of photos Miko left to Cherry Rose, along with a zippered pouch containing all of Kim Beraku's personal papers. There were also several loose receipts from Seoul and Body Baths, bearing silent witness to Toshiko's stalking of Kim. I remembered how quickly she'd left the kitchen after noticing Pat. Undoubtedly, she had been one of Kim's "cronies."

As I was closing the dresser, a silver brush crashed to the wooden floor, knocking off its ivory back. I picked it up and found myself staring at an old photograph that had been concealed behind the carved ivory panel, of a beautiful Japanese woman holding a fat, curly-haired baby.

And the side border had been ripped off...

"Speaking of photos, Davida," I said as we trooped downstairs to tackle Rikka's boudoir. "I've been carrying those fashion show pictures of yours around for weeks, now. You still want them, or what?"

Davida shrugged. "May as well take a look," she said, resolutely leading the way into Rikka's former lair.

I was glad to see the bed had already been dismantled and the rug rolled up. Davida explained Nobuo had his housemen take care of it as soon as decently possible.

By common consent, we worked as fast as we could, piling things from drawers directly into boxes, throwing cosmetics and toiletries directly into the large garbage bags provided for our convenience.

I tossed the velvet roll filled with simple and costly jewelry to Davida.

"I don't care what Nobuo said," I told her, "you'd better get him to look at this stuff."

Lil was buried in the depths of a walk-in closet. "Help!" she called in a muffled voice. "I'm being smothered in fur!" There was a series of thumping noises, then suddenly, she yelped in anguish. A moment later, Lil emerged from the closet, holding a bleeding right hand.

"What happened?" I yelled, while Davida snatched the few remaining tissues from the box depleted by Tia.

Lil looked dazed. "I'm...not sure...I was sitting on the floor, gathering up a bunch of shoes to throw into the box, and all of a sudden, something cut me."

I ran into the lighted closet and peered down at the blameless-looking pile of expensive footwear. Beyond spotting a pair of green Maude Frizons that filled me with lust, I noticed nothing unusual. Certainly nothing capable of inflicting a deep wound on Lil's hand.

Squatting down, I scanned the cedar for possible protruding nails or a loose piece of metal molding, but there wasn't so much as a splinter marring its smooth, fragrant surface.

Thoroughly stumped, I turned to go back into the bedroom, glancing down at the designer jumble as I passed, and a deep, dark chill shot through me. Because this time, I saw something that clicked.

Davida had succeeded in stanching the blood flowing from Lil's palm with a tourniquet fashioned from a twisted rope of Kleenex.

"Davida, I think we ought to take a look at those pictures," I said.

She and Lil stared up at me from the floor as if I were nuts. "You mean, like now?" Davida was incredulous.

"Like, right this minute," I replied. My voice felt thin and reedy in my throat. That ventriloquism thing again.

I dug the manila envelope out of my bag, fumbled it open, then dumped the pictures onto the ottoman. Like a blackjack dealer, I fanned them out.

"Tell me what you see, ladies," I invited.

Davida stared at the photos as if hypnotized. Lil glanced at me first, then focused upon them in frowning concentration.

"Lil, what did you and Russ say to Rikka, right before she went into the water?" I asked.

Lil closed her eyes. "Russ and I agreed never to mention it because of what happened," she answered sadly. "You know, we prayed every day for the work, the cast, crew, and everybody connected with the picture?"

I nodded, but she didn't see me.

"Well, that morning when we prayed, Russ and I both felt that Rikka had something very dark on her soul, and if she didn't make it right, she was leaving herself open to something terrible."

Tears slid down Lil's cheeks. "We knew we were obligated to warn her. Just for a moment, it seemed like she was going to tell the truth. But then she laughed, and walked away. The next thing we knew..."

Davida's olive skin suddenly faded to white. She pointed at two pictures. "There. And there, Ava," she managed to choke out.

I went back into the closet and used the wooden handle of an umbrella from the Hong Kong Peninsula Hotel to gingerly separate first one, then the other, of those black satin mules Rikka had worn through the fashion show, from the rest of the pile.

I took off my own shoes and cautiously slipped my feet into them while Lil gaped at me.

"Ava! What on earth?"

Davida, who looked like she was about to throw up, didn't comment.

"The trouble is," I mused, trying to balance on the four-inch heels, "everybody, including the police, was only too willing to lump Miko in with Hanae Joon and Rikka Tring as one of Toshiko's victims, but she wasn't.

"That's why, when she was busily dumping forty-plus years of hatred and bitterness on Nobuo and bragging about knocking off Joon and Rikka, she merely remarked—in passing—that it was a good thing Miko died.

"What's more, I'll bet if anyone had bothered to check up on her whereabouts the night of the fashion show, the other servants would've sworn she never left the house."

"Then who?" Lil asked.

"It's right here in black and white," I said, picking up the two pictures.

The first showed Rikka, the Dragon Lady, posing to kick Miko, the masochistic rickshaw driver. "The reason they never found the weapon," I said, "was because the killer wore it out of Bonsai. Allow me to demonstrate."

I stamped my right foot, then took aim and kicked at the side of a filled cardboard carton. Lil shrieked and Davida gulped nauseously when they saw the gash left by the three-inch blade concealed in the sole beneath the toe, which retracted after another stamp like a snake's tongue.

"I was whacking the shoes on the floor to get dust out before I boxed them." Lil's voice was faint.

"Rikka killed Miko right under my nose," Davida said dully.

I agreed. "Yep. The poor girl was already dead and didn't know it when she popped into the sedan chair to do coke with Woo. Remember, Weinberg said that people who've been fatally stabbed have been known to function for amazing lengths of time?"

"Okay, that explains the stabbing and the heart attack, but not her broken neck," Lil pointed out.

Davida hauled herself to her feet and took the other picture from me. "This does, though," she told Lil.

At first, the photograph appeared to be simply an amusing shot of the exotic little band of musicians posing with their instruments against the long clothes rack.

But a closer study revealed to the far right and behind the rack, one curtained edge of the sedan chair. And Rikka Tring was leaning inside.

Off to the left, evidently in the process of hanging something on the rack, was Guido. Watching Rikka.

"After Rikka had stabbed Miko, she must've lost track of her in that madhouse," I surmised. "So when she spotted Woo sneaking into the sedan chair, she figured Miko had arranged to do drugs with him there.

"By the time she was able to work her way over without being obvious, Miko's weakened condition had already brought on the cocaine heart attack, and Woo had flown the coop."

Davida nodded. "But I'll bet Miko wasn't dead when Rikka peeped in to see what was going on. She knew Cherry Rose was due to change in there any minute, and couldn't afford for Miko to be found in time to save her. So, she just simply ducked in and snapped her neck."

The reason Miko had had to die was because Rikka thought she was the only person who knew she'd had her tubes cut and therefore couldn't possibly be pregnant by Nobuo. Or Guido.

We could only speculate as to what the scenario had been, but I thought we came pretty close.

Guido could not have resisted boasting to Miko that he'd gotten Rikka pregnant.

Rikka must've kept Guido on the string by convincing him that Nobuo had used his power and money to seduce her, but they could get revenge by making him think the child was his, and make him pay up, bigtime.

That would tie in with Guido's direct accusation of Nobuo, as well as what Woo Kazu remembered Miko saying about Rikka running a scam on her father and "looking for a star in the east." And, that her poor brother was so dumb he'd believe anything.

Miko would figure the only reason Rikka was keeping Guido around was to use him to kill Nobuo. After they were married and she was in the will, all she'd have to do would be to stage a convenient miscarriage, then go running to Guido and accuse Nobuo of causing it.

This, of course, would send him over the edge and he'd be ready to tear Nobuo apart. Nobuo himself had implied this to Guido, when he'd told him there never had been a baby.

Toshiko had successfully poisoned Miko's mind against Nobuo, so she didn't care what happened to him. But Miko was determined Rikka must not be allowed to carry out her plan. Not only because she intended to sacrifice Guido, but it would interfere with Toshiko's program of revenge.

Most likely, Miko confronted Rikka and threatened to expose her, thereby sealing her fate.

Guido was probably dumbstruck when he realized he'd actually witnessed Rikka killing his sister. For the second time, only he couldn't have known that.

How could she possibly have explained it to him?

The only thing I could think of was that she'd told him Miko was going to tell Nobuo the baby was Guido's.

Lil said reflectively, "Then, Nobuo upset all Rikka's plans by putting her in the will before they were married, specifically including that nonexistent baby! That had to make her afraid he knew something, so from then on, she was walking on eggs."

"Your husband is no fool," I told Davida.

"Not completely, anyhow," she amended sardonically. "But believe me, he's the first to admit he left himself wide open for the whole thing."

All at once, I realized I still had Rikka's killer shoes on. Immediately, I kicked them off. Their maribou poufs wafted like the wings of two dark, evil birds as they soared across the room.

Where on earth had she found them?

I looked at Davida and Lil. "Well, what do we do about this?"

Davida shrugged and looked down at her strong, brown hands.

"That is a tough one," Lil admitted.

"So? All of a sudden you're not getting special instructions from Above?" I challenged.

Lil glanced at Davida before speaking. "You said it yourself,

Ava. Undoubtedly, Nobuo pretty much stayed a couple of jumps ahead of Rikka. But somehow, I don't think he could face such solid confirmation of his worst suspicions."

Davida raised her head and there were tears in her eyes. "I agree. As much as Rikka hurt him, as much as she hurt me, I think she more than paid for it."

So, on our way back to Encino, Lil and I made a slight detour. To the Pacific Ocean.

FIFTY-TWO

"FRANKALA! WHAT'S THIS I'm hearing about Barry going to become a father? Oy, that Sonia can talk of nothing else. A father? I tell her Barry should be a grandfather by now. And she should be a great-grandmother. At all their ages, it's ridiculous. Meanwhile, I suppose we'll have to have a bris and a baptism and whatever the Japanese do. Which I can't imagine what it is. By the way, Frankala, did you know you're six months younger than Barry? Please! Don't think I'm upset because Sonia will have a grandchild and I won't. I've gone this long, I'll survive..."

ROSEWOOD'S ASHES

by
AILEEN SCHUMACHER

New Mexico engineer Tory Travers is summoned home to Gainesville, Florida, where her estranged father lies in a coma after a hit-and-run accident. While preparing to face the demons of her past, Tory finds herself unwittingly embroiled in a complex, emotionally charged and deadly conspiracy connected to a 1923 racial massacre—the torching of a town called Rosewood.

Available May 2002
at your favorite retail outlet.

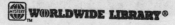

KEEPING SILENT

CARLA DAMRON

A CALEB KNOWLES MYSTERY

Acclaimed sculptor Sam Knowles, deaf since sixteen, is accused of murdering his fiancée, Anne. She's found bludgeoned to death with a newly completed work of art, her lifeless hands signing the word *no!*

South Carolina social worker Caleb Knowles believes in his brother's innocence, knowing Sam would never harm the woman he loved. But Sam, battling demons Caleb cannot understand, retreats into a hard shell, leaving Caleb to sovle the crime—and save his brother.

*Available May 2002
at your favorite retail outlet.*

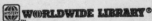 **W⊕RLDWIDE LIBRARY®**

WCD421